Somebody Tell Aunt Tillie We're In Trouble!

Christiana Miller

Somebody Tell Aunt Tillie We're In Trouble!
Christiana Miller

HekaRose Publishing publication date:
August 2014

HekaRose Publishing

www.hekarose.com

ISBN-13: 978-0692292563
ISBN-10: 069229256X

To my little muse, whose songs of love, wisdom and creativity inspired me to dance,

May your life be filled with music, magick, laughter and love!

Acknowledgements

A big THANK YOU goes to:

Griffin and Mark, for everything you do.

My beautiful AR, I'm in awe of your boundless creativity and imagination and I love you so much.

My grown-up kids, for being so awesome, and to my Mom, who always asks me when the next book will be out.

Troy and Stephanie, for your unwavering support and for allowing me to immortalize Lord Grundleshanks.

A big thank you to Nicole Brooks for coming up with the title, Somebody Tell Aunt Tillie We're In Trouble!

Donna McCue, Karen Ann Coffey, Carrie Wolf, Terry Parrish, Mickey Claus, Debbie Clayton, Tawnya Murphy, Cyndi McCormick, Jennifer Krause, Michele Clement and Karen Ann Sturgen for playing the name game.

But most of all, I want to send a big thank you to the Universe and the Muses for coaxing me onto this path, to my amazing readers, who've been so incredibly supportive, and to all the children in the family, for giving me hope for the future.

Somebody Tell Aunt Tillie We're In Trouble!

Mara's in hell! Neither one of the guys in her life is talking to her. Paul, her ex-boyfriend, is afraid she's going to give birth to a baby demon—complete with horns and hooves. He wants proof that he's actually the father. And her best friend, Gus, is so obsessed with his new boyfriend and his plans for the late, great, Lord Grundleshanks the Poisonous Toad, he has no time for anyone else.

After Gus flips the seasons and manages to bring summer into winter, everything starts going weirdly wrong. Summer refuses to leave. Household electronics start going haywire. When J.J., a local boy, vanishes from Mara's car, Mara begins to suspect he's been turned into a rat. But it's such a crazy idea, who could she possibly talk to abut it? Then, her dead Aunt Tillie shows up to warn her that Gus is in trouble—big trouble—and it's up to Mara to save him.

Before Mara can stop him, Gus opens up a portal to Hell and the Devil comes calling. Now, she's got her hands full, trying to find out what happened to J.J., assure Paul she's not going to give birth to a mythological creature, and broker a truce between Gus and the Devil before Gus becomes Hell's newest resident.

(*Note*: This story takes place after *Somebody Tell Aunt Tillie She's Dead* and before *A Tale of 3 Witches*).

Somebody Tell Aunt Tillie We're In Trouble!

Chapter 1

When Gus told me he was going to do the Toad Bone Ritual, I should have cremated the toad and saved us all a whole lot of misery. But it seemed like a perfectly good idea at the time. After all, Grundleshanks wasn't just any toad. He was something special.

For people who are just tuning in, my name is Mara Stephens and I'm a witch. Not one of those fantasy witches who can wiggle her nose and turn your uncle into a carrot. An actual witch. Which means the Otherworld tends to kick my ass and laugh at me about twice as often as I get to score any wins.

The guy I'm living with currently, is my best friend, Gus. He's a witch too. (And no, warlock is not the *defacto* term for male witch. A warlock is a witch who's betrayed their oaths. To be warlocked is to be shunned and cast out. Although there is a guy in England who's seeking to reclaim the word as a term for male witches. But that's a whole other story).

Anyway, Gus is... Think Jack Sparrow meets Harry Potter. He's all attitude, fashion, magick and mischief. Although lately, he's been a huge pain in the butt. I blame the toad. Lord Grundleshanks. Or, more precisely, Lord Grundleshanks the Second. Apparently, Lord Grundleshanks the First is living with Gus's childhood friend, Andwyn, out in Utah. Who knew? I only found out when Gus called him, asking about the odds of getting another toad out of the Grundleshanks line.

But our Grundleshanks is currently residing in the spirit world. Or, at least, he was. Until Gus got the bright idea in his head of immortalizing him through the Toad Bone Ritual. *Ha!*

I should have stopped him right there. Or tied him up and locked him in the attic until he got over it. But I didn't think he could possibly get into as much trouble as he did.

I should have known better. Gus is kind of impulsive and the last time I did an impulsive ritual that sounded like a good idea, I wound up accidentally killing my Aunt Tillie, having to fight off an evil-minded ancestral spirit for control of my body and getting knocked up by a demon who had possessed my boyfriend.

I should have realized that this wasn't going to turn out any better. But like I said, it all started out innocently enough...

* * *

The sucky thing about being pregnant—other than morning sickness—was not being able to take anything stronger than Tylenol for headaches. I was sprawled out on the couch with a bag of frozen peas over my forehead, massaging my scalp to ease the tension, when Gus crashed through the front door with all the energy of a tornado.

"I'm hooooome!" Gus hollered, a blast of arctic wind ushering in his arrival. He was dragging a giant rolling suitcase behind him and looked… different. He had been in Chicago for what seemed like forever, indulging himself in some quality boy toy time, since he had yet to crack the gay scene in Devil's Point. Which, to be honest, kind of surprised me. Normally, his gaydar was humming 24-7. The boy was definitely off his game.

Our two Dobies, Aramis and Apollo, eagerly jumped all over his legs, panting and barking in long-legged puppy happiness.

Just in case I had missed Gus blasting through the door, Aunt Tillie shimmered into view on her rocking chair. "Alert the media," she said sarcastically, while she knitted a pair of baby booties. "Little Lord Fauntleroy has found his way home."

Then, the baby started kicking my kidneys, in some kind of embryonic happy dance. You may think that my soon-to-be child shouldn't be able to hear people talking inside her liquid-filled womb or sense the world around her, and you'd be right.

But thanks to a combination of witchblood and demon seed, my baby who, according to pictures in baby magazines, currently resembled a miniature Creature From the Black Lagoon—was aware, responsive and mobile. Way more developed than any of the books said was possible. Even in her current micro-me size, I could feel magic radiating from her.

"Could you take it down a few notches?" I asked, exasperated.

"Nice to see you, too." Gus responded.

A shaft of sunlight bounced off the snow outside and rudely shoved its way into the living room. I dropped the bag of frozen peas on the side table and squinted at Gus, shielding my eyes. "Can you close the door? You're letting out the heat."

Gus mercifully complied.

The baby head-butted my belly, irritated at my lack of enthusiasm.

"Ow! And you can knock that right off." I snapped.

"What is wrong with you, woman?! I didn't touch you." Gus protested.

"Of course, *you* didn't."

"Then *who* are you talking to?!"

"Who else is using my organs as makeshift soccer balls? I'm talking to the baby." I said, rubbing my belly in a circular motion, trying to soothe the little monster.

"I have been gone for weeks. Weeks. Nay onto months. Practically years. I wasn't just away for the day. You should be thrilled to see me. Dancing and showering me with offerings. At the very least, have a Scotch and water waiting my arrival. Where's my smiling, happy *'welcome home, I've missed you so much'* face?"

"I'm pregnant. Nauseous and stressed *is* my happy face." I said, and felt my eyes filling up with tears. *Damn hormones.* I sniffled and reached for a tissue from one of the many boxes I had on the coffee table.

"You certainly have an odd way of showing it."

"What do you expect? You left me alone with Aunt Tillie for too long," I pouted. "I think she's rubbed off on me."

"One can only dream," Aunt Tillie snorted. "You'd be better

off."

Gus raised an eyebrow.

"I should buy stock in Kleenex. I can't even watch TV commercials without breaking down." I sniffled and blew my nose. "I'm happy you're finally back. I'm just a bit cranky today, okay? I'm sorry. Why didn't you text or call to tell me you were on the way?"

"Seriously? You need advance notice to find warmth in your heart? Okay, Wicked Witch of the Tundra. Next time, I'll send flying monkeys to announce my arrival."

I laughed and felt some of the tension in my head release. I had had a tingling feeling all day, like Gus was on his way home, but since I hadn't heard from him, I had tried to shake it off as wishful thinking. The constant anticipation had worn on me though, until it triggered a headache.

"If it makes you feel better, the baby's thrilled to see you. She's dancing a jig on my bladder and kicking me in the kidneys."

"You mean *he*," Gus said, grinning. "That's my boy."

"Boy, shmoy. I'm getting a lot of girl energy."

"Obviously, we can't both be right."

"Maybe it's a butch girl," I said.

"Or a femme boy."

I thought about it. "I can live with that."

And I could. Either would be fine, because honestly, the one thing I wouldn't know how to raise was a testosterone-heavy male. They had generally brought me nothing but grief.

"Hold the phone! What if it's twins?" Gus asked, clapping his hands. His eyes beamed. "Wouldn't that be something? One for each of us!"

I groaned. One unexpected baby was going to be work enough. I couldn't imagine raising twins.

Aunt Tillie clucked in disapproval. "Tell the idiot that babies are not toys. They're living beings."

"You tell him," I said.

"Now, who are you talking to?" Gus asked.

"Aunt Tillie. She's sitting right there," I pointed to her rocking chair. "Can't you see her?"

Gus looked a little stunned. "No…"

"Seriously?" I sat up straighter, surprised.

Gus shook his head. "Seriously. That's just… Weird."

"You used to be able to see her though, right? Before you left?"

"Not as solid as you, but well enough."

"Aunt Tillie, how are you blocking Gus?" I asked, curious and a little concerned.

She shrugged and continued knitting.

I mean, it was one thing when we were both seeing Aunt Tillie. Gus was like a check and balance for me. But if it was only me… I had to wonder, was I really seeing Aunt Tillie, or was my imagination on overdrive?

When I looked at her again, she was gone. All I saw was an empty chair.

Chapter 2

After Gus deposited his stuff in his room, he came back downstairs. When he found me in the kitchen, he grabbed his chest and gasped, as if he was having a heart attack.

"Knock it off," I said, throwing a green bean at him.

"Barefoot, pregnant and shackled to the appliances. I love it." He whipped his iPhone out of his pocket. "I'm going to commemorate the occasion."

I stuck out my middle finger, just as the tiny camera clicked.

Gus slid the phone back into his pocket. "I knew if I left you on your own long enough, you'd befriend the kitchen. Have you figured out how to turn the stove on? Or are you just teasing me with promises of nosh?"

"Watch it, buddy." I warned him. "Or you'll be eating your dinner raw."

"Oh, come on. I've been traveling for hours and hours to get back to you. Spoil me a little."

I opened the fridge and scanned the shelves for quick-fix carnita meat. "You're lucky I like you."

"I'm lucky you finally learned how to cook. The steady diet of microwave dinners was getting old."

"Is that why you left for so long?" I asked. To my dismay, tears started pricking my eyes.

Gus came up behind me and kissed my shoulder. "Isn't that sweet? You missed me. Who would have thought?"

I closed my eyes for a minute and didn't say anything, until I got my equilibrium back. Then I pulled out the carnitas, a bag of salad and a bottle of dressing.

Gus started setting the table. "I like what you've done with the place. Holiday decorations, Yule tree. How'd you get a Yule tree in here, on your own?"

"I ran into Paul at the Christmas tree lot and he offered to help me bring one home, since you were out of town." Paul was my on-again, off-again boyfriend and the unknowing father of my baby.

Gus nodded and looked around, impressed. "It's almost like we're real grown-ups."

I shrugged. "Baby on the way. One of us needed to started acting like an adult."

"Yeowtch. Sheath those claws, bitchy kitty."

"Just putting you on notice. The miniature human will be taking over the spoiled child role for the next eighteen years. You'll have to relinquish your crown."

I dumped the carnitas into a pan and started heating them up. The microwave would have been easier, but I had stopped using it once I found out I was pregnant. I was probably being paranoid, but I didn't want to take any chances.

"Of course, he will," Gus said, soothingly. "I'm not greedy. I can share the role of irresponsible youngster with him."

"With *her*," I said, stirring the pan.

"Just think of all the trouble we can get into together." Gus said as he started working on the salad. "I can take him *or her*, to their first drag queen show. We need to get a baby backpack. Do we have any bleu cheese dressing?"

"Sorry, buddy. It's on the no-no list for preggie ladies. You'll have to deal with French until I go shopping."

"I wonder if they have any baby glitter backpacks on the market with crystal designs? Maybe a little sparkly pentacle? Or a triple spiral?"

I snorted. "I think you'll have to bedazzle your own witchy

backpack. That's definitely a missing niche in the baby items business."

* * *

After dinner, Gus took care of the cleanup, while I settled down with a book.

"The kitchen is now spotless milady," he said with a flourish, as he flopped down on the couch next to me.

I squeezed over to give him more space.

"I even got rid of the coffee stains on the counter. You really need to clean those as they happen." He popped open the top button of his jeans and took a deep breath. "That's better."

I glanced at him. "Between your belly and mine, we're going to need a sturdier sofa."

Gus narrowed his eyes. "I may have put on a few pounds, but I'm not that big."

I snorted. "Have you looked in the mirror, lately?"

"Motherhood has made you mean. Knock it off."

"Sorry," I said, smiling.

"Besides. It's your fault."

"How do you figure?"

"I blame your pregnancy. I have never been so famished in my entire life. I swear, I've been eating for the three of us."

"I can tell," I laughed.

"Glass houses, honey." Gus stared at my stomach as I stretched and rubbed my lower back. "You didn't have a baby bump when I left, did you?"

I groaned. "You've been gone a long time."

"Surely, not *that* long."

"Last week, I dreamt that instead of giving birth to a baby, a seven-year-old dictator walked out of me, demanding the car keys. The next morning, my pants wouldn't fit."

"You woke up with a belly?" Gus hooted with laughter. "That's impressive."

"I already had a little belly. I just woke up with a bigger one. Check this out." I held up my shirt so he could see the wide elastic band supporting my baby bump.

9

Gus made a face. "That's spectacularly unattractive. What is it? A slingshot?"

"Pregnancy band."

"I have a better idea. Let's hire an Oompa-Loompa to walk underneath you and support your belly on his head."

I laughed. "I think I'll stick with the pregnancy band."

"Don't be hating on my little orange men. They may be small, but they're mighty."

"You just have a thing for dwarfs."

"Don't judge me. I'm all about equal opportunity," he said, lifting my legs on top of his and massaging my feet. "So, how's our toad doing? Have you been checking on him?"

Gus had made a stone cairn for Grundleshanks outside and enclosed him in it, so he'd be protected from predators while ants and beetles helped him decompose. At least, that was the theory.

"Are you kidding me? I'm pregnant. I can't check on frying eggs without hurling. There's no way I'm going to check on a decaying corpse for you. No matter how much you rub my feet."

Even thinking about it made me nauseous. I shuddered and tried to get the image out of my head. When I opened my eyes, Gus was giving me a pained look and holding out a piece of candied ginger.

"Thanks." I popped it in my mouth. "If it helps, the weather's been a bitch since you've been gone."

"It is winter."

"It's been beyond winter."

"Morgue-cold, by any chance?"

"More like Antarctica, igloo-building, and the Poles flipping. There's cold and then there's Devil's Point cold. Did you see the six-foot drifts of snow out there? They're frozen solid. It's gotten too cold to snow anymore. The only thing that's keeping me from turning into an ice sculpture is that this baby has turned my insides into a furnace."

Gus frowned. "That's not good. That means Grundleshanks is probably more toadsicle than he is decomposed pile of bones. Maybe I should bring him indoors."

"Oh, no you don't," I said. "How long does it take a toad to decompose anyway?"

Gus looked stumped for a moment, then he stopped rubbing my feet and whipped out his iPhone. "The magic of technology..."

Chapter 3

A few minutes later, Gus was frowning at his phone. "Fifty years. That can't be right."

I hooted with laughter and almost choked on the ginger. Gus's patience was taxed if he had to wait half an hour for his meal at a restaurant. Fifty years might as well be three lifetimes.

I got a sudden mental image of Gus at eighty, camped out at the cairn in a pentacle bedazzled folding chair, with a stopwatch in one hand and a blackthorn cane in the other.

"Didn't your mother ever teach you that it's rude to laugh at frustrated people and Internet misinformation?" Gus's frown deepened.

"I'm sure that's not right." I said, patting his arm. "They must be thinking of fossilization, not decomposition."

He made a noncommittal noise and kept scrolling through whatever website he was on. "Weird. Have you ever heard of exploding toads?"

"Spontaneously exploding?"

"Yeah. Boom." He said, gesturing with his hands. "It's a bird, it's a frog, it's a toad bomb. A domestic toadarist. A whole new definition for Toad in the Hole."

Well, that didn't help. I started laughing all over again.

"I'm trying to have a serious conversation," Gus said, grinning.

"So, knock it off, Chuckles."

I took a deep breath and tried to think about Grundleshanks and what a special toad he was.

"No," I said, in my most serious tone of voice. "I've never heard of toads spontaneously exploding."

I tried to look over his shoulder at the phone screen, but my eyes were still light-sensitive.

Gus noticed and darkened the screen for me. "Toad liver is a delicacy for crows in Hamburg, Germany."

"I know where Hamburg is."

"Of course you do." Gus said, patting me on the arm.

I rolled my eyes and felt a stab of pain. I really needed to stop doing that, before my eyes got stuck in that position.

"Wouldn't it be a delicacy for crows everywhere?" I asked.

"You would think. But I haven't heard of anything like this happening in the U.S. Maybe German crows have a more advanced palate. *Anyway*. The birds figured out how to get livers out of living toads."

"Wait. Living toads? As in *alive* toads?" I asked, trying to catch up.

"Is your brain ticking along two beats slower than normal?" Gus looked at me, one eyebrow raised. "Generally, yes. That's what living means. I have yet to run into it as a synonym for dead. Alive, living, non-dead. Undead. Hey! The crows created an army of undead toads!"

"That's just... gross."

"Gross and cool. Oh, hold up. You're going to love this," he said, and continued reading. "In retaliation, the toads would swell up to three times their size and explode, spewing their innards up to one meter."

"Ewwww! That's disgusting."

"What's even freakier is the toads were still alive after exploding."

"Are you kidding me?!" I screeched. "That's not even possible. They were alive after getting their livers plucked out?"

"Apparently."

"And then they were still alive after their innards exploded?"

"That's what it says."

"For how long?!" I asked, fascinated in spite of myself.

"All it says is 'a short time'." Gus replied.

"That's just... insane. Freaky. Freakily insane. Attack of the Zombie Toads."

Gus kept reading from the tiny screen. "A thousand toads exploded over three days."

"Holy crap. And then it just stopped? That can't possibly be right. No way can anything still be alive after having their livers plucked out and their innards exploded."

Gus grinned. "Demon Crows vs. Zombie Toads. It's an Otherworldly Smack-Down. There's no other explanation. Crows and toads are both messengers of the underworld. There had to be something supernatural at work. Besides, if birds suddenly developed the ability to pluck their favorite yummies out of living creatures, with surgical precision, why would they stop?"

"Maybe they ran out of toads?" I said, guessing. "Or they got tired of being drenched in toad entrails?"

Gus shook his head. "We're not talking normal toads and crows here. We're talking demonic. Or Daimonic. What if it was Voodoo? Voodoo practitioners can create all sorts of unnatural phenomena."

I shuddered. I had experienced some of that kind of power first-hand recently, thanks to Mama Lua and her zombie powder.

I suddenly got a mental flash of Gus, terrified, ducking, his hands trying to protect his face, as a giant black bird came barreling at him. I shook my head to clear the image out and tried to replace it with a visual of happy Gus, walking through a field of flowers, on a sunny day.

Gus rubbed his hands with glee and raised his eyebrows. "Or... what if toads and crows are just a front? What if the words are code for something else? Like Templars and Crusaders? Hey, maybe we can—"

"—Stop right there," I said. I knew where this was going. "I don't care how bizarre it is, or how Voodoo-ish, or what they actually mean by toads and crows. I am not getting on a plane to Germany to go check it out. You'll just have to let this one be."

Gus shrugged. "If it happened once, there's a good chance it'll happen again. Just in case..." he pointed at me. "Keep one eye on the skies, and one hand over your liver."

I looked down at myself and tried to figure out where exactly my liver was...

Just in case.

Chapter 4

The next morning, I was startled out of a sound sleep by a subsonic *boom*. I felt it, more than heard it. Like my body was a drum skin, stretched taut over a kettledrum, and someone had struck a warning thud.

My heart raced. My mind tried to swim through its morning fog. Where had I felt that sensation before?

The house wards.

I jumped out of bed and raced downstairs, the Dobies at my heels. My cottage was known for having a magickally proactive defense system, with a history of having turned at least one would-be arsonist into a rowan tree. There was no telling what the wards would do if they were triggered.

*   *   *

I tore open the front door and was practically knocked over by the wind chill. My eyes teared up from the cold and I tightened my robe around me.

There was a large box on the front porch.

That would explain the wards going off. Someone must have thrown the box on the porch, instead of gently placing it.

I looked around, trying to spot a hapless delivery person sprawled out on a bush, or an additional piece of shrubbery that hadn't been there before, but everything looked normal.

There was a *Sunset Farms* logo on one side of the box. This must be the organic fruit and veggie bi-weekly delivery Gus had ordered while he was in Chicago.

I made a face. When I tried to talk him into an all-fruit box, Gus accused me of being a sugar junkie and lectured me about fruit addiction.

I picked it up and carried it into the kitchen, trying not to trip over the Dobie menaces who, for some unknown reason, were feeling compelled to do figure eights around my feet.

After I started a pot of decaf coffee brewing, I fed the Dobes, put winter sweaters, hats and doggy booties on them, and let them out into the run Gus had built for them before he left for Chicago, so they could play. Gus would be laughing his ass off when he saw their wardrobe, but it was ridiculously cold outside.

How did people deal with this kind of cold year after year? I'd only been dealing with it since Samhain, and the novelty had definitely worn off. If I could pick up the cottage and grounds, and move them to Los Angeles, I'd be on the first plane back to sunny California.

I tossed a starter log into the fireplace and lit it. Once the flames were merrily crackling away, I went upstairs to check on Gus and tell him his delivery had arrived. But he wasn't in his room.

I looked around, surprised. I couldn't imagine where he would have gone so early. Gus was a big believer in getting his beauty sleep. I quickly searched the rest of the house, but he was nowhere to be found.

I started feeling anxious. I know he's a grown man, but I'm a worrywart and this was Gus we were talking about after all. If anyone could figure out a way to get into trouble, it would be him. So I went to my bedroom, sat on the carpet in front of my altar, and did a quick check of the web using my sixth sense.

* * *

It took me awhile to locate Gus. For me, Gus was usually a gold light on a glimmering green/gold string. Today, his light was partially hidden by a dark cloud. It didn't feel immediately menacing, but that cloud worried me. I'd never seen anything like it before. I tried to poke at it, but my attempts were completely blocked.

The alarm on my clock/radio went off, shooting me back to reality with a nasty screech. I stood up and half ran, half hopped over to the nightstand, my right foot all pins and needles from being under my body.

I slapped at the alarm to turn it off, but—like most electronics—it totally defied me. Every time I turned it off, it would turn itself back on. Finally, I gave up and pulled the plug out of the wall.

Great. Gus was being stalked by something that looked like it was out of the Abyss, my concentration was shot, and according to the alarm, it was time to get ready for my breakfast date with Paul.

I sent up a prayer to the Goddess to watch over Gus, then quickly showered and dressed in my best *hide-the-baby-bump* fashion.

*   *   *

I don't know how I managed it, but I was actually ready to go twenty minutes before I needed to leave. So I stopped in the kitchen, poured myself a cup of decaf and unpacked the box. Of course, the good stuff—oranges, plums, apples—were at the bottom. I had to dig through all the veggies first.

Fennel bulb after fennel bulb. How much fennel can two people eat? And since when did fennel become a vegetable? I always thought it was an herb.

Green peppers.

A head of lettuce.

A bunch of weird-looking green stuff—I checked the invoice, and it was kale.

Small oblong heads of endive.

Human head.

I dropped the head and screamed. From the floor, Gus's face looked up at me.

"*Help me,*" it said.

I screamed again.

Chapter 5

G us slammed through the back door.
"Why does your cottage have to be this far north?" He grumbled.

I looked at him, shocked. "What…?"

"In its next life, I expect it to reincarnate itself south of the equator. Brazil would be nice."

I looked down at the floor, where a head of cabbage rolled against my feet.

Cabbage?

I looked back up at Gus.

"I'll have a talk with the Daimon of the cottage," I said, trying to keep my voice from shaking. "I'm sure, by its next lifetime, it'll be ready for a warmer climate."

I hadn't thought about it before, but it wouldn't surprise me if the cottage did actually have a resident Daimon.

"Thank you." Gus replied.

I nodded and looked back down at the head by my feet.

Still cabbage.

I picked it up and put it on the counter.

What the hell just happened?

"Hey! My delivery is here." Gus said.

I turned to Gus, uneasy. "Gus, what are you up to?"

He looked at me, blankly. "Trying to give you a balanced diet? You can thank me at any point. I'm sure the baby will appreciate it."

I narrowed my eyes at him and concentrated. He had one hand on the counter, and the other behind his back. "What are you hiding? I don't think it's a grapefruit."

He gave me a sheepish grin.

"Seriously." I said. "What are you up to? There's some massively dark energy around you and it's freaking me out a little."

Gus reluctantly held up a perfectly preserved Grundleshanks, encased in a clear brick of ice. "Necromancers-are-us. Care to dance with the dead?" he said, waving Grundleshanks at me.

I yelped and jumped back as a drop of melting ice water hit my arm.

"Knock it off," I batted Gus's arm away. "Put him in the sink before he drips on the floor."

Instead, he thrust Grundleshanks closer to my face and, doing his best Al Pacino impersonation, said: "Say hello to my little friend."

As the smell of decomposing toad and melting ice hit my nose, I felt my stomach turn and heave. I barely made it to the kitchen sink in time.

Gus sighed. "Seriously, is it too much to ask for you to be a little less disgusting? All this vomiting is making me queasy."

"You're standing in my kitchen, waving a dead body at me, and I'm making *you* queasy?" I said, running water down the garbage disposal side of the sink to clear it out.

"There is no possible way you can smell him. You can barely see him. He's an amphibian Han Solo, dipped in watery carbonite. Look at him. I'm never going to get this ritual done."

I ignored the toad and rinsed out my mouth. When I looked down, I noticed I was going to have to change my clothes.

"Crap. This is my nicest shirt. Now what am I going to wear?"

"It's not my fault." Gus said, defensively. "You can't blame me if being pregnant has turned you into Super-Smeller Girl. I wouldn't have brought Grundleshanks in if he was decomposing and stinky to *normal* noses."

"Sure you would have." I scrubbed at the stains with water and dish soap, but I only succeeded in making the shirt slimy and sudsy.

He thought about it for a bit and nodded. "You're probably right. A boy's got to get his kicks somehow. If you're done, move over so I can thaw him out."

"No way! You are not using the sink!"

"Why not? You do disgusting things in the sink."

"*I* have morning sickness. I'm not playing animal coroner. Forget about it."

Gus looked around, frustrated, his gaze landing on the microwave.

"No!" I hollered. "New house rule. *No Dead Animals in Any of the Kitchen Appliances.*"

"Oh, relax. Just on defrost. Just for a few seconds. I'll even wrap him in a paper towel and put him in a ziplock bag."

"I will scalp you in your sleep." I said, glaring at him.

"Well, that's not very generous. Whatever happened to 'love thy roommate as thyself'? Isn't 'thy shalt not be selfish' one of the commandments, Miss EpiscoPagan?"

"You know what your problem is? You are incapable of sharing a kitchen with normal people. Maybe your next boyfriend should be a vet—or a coroner."

"I'm sharing just fine, missy. You're the one having the hissy fit."

"Whatever," I said, rolling my eyes. Then I winced. I really needed to stop doing that. It kinda hurt.

"Some days I wonder if you even remember you're a witch. If you're going to be pissy and possessive about the kitchen, you should put a personal fridge and small microwave on my list of approved Yule gifts for Gus."

I took my hand off my eyes and glared at him. "How many brain cells did you kill in Chicago? If burying makes bones fragile, what do you think microwaving's gonna do to them?"

Gus finally gave in. "Fine. With the way things work in here, he'll probably explode anyway, and we'll have toad guts all over the place."

Oh no! My stomach started heaving at the thought. I quickly squeezed down on an acupressure point on my wrist that was supposed to control nausea.

Gus must have seen the look on my face. "Oh, my Gods. Please, put a lid on your gut volcano. Fine. I'll take him back outside. Maybe sealing him in a plastic bag will help things go faster."

He shot me a disgusted look, grabbed a plastic freezer bag and hustled outside.

Chapter 6

Surprisingly, the acupressure worked. I took a deep breath and felt my stomach settle. Before I went upstairs to change, I poured an offering of sweet white wine into a shotglass and placed it on the kitchen windowsill for the cottage Daimon. Just in case.

I got back downstairs, just as Gus was returning.

"Where's the Yellow Pages, Princess Vomitron?" Gus asked, coming back in. "The toad and I have business to attend to. Are there any entomologists in this rinky-dink village?"

"Why don't you just order some corpse-eating beetles online and get it over with? Wasn't that your original plan?"

"I tried. They're an endangered species."

"Meaning Amazon doesn't carry them?"

"Bingo. I need a Plan B. So… phone book?"

"In the drawer, under the phone."

I glanced at the clock. If I hurried, I could still make it on time. From the counter, Grundleshanks's spirit gave Gus a baleful look.

"You might want to clear your plans with Grundleshanks, first. He doesn't look very happy." I said as I got my coat from the coat rack.

"Seriously? He's here? Where?" Gus looked around.

That stopped me in my tracks. "You can't see Grundleshanks either? For real?"

Before I could stop it, a grin started spreading across my face.

Gus gave me an annoyed look. "Don't look so smug. Just because you're freakishly gifted at seeing the dead, doesn't make me a lesser witch."

Ha! Finally, something I was better at than Gus.

"I'm going to write this day down on my calendar. Gus Andrakis admits a weakness." I pointed. "He's on the kitchen counter, next to the bowl of apples."

"And dead Grundleshanks by the food doesn't turn your stomach?" Gus scoped out the counter.

"I can deal with spirits. It's the flesh they leave behind that gives me the heebie-jeebies. If you really want to see him, try closing your eyes."

"Teach your grandmother how to suck eggs," Gus snapped. "I know how to sense spirits."

"Okay, *boss*. You da witch."

"Shut it," Gus looked around, frowning. "I'm not getting anything by the apples."

"Because he's moved. Try looking over by the coffee pot, witch boy."

"You made real coffee?" Gus asked, giving up on Grundleshanks spotting. "I have been up since ridiculous-o'clock in the morning. I could use a whole pot of coffee right about now."

"Sorry. It's decaf. Fresh-brewed though."

He shuddered. "Get back, you evil woman. The only point to coffee is the caffeine."

"If I have to drink decaf for nine months, you can suffer along with me."

"In case it escaped your notice, I don't have a womb. And that wasn't by accident." Gus said, presenting his mid-section with a flourish. "That was a conscious decision, made in my pre-fetal state. So I could drink real coffee and mingle with the superior sex."

I rolled my eyes. "If by superior, you mean arrogant and condescending, I'll give you that one. Besides, it's not that bad. Decaf tastes just like regular coffee... mixed with essence of peanut butter."

He snorted. "Not a selling point. While you're writing up my gift list, add an espresso machine. Thank the Gods for English Breakfast Tea." He said, grabbing the tea kettle off the stove and filling it with water. "A winter of no caffeine would kill me. I'd have to learn how to hibernate."

"Welcome to my world." I said, putting on my parka.

"Where are you going, anyway? Is it a doctor's appointment? Are you having an ultrasound? Can I come? I want to see the baby."

"No, to all of the above. Except maybe, yes, to the last one, next time I go."

"Is there a reason you're avoiding telling me where you're going?"

I sighed. "I'm meeting Paul for breakfast. And thanks to you, I'm going to be late."

"How is that my fault?!" Gus asked with faux outrage. "You ceding control of your stomach to the baby isn't my doing. That would be *your* fault. And Paul's. I am the sole blameless one in this entire arrangement."

I waved him off and unlaced my warm winter boots.

"I don't know what you see in that wussy, wanna-be ghostbuster, anyway." Gus said, all pouty. "You can do so much better."

"He's the father of my child." I replied, struggling to slide my swollen feet into the boots.

"More's the pity," he muttered. He came over, took the boots from me and grinned. "But I promise not to hold that against the baby."

I balanced with one hand on his back, as he slid one boot then the other, onto my feet.

"He's not that bad. He's easy to look at, he's got a bod that can stop a truck, he's smart and unlike you, he prefers oysters to snails." I said, borrowing the reference from the film, *Spartacus*, and waggling my eyebrows suggestively.

"That doesn't mean he's right for you."

I looked at Gus, askance. "Are you feeling all right? You're the king of superficial lays."

"Honey, have sex with him all you want. Just don't fall in love. He's not good enough for you. Branch out, little tree." He laced up one boot and started working on the next.

"If you really want to have a say in my love life, you're going to have to learn to switch-hit."

"Hey! I like women," Gus protested. "As long as they understand that their role in life is to serve me and tell me how amazing I am, while I get ready for one of what will be my many dates—with men. Many men."

I shook my head. "Whatever happened to monogamy and commitment?"

"They went the way of the rotary phone. How can I possibly let all this awesomeness," he said, gesturing at himself, "be confined to one person? It just wouldn't be fair to the world."

"You do know you're impossible? If your ego gets any bigger, it's going to need its own zip code."

He finished lacing up my boots and stood up, grinning. "But I'm not against tossing a woman in there, now and then, just for a change of pace."

I snorted. "You're such a tease. If you were into women, my life would be much more interesting."

I kissed his cheek, put on my scarf and gloves and headed out.

* * *

In the car, I couldn't shake the image of Gus's head, rolling on the kitchen floor, pleading for help. *What the hell was he up to?*

The image made my stomach cramp with anxiety. There had to be something going on with him that he wasn't telling me. Unless it was meant to be a warning about the toad ritual he wanted to do. But why would that cause ripples in the Otherworld?

The toad bone ritual was something he had found in an old George Ewart Evans book. It had been practiced over a hundred years ago, by an esoteric sect known as the Horsemen. The bone was rumored to give them the ability to calm or bedevil horses, with just a whisper.

Since life back then had been dependent on horses, people who were able to control them were in high demand. But nowadays, very few people even rode horses anymore. It was a sport practiced by choice, rather than a daily necessity. So why would anyone—on either side of the Veil—care what Gus did with the toad bones?

I shook my head to clear it and carefully backed out of the driveway. I was running too late to think about it now. Besides, even with the constant snow plow activity all winter, and the reapplications of Devil's Point (rapidly diminishing) supply of rock salt, the road was still slick with snow and ice in patches, and it soon demanded all my attention.

Chapter 7

B y the time I got to the diner, Paul was already eating.

"Sorry, I'm late," I said, giving him my most charming smile.

I took off my parka and hung it on the back of my chair. The diner looked cheery and Christmasy, with twinkle lights along the ceiling and walls. But it was ridiculously warm.

What was the point of dressing for the season if businesses insisted on turning the heat up to eighty in the winter and the air conditioning down to sixty in the summer?

"I figured you weren't coming." Paul said, barely looking at me.

I picked up a menu and sat down. "I tried to text you, but I kept getting an error message."

He raised an eyebrow. "What *did* people do before the world of texting?" He turned his focus back to his eggs, his face tight.

"I'm not *that* late. If you were running on pagan standard time, this would be considered punctual."

He frowned. "I don't even know what that means."

"It's a joke," I explained. "Because pagans are usually late?"

"I picked up that much."

I sighed. Gus would have thought it was funny. Too bad he wasn't here.

I tried to read the menu, but the waves of annoyance and

impatience rolling off of Paul were practically visible.

I put the menu down. "All right, out with it. I know you're pissed."

He gave me a hard look. "I just find it disrespectful. It's like your time is more important than anyone else's time, so it doesn't matter if people have to wait for you."

"That's ridiculous. I'm not disrespecting you, I had extenuating circumstances." I protested.

"I'm all ears." He said, attacking his eggs with his fork.

"I did try to text you," I repeated. "But I kept getting *message not sent*. What the heck's up with that?"

He sighed. "I reached my texting limit, so I've disabled it for a few days."

"Seriously? You can do that?"

"Yes. Everyone can do that," he said, still looking annoyed.

"Wow. I wish I had known that sooner. I had to up my text messages to unlimited while Gus was in Chicago. He maxed me out the first week he was there."

Paul continued stabbing his eggs. "You have me here in person. Why don't you just tell me?"

I rubbed my belly and thought about how much I was ready to tell him. I was pretty sure Paul was the father of my baby—or, at least, he contributed the human DNA. And I was really hoping he was the only DNA contributor, other than me. With the odd way the baby was maturing, I had real fears about that last part.

But Paul was having a difficult enough time dealing with everything that had happened. Being possessed by a demon was hard enough on him. The last thing he needed was to find out that he had become a baby daddy in the process.

Besides, I really wasn't looking forward to that conversation. Maybe I could put it off awhile longer. Like, until after the baby started kindergarten.

Unfortunately, I was pretty sure that trying to brush Paul off with an off-the-cuff remark wasn't going to do much to improve his mood either. And since the best lies are rooted in truth... I decided I might as well go with nausea.

"I think I had a bad shrimp the other night. My stomach's still feeling rough. I didn't know if I was going to be able to make it this morning, but I really wanted to see you."

Just then, the waitress showed up with a pot of coffee. She refilled Paul's cup and turned towards me. To follow through on my half-lie, I ordered chamomile tea and toast.

Then I turned my attention back to Paul. "So, how are you doing?"

He sighed, put his fork down and ran his hand through his hair. "Okay, I guess."

I nodded, sympathetically. "Want to talk about it?"

"It's been kind of weird." He leaned over the table and lowered his voice. "The worst part is the dreams. How do you deal with them?"

"I think I have it easier. My dreams aren't like yours."

"Are you kidding me? You don't get nightmares?"

I thought about it. "Sometimes."

"Aha! So you do get them."

"Not as much as I used to."

I didn't need to revisit last summer in dreamscape. I had a constant reminder of the situation growing inside me. Paul and I had been possessed for a bit—long story!—and while I had been able to deal with it, thanks to my witchy genes, Paul was a normal human. Which left him with massive gaps in his memories and what I had come to refer to as PPSD (Post-Possession Stress Disorder). When he wasn't confused, haunted and plagued by nightmares, he was twitchy, jumpy and anxious. He went from having a sunny disposition to being short-tempered with occasional bouts of rage.

"What about those *deja vu* moments?" He pressed on. "Where you'll see something and it'll set off memory fragments? Something that you'd swear you've never seen, done or said before, but somehow, it's familiar? Like you're living through something twice? Don't those drive you insane? Or the crazy flashbacks, where you feel like you're trapped and you'll never get out?"

I put my hand on his arm to stop him. "I don't have the same problems. I remember all of it, so my mind's not reaching out, trying to fill in the blanks."

"Liar. You just said you have nightmares."

"Rarely. For me, living it was the nightmare. I don't get the *deja vu* moments. I get flashbacks sometimes, but I tell myself they're not real and they go away."

"What are you fucking made of? Teflon?" Paul shook his head. "I wish I could let things roll off my back like you do."

The waitress dropped off my order and I smiled at her. I took a bite of the lightly buttered toast and shrugged. "I made a conscious decision to not get stuck in time. I don't want to spend any longer back there than I have to."

"Good for you," he said, sarcastically. "Unfortunately, my conscious mind and my subconscious mind aren't cooperating with each other. And it's my subconscious controlling the horror show."

I looked out the window, remembering all too clearly what we had gone through and what it was like to be a passenger in my own body.

Outside, the sky was gloomy and full of the promise of snow. Gus wasn't going to like that one bit. If he couldn't have warmth, he had been pretty adamant about wanting sun.

Paul hesitated, his hands gripping his coffee mug. "I'm thinking of seeing a shrink."

"What?!" I said, taken aback, my attention abruptly returning to him. "You can't do that."

"I can. I have the right and the ability, and I already did," he said, the tension visible in his jaw. "I figured I owed it to you to tell you. That's why I invited you to breakfast."

So much for my idea that we were here to attempt a reconciliation.

"But... but..." I sputtered. "What the heck are you going to tell him? You can't tell him the truth. He'll lock you up in a loony bin."

"I know," Paul snapped. "I'm trying to be as vague as possible. I told him I was in a car wreck. He thinks the accident is what I'm having nightmares about. He gave me a prescription for anti-anxiety meds."

I grimaced. "Those things can be lethal."

"It's either meds or insanity. Which would you suggest I settle for?"

I sighed. "I see your point. Do me a favor. If you start feeling suicidal, stop taking the drugs and give me a call."

Paul nodded and glanced at his watch. "I need to go."

"But... we haven't been here that long. I mean... this is Saturday. It's the weekend. People are supposed to be able to slow down and enjoy life on the weekends."

He stood up and tossed a wad of cash on the table. "Unlike some people, I don't want to be late for my next appointment. Maybe next time, you'll be more punctual."

I turned and watched him as he walked out. He was still as sexy as ever, but wow, talk about distant and hostile. It was like he blamed me for everything. I guess a lot of it *was* my fault.

*   *   *

When I turned my attention back to the table, I was startled to see a man sitting in the seat Paul had vacated. He had blazingly-bright blue eyes, black hair just going to silver and a charming grin.

"Talk about rude. Today's young people have no manners." He said, nodding his head in Paul's direction.

"I'm sorry. Do I know you?" I asked, trying to place him.

He smiled. "Not yet. But you will."

I drank my tea as I pondered that. If I was back in Los Angeles, I would have pegged him as an actor. There was something so familiar about him. And kind of creepy at the same time.

"I'm sorry," I finally said. "I don't mean to be rude, but I'm currently under a male moratorium. I have way too many men in my life right now."

He smiled, flashing deep dimples and unnervingly sharp, white teeth. "Unlike them, I have all the patience in the world," he said, winking at me. "I'm willing to take a rain check."

Outside, the sky darkened and lightning flashed. Thunder hit so hard and so close, the windows of the small diner shook. I turned, halfway expecting to see a crack in the glass.

What in the world was going on out there?

There was no way it was warm enough to rain. And I had never seen an electrical storm in winter.

When I turned back to the table, the stranger was gone.

Chapter 8

I hurried home to tell Gus about the strange guy at the restaurant and the weird lightning storm. When I got there, Gus was out in the back yard, laying on a blanket on the snowy ground. He was bundled in a parka and ski mask, and surrounded by a giant circle of jar candles, pushed into the snow.

As I got closer, I noticed Gus's eyes were closed and he was humming and waving his gloved hands.

"What are you doing?" I asked.

"Weather magic," he said, opening one eye. "Either I thaw Grundleshanks out in the house, or I need warm weather."

"Wait until summer."

"Bite your forked tongue. Patience is not a good color on me. I want that toad bone and I want it now."

I sighed. "You do realize that for every action there is an equal and opposite reaction, right? That's got to be even more massive when it comes to weather."

"Hush, woman. You're interrupting a genius at work." He sat up. "Would you tell Michaelangelo his ceiling mural could be mistaken for graffiti? Or DaVinci that his helicopter plans would anger the Gods?"

I rolled my eyes. "There's got to be a twelve-step program somewhere to wean you off your ego." I looked around "Where are the dogs?"

"They were distracting me. So I took off their ridiculous winter wear and put them in the house. Hats? Really?"

"I didn't want their ears to get frostbit."

He snorted. "Good thing you're having a baby or you would totally turn into one of those people who dress up their pets and make them pose for pictures."

I debated kicking him. "At least I'm not a public menace. You seriously think it's a good idea to bring summer into the middle of winter?"

"If I pull it off, you'll be the only person in this entire state complaining."

Somehow, I had my doubts about that. "Does that mean you were responsible for that freak lightning storm this morning?"

Gus grinned, pleased with himself. "*See?* I knew I could do it."

"That was weird," I admitted, impressed. "Did you see it?"

"I wish. I was a little preoccupied causing it."

"On the other hand, it could have just been an odd coincidence," I said.

"No such thing. Meaningless coincidence only happens to mundane humans. That was a talented witch tweaking the threads of Fate, pinging divine synchronicity and bringing serendipity into play. Now move along and let the witch do his work." He laid down, closed his eyes and returned to his humming.

I snorted but did what he asked.

* * *

I meant to go back outside and check on Gus again, but after spending most of the day cleaning the house, I just wanted to sit and rest for a bit.

I curled up on the couch, in front of the fireplace. I was so toasty warm and comfortable, that I totally fell asleep reading the latest six-hundred page Stephen King novel.

I was in the middle of a very weird, icy-cold, watery dream when a loud crash woke me up.

I jumped up from the couch, my heart thudding. The Dobies, who had been sleeping next to me, immediately alerted.

While I had been asleep, the fire had gone out and night had fallen. The moonlight coming in through the window highlighted the ghost of my Aunt Tillie. She was sitting in her rocking chair, knitting. The puppies softly growled at her.

"You may want to go check on that," Aunt Tillie said, indicating the back door with her head. "Sounds like Captain Sparrow out there, is in trouble."

I bolted for the back, pulling on my coat as I ran.

* * *

When I got outside, the jar candle had sunk into the snow and it looked like the snow was glowing, with merry little flames dancing just under the crystalized surface, in a giant circle.

But I couldn't see Gus anywhere.

"Gus!" I hollered. "Gus!!!"

There was no response.

The back yard was still in ritual space. I could feel the energy humming.

I took me minute to find him. He was sprawled out in the middle of the circle, half-covered by snow, half-covered by a blanket.

I cut through the circle and rushed to his side.

He was unconscious and his breathing was shallow.

Despite his winter wear, his skin was freezing cold to the touch.

At least he was still alive.

* * *

I dragged Gus between two of the candles, into the house. When the puppies saw us, they gave happy little yips.

But those yips soon turned into whines as we got closer.

They slowly backed away, growling.

I shook Gus, trying to wake him up.

But there was no response.

It was like his body was there, but whatever it was that made Gus who he is, his *essence*, had vacated the premises.

And he was cold.

So cold.

I tossed all the blankets I could find on him and then used a starter log to get a fire going. But the warmth from the flames seemed to glide right over him, without touching him.

It was like Gus was encased in a block of ice, just like Grundleshanks had been.

Chapter 9

The puppies growled from underneath the couch.

Gus's skin and lips were turning a light shade of blue. I put my hands on his face, to try and warm it up.

I was immediately hit by an intense cold, like I've never felt before. Tendrils of frost snaked around Gus's skin and creeped up my hands, freezing my fingers.

I gritted my teeth and ignored the pain. I concentrated until I found the golden thread of energy that extended from Gus's body to his spirit and followed it out into the ethereal plane.

That's when I realized that energetically, he was still connected to the circle in the yard.

That must have been what the weird rolling head image had been about this morning. Gus's weather magic had obviously been a colossally bad idea.

It took all the strength I had to break through the thickening frost and wrench my hands off his face.

My fingers were painfully cold.

I could see my skin starting to turn blue.

I looked around for something I could use to cut Gus from the circle, before he sucked me into whatever he had been doing. My gaze landed on a ritual sword that Gus had made and mounted on the wall.

Gus worked a lot with the Faery realm and if there was one thing the Fae didn't like, it was iron. Fae energy was like gossamer threads on the wind, or a spider web, twinkling with dew. Iron, on the other hand, directed, blasted and cut energy. Nothing annoyed the Fae more than humans blasting energy around, reconfiguring or destroying the Fae's carefully laid work, or forcing their portals to slam shut.

Which was exactly what I was going to do. I was going to use the sword to slam that circle down fast, sever the working and shut the portal to the Faery realm.

But when I tried to take it down off the wall, the sword slipped out of my useless grasp and clattered to the floor.

Damn it!

I put my hands as close to the fire as I dared, to thaw out my fingers. But the blue color was spreading from my fingers up my hand, to my wrists.

The sword's hilt end was slightly off the ground, so I pushed on the edge of it with my foot. As it went down, the blade went up enough for me to slide my arm underneath it. I stabilized the blade and hilt between my forearms and elbows, and slowly stood up.

I didn't want to risk dropping the sword, so I carefully hurried outside to power down the space, reel Gus back in and call an end to whatever hellish rite he had started.

*   *   *

The back yard was still glowing, a sea of flames lighting up the snow. I picked my way through the candles, to where I had found Gus and prayed I was doing the right thing.

While I hoped that when I cut Gus's connection to the rite, it would bring him back, my fear was that cutting it could strand him in the world of the Fae.

But I had to do something. Turning, so that the sword moved in a wide circle, I chanted:

"Red threads and black threads, white threads and grey.
Spirit of Gus return, as fast as you may.
Gold, silver and bronze, threads of spirit and soul.

Gather Gus's heart and head, back where you belong.
Back to blood, back to bone.
With the song of this sword,
and my Will alone,
This rite is done."

As I brought down the circle with the sword, the candles whooshed out, and the intense, burning cold released its grip on my fingers. I drove the sword deep into the snowy earth and felt the circle's energy collapse and get sucked down, into the ground.

*   *   *

I ran back into the house, my heart racing. Gus was right where I had left him. Next to the fireplace, completely unconscious.

My heart skipped a beat. *Please, tell me I didn't screw that up.*

I turned on the lights, but nothing happened. We must have lost power at some point.

I walked over to Gus. In the firelight, his face didn't look as blue as it had before. That had to be a good sign, right?

I laid down on him, on top of the blankets, trying to warm him up with my body, rubbing his arms, his face.

His skin was ice cold and rigid.

"Come on, Gus. Get back here," I pleaded.

I pressed closer into him, holding my breath, looking for signs of life.

I felt for a pulse.

But he was still.

So still.

Corpse still.

Chapter 10

Oh, hell! I ran to the desk and fumbled for the phone to call the paramedics.

No dial tone.

Damn it. The phone was tied into the electricity. Where was a rotary phone when you needed one? Where was my cell phone?

I quickly emptied out my purse, in the circle of light by the fire. The cell phone was dead. I had forgotten to plug it into the charger.

I had to get Gus back, quick, before he suffered the same fate as the phones.

But from where?

Where had he gone?

Did I still have time?

Or was it already too late?

In my desperation, I could feel magic building up in me, like electricity. I rubbed my hands together, faster and faster, concentrating and building the power, until I could feel it, like a physical force, between my palms.

I directed the energy at him. *"Gus, I command you, by the power of the Dame of the Crossroads, you return to me this instant."*

Nothing. There was no response.

I thought it through as quickly as I could. If Gus was asking winter to take a holiday, he would have gone to the Winter Queen, or to the Callieach, to bargain.

"To the Winter Queen of the realm of Faery, I apologize for this intrusion. Kostas Yianni Andrakis, I humbly request your spirit be released. By blood and bone, by womb and tomb, return here to me, return home."

I could feel a small sigh, a release of tension in the Web, but Gus still wasn't back.

Damn it.

By now, my hands were buzzing with power.

"Gus, you son of a bitch, you get your ass back in this body now, or I'm dropping the toad in the lake and you'll never get that bone."

I clapped one hand on his forehead and the other one I slammed down on his chest, as hard as I could.

Gus's body rocked from the shock, as electrical currents sparked and coursed through him.

What the hell?!

I let go of him and looked at my hands.

That had never happened before.

I looked back at Gus.

His nostrils fluttered.

He was breathing.

He was *finally* breathing.

"Thank you, Lady," I said to the heavens, feeling a huge wave of relief wash through me.

I touched Gus's face. It was still cool, but that was a huge improvement over 'covered in icy frost'.

And this time, I was able to detect a slow pulse.

I bent forward, warming his cheeks and nose with my breath and hands.

Finally, he stirred and groaned.

"What did you have for dinner? Garlic sardines with a side of sauerkraut?" He said, turning his face away from mine.

I laughed, relieved, and sat back.

Gus had returned.

"No, but that sounds weirdly good. I might have it for a midnight snack. What the hell happened to you?"

"Why did you stop me?" He asked, frowning.

"You were unconscious. No, wait, unconscious doesn't even begin to describe it. You were beyond that. You weren't freaking breathing. Your heart wasn't beating. I thought you were a goner."

"I beg to differ. I had momentarily vacated the body, is all. I'm sure my systems slowed down to protect my organs."

"You were covered in *ice.*"

"I was *working.*"

I smacked his arm, irritated. "You say working. I say, *three seconds away from calling an undertaker.* You're lucky you didn't wake up in a body bag."

"If you ever think I'm dead again, get that verified by a doctor before you do anything irreversible. Like with a stethoscope and an EKG machine."

"You'd better not ever do this again, okay? My heart can't take it." And then I smacked him some more.

"Owww. Stop beating me, woman. I had to go there. It was the only way I could negotiate with the Winter Queen. Besides, you got me back."

"Barely. You scared about three years off of my life span." Finally, curiosity got the better of me. "So, what was it like?"

Gus grinned and sat up. "A lot like outside, but without roads or houses. Just acres of land, covered in snow and ice. Massive forests, but it's perpetual winter, so the only green comes from pine trees. All the rest of the trees are bare, their limbs covered in snow. And her castle... is this glorious monument to winter, made entirely of ice. But it's like a living thing. Even in the moonlight, it sparkles like you wouldn't believe. It's gorgeous."

"Let me guess—you got handsy with it, didn't you? That's why it started converting you into an ice sculpture?"

Gus looked so guilty, I knew I was right. That's the nature of the Otherworld. When you reach out and touch it, it can reach out and touch you right back. Although, usually not quite so dramatically. But it has its moments.

"I have to say, since we moved out here, the magick has been—in general—off the charts. Color me impressed. The weather may suck, but the leylines are buzzing with power. We're both evolving to something that's way beyond normal. *It's an owl, it's a broom, it's SuperWitch!*

"It's not us. It's Themselves." I said, pointing at the sky. For witches, the term 'Themselves' covered a lot of territory, from deities to faeries to fallen angels. "I don't know what's going on, but the Veil between worlds seems to be pretty non-existent out here."

"It's this place," Gus agreed. "I love this place. If we could pick it up and move it to Los Angeles, it would be absolutely perfect."

"Preaching to the choir. I was thinking that this morning."

"Do you think you could talk to the Goddess of the Crossroads about that? You seem to have a good relationship."

"Are you kidding? I'm sure She's racking up some kind of scoreboard, every time I have to call on Her to help. It's not going to be so good when She calls in those chips."

The lights flickered and came back on. Gus stretched and sat up. "Do we have any whiskey left? I could use a drink."

"You?" I snorted. "I'm the one you put through hell."

"You have a point. Consider it payback for the hell you put me through when you moved out here." He looked at my belly and raised an eyebrow. "Chocolate milk?"

I sighed and nodded. "Extra chocolate. Double marshmallows."

Gus walked into the kitchen, while I sat next to the fire and fretted. He had really scared me. Especially after the visions I had been seeing lately. When I checked the Web (of Wyrd not the Internet), that black cloud that had been dogging him, was covering more and more of his light.

I could feel that he was getting deeper and deeper into something dangerous, but I couldn't quite see what it was. The only thing I knew for certain, was that whatever it was, it wasn't good.

Chapter 11

By the time Gus came back with a hot cocoa for me and a hot toddy for himself, the puppies had finally crawled out from under the couch and were laying down next to me.

When my heart rate returned to normal and I could sip my drink without feeling like I was going to drown, I was ready to talk.

"So, after everything you just put me through, how did your negotiations turn out?" I asked.

"We'll have to wait and see. Weather magic isn't an exact science, you know."

"Is any magic ever?" I shivered as the winter wind buffeted our cottage.

As the gust crested in power and howled, a quiet voice wrapped around me like an icy-cold serpent.

"*It's turning out just fine for me,*" it hissed, before dissipating into the walls.

"Did you hear that?" I asked Gus, my eyes darting around the room.

The Dobies sat up, alert and on edge, growling and looking around.

"The only thing I hear is the chattering of my teeth." He got up to toss another log onto the fire.

Soft laughter reverberated through the room.

"Tell me you heard *that*?!" I yelped, gripping my mug.

The back door slammed open. A blast of freezing cold air whooshed into the cottage, blowing out the flames in the fireplace, and smashing the lamp to the ground.

The Dobies ran for their hiding spot, under the couch, and wedged themselves in together.

"What the fuck?!" Gus hollered, forcing the words out as a windstorm invaded our cottage. Over the roar of the wind, I could hear the puppies howling and barking from their hideaway under the couch.

The back door slammed shut, but the wind continued blowing inside the cottage, spiraling faster and faster.

As the currents grew stronger, it was a struggle to stay upright.

Bottles, pictures, tchotchkes crashed onto the floor.

Gus anchored himself to one of the stone columns that buttressed the fireplace.

I pushed my way through the tempest, trying to get over to him, but I had to fight for every step.

Before I could reach a stationary object, the whirlwind lifted me off the ground and sent me hurtling through the air.

I screamed, but the sound was ripped out of my throat by the sheer force of the wind.

I was an inch away from slamming into the wall, when the wind gently and unexpectedly died down.

I half-fell, half-slid to the ground, amid a pile of overturned chairs and shattered ceramic.

Gus was at my side in a matter of seconds. "Are you all right?"

I gingerly moved one limb at a time.

Everything was working.

I turned my focus inward to the baby.

Move, baby. Show me you're okay.

Nothing.

Honey, please. You're freaking your momma out here.

Slowly, I felt a stirring.

I breathed a sigh of relief and looked up at Gus. "We're okay."

Gus opened the front door and looked out over the porch and yard. "What the fuck just happened?" He asked, looking around. Everything was calm. None of the snow had shifted, not even an inch.

"How should I know? You're the one who caused it. What did *you* do while you were in the Realm of Faery?" I snapped.

"It wasn't me," he protested.

"Right. Because indoor tornadoes happen all the time in Wisconsin."

"Maybe," he said.

"Bull," I looked around at how badly the wind had trashed the room. It was in total chaos. "We got slammed by a freaking *Gus*nado."

"It wasn't me—at least, not *just* me. I thought we agreed, it's this place. It's not my fault your cottage takes a simple little magical working and multiplies it tenfold."

"Simple working, my ass." I gingerly stood up. "Simple-minded, maybe."

"Don't jump on my shit, woman. You're the one letting a golden opportunity go to waste."

"What are you talking about?" I asked, still glaring at him.

"Earth to Mara. Do you know how many witches would pay to do their rituals at a place like this? This cottage is sitting on some wicked powerful leylines. You could make a fortune."

I snorted. "Sure. That sounds like a really great idea. That way, I can have every witch and wanna-blessed-be contacting me at all hours, from all over the globe, trying to get in here and cause all sorts of havoc, just like *you* do. Destroying my house and trying to kill themselves—and possibly us—in the process. I don't think so. You know what sounds like a better idea?"

"What?"

I felt a growl rising in my chest and before I could stop it, I was yelling at the top of my lungs. "Tone down your fucking rituals!"

I was so mad, every muscle in my body was shaking.

The thing was, Gus actually did have a point. Locations that would make most people run screaming, are like heaven-sent manna to witches. It was one of the reasons I wasn't about to give up the cottage. Sitting on top of an open portal to the Otherworld, is beyond awesome—if you're a witch. If you're not, you need to get the hell out before the place destroys you. Sell and sell fast. Advertise it to witches and you'll be able to unload any kind of haunted locale in a heartbeat.

But, as a witch, you also had to be super-careful what kind of mayhem you called up when you were living in an open portal. And Gus seemed incapable of understanding that concept. I'd bet he'd feign complete ignorance of the word *careful,* even if I tattooed it and its definition on his ass.

"You should try some meditation." Gus said, shaking his head. "All this stress can't be good for the baby."

"Meditation isn't my problem," I snapped, when I could talk again. "You are. Instead of driving me crazy and courting the wrath of the Weather Gods and the Winter Queen, why don't you try being patient for a fucking change?"

"Because fifty years is a geological pace," he snapped. "Not a Gus pace. "Think of it as helping a good cause."

"It's the Internet, Gus! Not everything you read is fact. In fifty years, Grundleshanks won't be decomposed, he'll be a freaking fossil."

I stomped off to my bedroom, followed by the (understandably anxious) puppies. Right now, they were the only company I wanted to share a room with.

Chapter 12

The next day, I woke up to parka weather, a cleaned-up living room and a depressed Gus. We were out of milk, but he was so contrite about the damage he had caused, when he saw me pouring decaf coffee on cereal, instead of poking fun at me or lecturing me about the evils of carbs, he ran out to the grocery store and completely restocked our kitchen.

As the week progressed, the weather warmed up. The first few days, we went from a wind chill of 120 below—so cold that the brakes in my car froze—to 30 degrees. It was so warm, it actually started snowing again. From there, the temperature kept climbing and the sparkly snow turned into wet, melted slush. Soon, the snow was replaced by a light rain. As it gently washed away the last of the slush and nourished the earth, winter was starting to feel a lot like spring. Especially when I took the puppies out in the woods and the mud was so deep, it almost pulled one of my hiking boots off. We all needed a bath after that walk.

Thankfully though, we had no repeat occurrences of indoor weather or that eerie voice. Since Gus swore he hadn't heard it, I was starting to wonder if it had been my imagination.

Gus, however, was still moping around. He wanted a ninety-degree heat wave and he wanted it now.

I almost felt sorry for him—until he waltzed into the kitchen one morning, throwing around attitude and judgmental looks.

"We need to replace the furniture."

"The furniture is fine. What we need to do, now that you're back, is nail it to the floor." I said. "There's no telling what kind of weather phenomenon you're going to call up next."

"It's dated."

"It's antique."

"It's too tacky to be antique."

"So says the King of Tacky. Wasn't your last coffee table a naked mermaid holding a glass disc?"

"That wasn't tacky. That was kitsch."

"What's the difference?"

"Kitsch is fun."

I snorted and took a carton of eggs out of the refrigerator. I was having mega-cravings for French Toast with powdered sugar.

"Oh no, you don't," Gus said, taking the carton out of my hand and putting it back in the fridge. He opened his wallet and pulled out a twenty. "Take your bad attitude and get ye gone, daughter of Eve. Forrest will be here any minute."

"Who the heck is Forrest?" I asked, confused. "And what happened to depressed Gus? Who let perky Gus out of his cage?"

Gus waggled his eyebrows at me. "That would be Forrest. He's the giddy-up in my go-go-go. He's the sugar in my lemonade. The color red in my crayon box."

"The cog in your cliche-machine. Got it. What happened with that Jack guy you hooked up with in Chicago?"

"You've got to keep up, girlfriend. Jack was so three weeks ago. I met Forrest at the gas station before I left for Chicago. I didn't think about him again, until I met him at the grocery store this week. Who knew your lack of domestic skills would land me a sweet thing like him? Decaf coffee on your cereal? Really?"

"Hey! It's a liquid."

"It's disgusting. Anyway, we went on our first date last night," he said, looking happier than I had seen him in awhile.

"And you didn't tell me?"

"You were asleep. That's all you do anymore. When you're not bitchin', you're sleepin'. Or eatin'."

"Baby on the way, hello." I said, pointing at my belly. "Cranky, tired and hungry pretty much defines my pregnancy."

"*What-evs,* baby mama. Besides, I didn't want to get your hopes up, if it didn't work out. Not to change the subject, but did you notice the outdoor thermometer? Sixty and climbing."

I sighed. "I really hope this weather thing doesn't bite us all in the ass."

There was the sound of a car horn outside.

"Speaking of ass-hickeys…" Gus ran to the front room to look out of the window. "There's my guy. Gotta go."

"Seriously? Are you providing drive-thru blowjobs now? Is that why he's not coming in?" I asked, following him. I felt snappish and surprisingly, more than a little jealous that someone new was now going to be taking up all of Gus's time.

"Get your mind out of the gutter, you nasty girl." Gus pulled out his cell phone and texted Forrest. "*Be right out.* Oooh, he says he's got a surprise for me."

"I hope it doesn't involve penicillin." I handed him back his twenty. "Can I go ahead and make my breakfast now? Since your new boyfriend doesn't have enough manners to come inside and pick you up?"

Gus made a face and blew me a kiss. "Try not to set the house on fire while I'm gone, Sybil. Maybe you could let one of your nicer personalities come out to play by the time I get back."

I flipped him off as he slammed out the front door.

*   *   *

After breakfast, I opened the windows to air out the house, then sat down at Aunt Tillie's desk. Although, I guess it was my desk now. I was still getting used to that idea, because the furniture still felt so much like Aunt Tillie. Maybe Gus was right about replacing it.

The puppies settled in by my feet for an after-meal nap and I booted up my laptop to see about getting him his own mini-fridge as a Yule present. I wondered how much it would cost to hire someone to build Gus his own little cottage get-away in the back yard. That way, he could move in there and stop annoying me so much.

After spending way too much time on shopping sites—mini-fridges weren't anywhere near as expensive as I thought they'd be, but custom-built sheds that looked like miniature log-cabin houses were *way* more than I could afford—I checked my bank account. It was dwindling at an alarming rate.

The online store wasn't making anywhere near the profit we had thought it would and with a baby on the way, money worries were burning a hole in my psyche. During my long month without Gus, I had gone out and tried to find a part-time job, but no one wanted to hire a pregnant woman. I was starting to feel the familiar cold fingers of fear and desperation wrapping around me, and I didn't like it one bit.

Chapter 13

As I searched online job sites, the room grew ice cold. The puppies stirred and looked around. They focused on the rocking chair and started to growl, in unison.

I sighed and shut down my laptop. Witches were hard enough on computers—I didn't want to take a chance on a ghost blowing the motherboard.

"I know you're here, Aunt Tillie. What's up?"

Aunt Tillie appeared in her rocking chair. "Divine bliss and eternal happiness got old. So I thought I'd drop in. Your mom and I have been discussing decorating ideas for the nursery." She looked me over and zoomed her focus into my belly. "The baby's doing well. Oh, look at that face. So cute!"

"Hey!" I said, covering my baby bump. "Stop looking inside my body like that. It creeps me out." After a second, I added "Really? Is the baby really doing well? Is it a she? It is, isn't it? Or is it a he?"

Aunt Tillie sniffed. "You said stop. So I did." She looked around, frowning. The windows were open, and outside, birds were singing and flowers were starting to bloom. "What month are we in? Isn't this supposed to be winter?"

"I think Gus's experimentation with weather magic may actually be working. Come back in a few days and I'll be in shorts and a tank top."

Aunt Tillie turned to me, her mouth a thin, tight line.

"Hey! Don't give me the stink-eye. I told him it was a bad idea."

"Eating month-old fish is a bad idea. Manipulating the weather is a catastrophic idea. He needs to turn this around now, or mark my words, you'll both regret it. You have no idea what kind of forces you're toying around with."

"I know," I said. "Messing with Mother Nature, B-A-D. I'll tell him."

"You are such an idiot. Grow a brain, girl, and do the MacDougal line proud."

"Is it MacDougal or McDougal?" I asked. "I've seen it both ways in the paperwork."

She gave me an odd look, as if I had derailed her train of thought by lobbing horseflies at her. "It was MacDougal in Scotland, but it was changed to McDougal by a careless clerk at Ellis Island. Americans always think they know best when it comes to spelling. Personally, I prefer Mac to Mc, but a hundred years from now, what will it matter? Now can we get back to the topic at hand?"

"I was hoping we were done with that topic," I said.

"So was I. I was hoping you'd learned your lesson with Lisette and the mess you got us all into. But here you are, doing it again."

"How is Gus's mess my fault?!"

"We both know that boy of yours can develop unhealthy obsessions, and he never thinks out the consequences. Mark my words, this weather ritual of his is going to bite both of you. And what he's planned next is even worse."

I blew out a cross sigh. Of course. That's why she was here. The toad bone ritual. "Gus just wants to honor Grundleshanks."

"Oh, he wants more than that." Aunt Tillie snapped. "He wants the type of dominion humans are not allowed to have."

I raised an eyebrow and gave her my best *don't be stupid* look.

Aunt Tillie didn't appreciate my attitude. A stack of books jumped off a shelf and crashed to the ground.

"Would you knock that off?" I said, annoyed. "Other people have done the ritual."

"Not many. Not often. And definitely not with *that* toad. You stupid children. You know just enough to get you into trouble and not enough to get you out. Why do you think the practice stopped?"

"Let me guess. Witches who tried and failed died, right? Isn't that how the line goes? You really need to chill with the dire warnings. Been there, done that, got the hoodie. They're losing their effectiveness."

"No," she said, equally annoyed. "Witches who failed were driven into madness and despair. Witches who succeeded died. The last thing I want is you two nincompoops showing up on my side of the Veil, destroying the place."

I couldn't decide if that was an insult or a left-handed compliment. "We don't particularly want to cross over yet, ourselves. And are you talking *all* witches, *most* witches or *some* witches? It couldn't have been *everyone*. The Horsemen didn't go mad or die. Or by die, did you mean, *eventually*? Because *eventually*, we're *all* going to die."

She harrumphed and gave me a cross-eyed stare. "Don't push me, or you'll find the toad bone isn't the only thing that can confer a fate worse than death. I don't know why I even bother with you two."

I sighed. "I've already told him to pull back on his rituals. What more do you want me to do?"

"Take the toad away from him."

"And tell him what? A mysterious toad thief struck in the middle of the night?"

"Why do you need to say anything? Haven't you ever heard of pleading the fifth, child? Throw the damn thing in the lake, and deny, deny, deny."

While I was thinking how annoying it was that people kept telling me what to do, no matter which side of the Veil they happened to be on, I must have fallen asleep.

The next thing I knew, the puppies were climbing up on my shoulders, their little puppy tongues licking me awake.

I set the puppies down and glanced over at Aunt Tillie's quietly rocking chair. I opened my sight and could sense her still there.

"Aunt Tillie?"

Either she wasn't in a talkative mood, or she had used up her ectoplastic energy for the day, because she remained silent.

Outside, the sun was shining so brightly, it was heating up the house and I was starting to sweat. I got up and went to the back door, to check the thermometer. The temperature had risen to seventy degrees.

What if Aunt Tillie was right? What was Gus's faux summer going to do to the natural order of things? Even worse, what if she was right about Grundleshanks? Would Gus go mad? Would we have to go into hiding? Was there such a thing as a Witches Protection Program? How badly were we going to be regretting everything, a month from now?

Chapter 14

Gus didn't come home that night. By the time I let the Dobies out for their morning gallop the next day, it was seventy-five degrees. I thought about going on a Grundleshanks-finding mission with the Dobes, but if they found the toad, it would not end well. And if I found him, queasy wouldn't even begin to cover my reaction.

Aunt Tillie was just going to have to deal with Gus on her own. If any ghost was capable of being a huge pain in the ass, it was my Aunt Tillie.

*   *   *

I pulled on an oversized tee-shirt and maternity jeans, and went to visit Paul's great-grandfather, Daniel. Since he was well over a century old, I wanted to make the most of any opportunities I had, to spend time with him.

The nursing home was on the outskirts of town, surrounded by an acre of land. It was surprisingly peaceful. The staff seemed to actually enjoy the oldsters and constantly thought of new activities they could do. Right now, Daniel was the reigning tournament champ of Wii bowling, although he had to cede his title in Wii boxing to an 80-year old newcomer.

When I got out of the SUV, the sun was bright and hot and cheerful and my guess was that the temperature was hovering around eighty degrees. I wondered what Daniel was going to say about the unusual weather.

*   *   *

I walked into his room just as Raoul, one of the nurses and a part-time stylist/barber/make-over artist for the oldsters, was finishing Daniel's shave.

"Hello, Miss Mara," he said, cheerfully.

"Have a seat," Daniel said. "I'm getting prettified. This may take awhile."

I sat down on the edge of the bed.

Raoul gently placed a steaming hot towel on Daniel's craggy jaw. "Let me know if it's too hot, sir."

Daniel cackled. "I have elephant hide for a face. Can't be too hot."

"What would you like today, for your hair cut?"

"Make me look like George Clooney. I got some hot young honeys I need to impress."

Raoul ruefully shook his head, grinning. "Ayyy, too bad I'm all out of miracles."

Daniel cackled. "You used them up giving Mrs. Norbert a full head of hair, didn't you?"

Raoul grinned. "You know I don't style-and-tell. Client-hairdresser privilege. How about a trim and blow dry?"

Daniel winked at me. "Don't get old," he said. "Life becomes all about settling."

"It's better than the alternative," I replied.

"There is that," he nodded, then turned his attention to Raoul. "If you can't do Clooney, let's go for Cary Grant."

"Mister Daniel," Raoul protested. "I'm a nurse, not a plastic surgeon."

I laughed. "You don't need a barber, Daniel. You need a magician. Too bad Houdini's dead."

"Hey, now," Daniel frowned. "Respect your elders, you young whippersnappers. Or I'll put both of you in a time-out."

"I'll tell you what," I said. "If Raoul can make you look anything like Cary Grant—even if it's Cary Grant's great-grandfather—I'll take you both out for dinner. You pick the day."

"Did you hear that? We have a challenge on our hands." Daniel said.

Raoul laughed. "Don't you worry, sir. We're going to win this bet."

"I pick a Monday." Daniel said. "Monday dinners are disgusting. Okra. Who the hell ever looked at okra and decided it was supposed to be edible?"

"Mondays work for me." Raoul said.

"Dinner time around here is four p.m. It'll be like a late lunch for you two young-in's. They like us to be in bed by eight. You'd think we were toddlers." Daniel flipped through his daily planner. "I'm booked for the next four Mondays, but the fifth one is all yours, sweetheart."

I took out my smartphone and added it to my calendar. "Done."

"I'm looking forward to it. I've heard all about you youngsters and your menage-a-trois Mondays," Daniel said, with a grin, waggling his freshly trimmed eyebrows.

"Oh, now, there'll be none of that," Raoul said, faking shock. "You'd better be on your best behavior, missy." He winked at me. "I don't want people saying you're buying us lunch just to get in our pants. Especially this strapping stud here," he said, nodding at Daniel. "The ladies will be beside themselves with jealousy."

"It'll be difficult, but I'll try to restrain myself." I could feel my lips twitching as I tried not to laugh.

"Hell with that. I'll let you grope me a little." Daniel chuckled. "Maybe even more than a little. Gotta keep up my reputation as a lady's man or all the chickens around here will be looking for a new rooster."

The door opened and Paul walked in, clearly surprised and a little angry to find me there.

Chapter 15

"Mara? What are you doing here?" Paul asked, frowning.

"Don't you go running off my girlfriend," Daniel warned him. "She's here to see me, not you. You're not the only cock of the walk in this town."

I smothered another grin. "It such a nice day, I thought Daniel and I could take a stroll around the garden."

"I'll see if I can squeeze you in on my dance card, young lady." Daniel chuckled. "I'm pretty hot stuff. And I'll be the bee's knees as soon as Raoul is finished with his magic." He checked his day planner. "Sorry, cookie. I'm seeing Gladys after lunch, Ruthie's my dinner companion and then I have an evening date with Carolyn, to watch The Great Gatsby."

"See how you are? As soon as the women start lining up for you, you forget all about me." I teased him.

"Never," he grinned. "But how often is summer going to show up in the middle of winter? Gotta strike while the iron's hot and the piston's are firing. If you don't use it, you lose it. That's a medical fact."

"Hold on, there," Paul frowned. "Don't you think you're being a little ambitious? And by date, what do you mean exactly?"

Daniel's face hardened. I looked into his mind and saw exactly what the answer was. It wasn't going to make Paul happy. The old man actually did have three different dates, with three different women, and Daniel was looking forward to a little night-time nookie with at least one of them.

I stepped in and covered for him. "Paul, knock it off. Daniel grew up in a more innocent time. I'm sure his idea of date and your idea of date are completely different."

"Not to mention, I'm a grown-ass man," Daniel fumed. "I changed your dirty diapers, boy. If I want to go out and walk the streets, looking for a good-time girl, it's none of your never-mind."

"Let's everyone calm down," I said. "Paul's just trying to look out for you, Daniel. He didn't mean it the bossy way it sounded."

Paul was about to protest, so I shot him a dirty look to shut him up. I didn't know what would happen if they started fighting and Daniel's blood pressure got too high, and I didn't want to find out. So I pushed that thought as hard as I could at Paul.

Somehow, Paul got the message and shut up.

Daniel harrumphed a few times, but he settled down too.

Then it suddenly dawned on me: *I had looked into Daniel's mind.* Whoa!

* * *

While it had always been easy for me to tell if people were lying or not, this was the first time I had looked into someone's head and saw their thoughts as clearly as if I was watching a TV show, or reading a book.

It *had* to be Devil's Point. It seemed to magnify everything, from ritual work to pineal gland abilities. I know it was bad of me, but I opened up my sight and dipped into all the minds in the room—just to see if I could do it.

Along with wondering how in the world he was going to make Daniel look like Cary Grant, Raoul was thinking about going home to his family. His shift was going to be over in another hour, and his wife was making homemade tamales. They were expecting another baby, and his thoughts were a jumble of anticipation, nervousness, worry about money and nostalgia about his grandmother's tamales.

Paul, on the other hand, was fuming. And he was angry with both Daniel and me. He was scared Daniel's social schedule was going to kill the old man, and he was furious that I kept butting into his life. I was the equivalent of a one-night stand from hell, who would never go away. If he could do it over again, he would have totally accepted jail time and fines for texting and driving instead of giving me his cell phone and getting mixed up in my craziness...

I gasped, hurt and angry, temporarily drawing everyone's attention to me.

"Sorry," I said. "I thought I saw a spider."

Paul rolled his eyes.

On the other hand, maybe it was all my imagination. What if I was just supplying their thoughts, rather than reading them?

To test it out, I asked Raoul: "I heard your wife is expecting. Is it your first time having a baby?"

Raoul chuckled while he focused on Daniel's hair cut. "No, this is our second. My wife, she wants to stay home with the kids until they're in kindergarten."

"I can understand why. That's got to be hard on you though, if you're the only one working."

Raoul nodded. "But kids, they need their mama. So, if I need to take another job, it's what I have to do."

"Isn't that sweet? So, you have a traditional marriage? You make the money, while she stays home to raise the kids, clean the house and cook? Does she cook? I tell people I cook, but what I mean by cooking, is heating up TV dinners."

Paul gave me an odd look, but Raoul chuckled. "*Si*. Tonight, she is making chicken tamales, from my *abuela's* recipe."

"Why did you want to know that?" Paul asked.

"I just wondered if my lack of domestic skills was a female aberration or an evolutionary sea-change," I lied. "Looks like aberration is winning."

Huh. So, I had pegged Raoul's thoughts. Which meant that I also, probably, had an accurate read on Paul's thoughts.

Well, that was depressing.

Raoul finished up Daniel's trim, put talcum powder on his neck, and flicked away the cut hairs with a soft brush.

"You're all done, sir," he said, taking the plastic cape off Daniel.

"How do I look?" Daniel asked me, preening and pointedly ignoring Paul.

"Just like Cary Grant's… great-great-grandfather." I said.

Daniel mock-frowned at me.

"But I'll still spring for dinner," I quickly added.

"On to my next victim," Raoul said, winking at me. He was really cute and funny and sweet. I could see why his wife was so in love with him.

It was funny because, until I dipped into Raoul's head, I thought he was gay. Having spent so many years in Los Angeles, my basic assumption is that all guys are gay, unless they prove otherwise. I really had to knock that off though. I kept tripping over my assumptions out here and falling on my face.

When Raoul opened the door to leave, a waft of strong perfume knocked me back. I must have turned green, because the next thing I knew, Daniel was offering me a plastic vomit bowl and a cup of water.

"No, I'm good," I said, pushing the bowl away. "I'll take the water though."

"Is it still your stomach?" Paul asked, confused.

"I'm sure it is," Daniel cackled.

"What the hell are you eating?" Paul asked. "No one has food poisoning for that long."

"Here you go, honey," Daniel said, ignoring Paul. He opened the drawer of his bedside table and handed me a small bag of candied ginger. "Good for nausea. My wife used to swear by it when she was pregnant. I can't eat it anymore. Gets stuck in my dentures."

I felt Paul stiffen as I took the bag and popped a piece of ginger in my mouth. Before I got pregnant, I never thought ginger would work for nausea, but it totally does. I actually started feeling better.

"She's not pregnant," Paul said, woodenly. "She ate some bad shrimp."

"Oh, loosen up, boy," Daniel clapped him on the back. "You can't keep something like that a secret. Not from me. I may be old, but I have the sight of an eagle. An old eagle with trifocals. But an eagle, none-the-less."

I forced myself to smile. "Can't keep anything from you, Daniel."

Paul shot me a dirty look—well, dirty was simplifying it. It was more a look of questioning horror.

"So, do we know? Is it a boy or a girl? Nothing gladdens my heart more than having another wee one in the family."

"Speak for yourself, old man." Paul muttered, his face darkening.

"What did you say, boy?"

"Nothing."

"You'd better watch your step, you little whippersnapper." Daniel pounded his cane on the floor. "Speak up or hold your peace. Mumbling is just rude."

"I think it's a girl." I said, interrupting Paul before he could repeat his comment. "But Gus, my roommate, thinks it's a boy."

Daniel hugged me and kissed my cheek. "Mazel tov! Well, I'm off to see my next honey. You two behave yourselves. And if you don't, have them change the sheets."

He cackled and hobbled off, leaving us alone in his room to talk.

As soon as the door had closed behind him, Paul turned to me, furious. "Pregnant?!"

Chapter 16

I sighed. "I was going to tell you..."

"When?!" He exploded. "You were going to tell me, when?"

I shrugged. In the delivery room clearly wasn't the right answer. "Soon. I didn't want to screw with your therapy."

"Are you kidding me?! You just found out I was in therapy. How far along are you?" He ran his hand through his wiry blond hair.

I tried to do the math. "I don't know. Beginning of the second trimester, I think."

"Damn it. Still. Maybe it's not too late." Paul took his cell phone out of his pocket. "Hell, even if you were about to give birth, I'm sure we could find someone willing to fix things."

"What are you talking about? I don't need anyone to fix anything."

He ignored me as he searched the Internet on his phone, until he finally found what he was looking for. "Here it is. We can be there in twenty minutes. Let's go."

He reached out to grab my arm.

I plopped down on the bed and held onto the frame. "I'm not going anywhere with you."

"Yes, you are. I have a friend who works at the Planned Parenthood Clinic in Oldfield."

"That's ridiculous. Even if I was remotely interested, which I'm not, you can't just drop by doctor's offices unannounced."

"We can call while we drive, set you up with an appointment."

"No," I said.

He hit the call button on his cell phone. "Fine. I'll call him now. Our lives can be back to normal by tomorrow."

"Like hell," I said, tightening my hold on the bed frame. "I am not getting rid of this baby."

He hit 'end call' and frowned at me, exasperated. "It's not a baby. It's a... It's a... it could be a freaking demon for all you know."

"Or not. It could just be a normal, innocent baby."

"Innocent, my ass. You got pregnant when that... thing... was happening."

He couldn't even bring himself to say the words. I couldn't blame him. Being possessed was hard enough. Finding out that you impregnated someone while you were possessed had to be tough.

"My body, my choice. You have no say in the matter." I glared at him.

"Like hell I don't." He glared back. "My body was involved in that little transaction too. Unless it was some kind of immaculate conception, my say counts."

"Since the baby's growing in my body, I have two votes to your one."

He threw up his hands in frustration. "Grow up."

"Fine. Let's talk paternity. What if it happened during that one crazy night at the poly-party? What if it's someone else's? Why should you get a say if we don't even know for sure if you're the father?" I snapped.

He yelled, "What if it's got hooves instead of feet?"

"Then I'll buy a pooper-scooper instead of diapers." I folded my arms in front of my chest, giving him my most stubborn look. "The only thing we know for sure, is that I'm the mom. My body, my baby, my decision. You can butt the hell out."

We continued glaring at each other for a bit. Don't get me wrong, I'm a pro-choice kind of woman. But, in this case, I had made my choice and I would be damned if I let Paul bully me, just because he was scared.

I looked past him, out the window. Staring at Daniel and his date in the flower garden was easier than looking at Paul right now.

"You can make the choice whether or not you want to participate in raising the baby, but you can not make the choice whether or not I'm going to give birth to it."

He paced the small room. "Either I get an equal say, or you can forget putting my name down on the birth certificate."

"I'll put whatever the fuck I want on the birth certificate. You can have a say in things when you stop being a total jackass." I snapped. "Not being named on a birth certificate doesn't magically absolve you if this is your kid. You want to be an absentee father, that's fine. You're going to have to live with that decision. Whether or not I have this child is something I will have to live with for the rest of my life. And I've made my decision."

He sighed and sat down in a chair. "Fine. Let's start with getting a DNA test done. The sooner we find out what's going on with that baby, the better."

"As soon as it's born, I will pluck out a hair follicle for you, myself."

"No. Now. There's an O.B. in that new Medical Center in Oldfield. Let's go have him do an amnio. See what we're dealing with."

I gasped. "There is no freaking way."

"Why not?!" He asked, mystified.

"Because amnios can cause miscarriages. And I'm not having a CVS done either. I'm not having some hack, backwoods doctor accidentally lopping fingers or toes off the baby while it's still developing. So you can just forget about it. There will be no invasive testing, period. You can wait until its born, just like the rest of us."

Paul looked like he was ready to strangle me. "I am not going to be stuck supporting a baby with birth defects, genetic mutations or three heads. So you'd better do something. Or I will." He said, his voice thick with threat.

* * *

I jumped in the SUV and turned the radio up to an ear-splitting volume. I tore off so fast, the tires squealed. The oldsters and staff who were out enjoying the mild weather, shot me such dirty looks, I felt like I was going to be single-handedly responsible for a run on blood pressure meds.

By the time I left the grounds, the seat belt warning was screaming and I was starting to get a headache.

Aunt Tillie's voice yelled above the din. "Pull over and buckle your seat belt, young lady. Stop acting like a petulant child."

She waved her hand and the car promptly lost power.

I turned the key in the ignition, but got nowhere.

I glared at her. Damn ghosts. Once she found out she could control electronics, there was no stopping her.

"I'm not a child!" I protested, buckling up.

"And you're not going to live long enough to have one, if you keep driving like that. I can tell you from experience, the trees are not very forgiving."

"I'm just mad." I grumbled.

"So, do what other pissed-off pregnant women do. Go shopping. Don't you have a baby to buy for?"

She blinked out and the car started up again. I turned the radio down and thought about it. Aunt Tillie was right. Maybe I could channel my anger into a productive shopping trip. There were still a lot of things I needed. Especially since I didn't have family to turn to for hand-me-downs.

I drove over to the mall in Oldfield and blew a hole in my bank account, making the idea of the baby as permanent as I possibly could. Then I went home to cry on Gus's shoulder, but of course, he was out with Forrest.

So I loaded the Dobies in the car and we drove around Devil's Point to check out Christmas decorations. Between the businesses and cheerily-decorated houses, the town's collective light bill had to be astronomical.

Oddly enough, as much as I had complained about the winter weather, I missed the snow, now that it was gone. It wasn't the same, looking at Christmas decorations in grassy yards. Now that it was warm enough to wear shorts and tank tops, it didn't feel like Christmas anymore.

Chapter 17

The next morning, I heard Gus banging around in the kitchen when I woke up. He must have put the Dobies out in the run, since they weren't milling around my feet like they usually did. Most people think Dobies need a lot of space, but they're the perfect apartment dog. All they need is the three square feet of space around their owner.

I should get a tee-shirt made: "Owning a Dobe means never going to the bathroom alone—no matter how much you might want to." Not that I got much privacy with Gus either, but at least I could beat him to the door and lock him out.

I brushed my teeth and wandered downstairs in my pajamas.

* * *

"Hey, whatever you're doing in there, I hope it culminates in food hitting my stomach. I'm starving!" I said, walking into the kitchen.

The Dobes were on the floor by the stove, their eyes following Gus's every move. He was in *crazy chef* mode. The counter and kitchen table were cluttered with ingredients and cooking tools, the stovetop crammed with skillets and bubbling pots.

"A feast can't just be pulled out of thin air, Sleeping Beauty. It takes preparation," he said, stirring a pot.

A feast? Then I remembered. Gus had decided we needed to

celebrate Misrule early this year and he was going to kick it off with a Supper for the Dead.

"But that's not until tonight."

"You'll ruin your appetite by eating now." He grabbed a pan of melted butter off the stove and brushed it onto layers of thin *phyllo* dough.

"Can I get a corner of space for a tiny bowl of cereal?"

"You're out of cereal."

"What? I still had a full box of chocolate-frosted sugar squares."

"*Had* being the operative word. Do you have any idea how bad sugar is for you?"

"Are you serious? You tossed my cereal?! That's not fair."

"It's the Time of Misrule. Time to turn your eating habits on their heads."

"No, it's not. Wrong on both counts. You're fucking with the schedule, like you're fucking with my food. Misrule is the twelve days after Christmas, not the twelve days before Yule."

"I'm a witch, dear heart. Which means, if I want to bring the spirit of Misrule into play before Yule, I can."

I snorted. "You can *try*. Doesn't mean it'll work. There has to be a rule against moving holidays around to suit your whims."

"Rules are for sycamores. Witches are rebels and rule-breakers. Witches have ethics, not rules. And my ethics are fine with me moving it to any time between Samhain and Imbolc. If the Catholic church can demote saints, I can move Misrule to a more convenient date."

"Seeing as how freaking bossy you're getting, we should call this the Time of Gus's Rule instead of Misrule."

"I'm okay with that. In fact, I like it. Welcome to the Time of Gus's Rule. Get used to doing what I say. And what I say is... your diet is the first thing on the chopping block."

I rolled my eyes. "I've been trying to eat healthier."

"Not much," he snorted.

"This is Sunday. Whatever happened to 'eat-anything-you-want' Sundays? And I didn't make that up. It was in that article you gave me."

"You'll thank me when you don't have gestational diabetes."

While Gus checked on the spinach, I tried to get in the refrigerator, but he was quicker.

He moved me aside. "Excuse me, Chef working here. This fridge isn't big enough for the both of us," he said, digging through the shelves.

A rumbly growl sounded from my midsection. "My stomach is lodging a formal complaint. If I can't have food now, I'm going to start gnawing on the furniture."

"At least you'll be getting some fiber."

"Gus!"

"Tell your stomach to chill. I'm a little busy."

"I haven't eaten anything since last night. Move over and let me at the food or I'm not going to be responsible for what happens to you."

"You should have woken up while it was still morning. The breakfast bar is closed."

"Cut me some slack. I'm growing a baby. It's tiring and hungry work."

Gus was still shifting ingredients around.

"What are the odds of me getting lunch out of that fridge, before I knock you unconscious and toss you on the barbecue?"

"Depends on whether or not you want a sandwich."

"Gus! Don't tell me you threw out the bread!"

"Flour is the new sugar." He handed me a bag of baby carrots.

I wrinkled my nose. "Unless these are made of weird-looking Twinkies dipped in orange frosting, I'll take option B."

"You keep feeding that baby your normal Frankenwheat, partially-hydrogenated, high-fructose corn syrup diet and you're going to give birth to a Twinkie. Obviously, I didn't come home soon enough."

Ever since we found out I was pregnant, Gus had been e-mailing me articles on the evils of carbohydrates, sugar and gluten. I dutifully downloaded them into a folder on my computer. I just hadn't read them.

I bit into a carrot. It wasn't half-bad. Sweet and crunchy. "I can't live on carrots."

"Here, diversify," Gus said, tossing me an orange.

"This is cruel and unusual punishment. Humans weren't meant to live on fruits and vegetables alone."

He snorted. "Deal with it." But he went back in the fridge and pulled out a leftover piece of salmon from his dinner date with Forrest.

I was going to turn it down, but my stomach growled and the baby practically reached out for it on her own.

"Don't forget to chew," Gus said.

I consciously slowed down my eating. But, wow, did this baby like fish. Salmon and cream-of-spinach soup were at the top of my list of cravings.

"Why do we need to celebrate Misrule now, anyway? Why can't we wait until after Christmas, like normal pagans?"

"It's not Misrule. It's Gus's Rule. You came up with it. I like it. We're keeping it."

"So... we celebrate Gus's Rule now and Misrule after Christmas?"

"Nope. Sorry, love. Forrest is taking me on a trip to Hawaii after Christmas. So, celebrate Gus's Rule with me now, or not at all."

My jaw dropped. "You just got back from being out of town!"

"Life is short, Miss Thing. I intend to live it to the fullest."

Gus went to check on a delicious-smelling leg of lamb in the stove. Seeing my opportunity to get into the fridge and add something chocolate to my plate, I slid off the chair and walked over to check out the contents.

Dang it. Not only was the sandwich bread gone, so was my chocolate stash, ice cream, frozen pancakes, American cheese, hot dogs, frozen french fries, chicken nuggets, ice cream toppings and maraschino cherries.

I searched through the cabinets. No creamy hazelnut chocolate spread, no ramen noodles, no mac and cheese, no potato chips, no cheesy puffs, no cookies.

"Are you kidding me?!" I said, practically screaming. "Is that why you didn't want me in the fridge? So I wouldn't see that everything was gone? Did you leave me *anything!?*"

"What are you talking about? This kitchen is filled with healthy stuff. Protein, dairy, fruit, vegetables and legumes."

"I want my faux food back!"

"Processed sugar, salt and fat are not only addictive, they're toxic. Your body is your temple. Stop desecrating it."

I glared at him. "You're taking your life in your hands, getting between a pregnant lady and her comfort food."

"I'm doing it for your own good. Besides, even if you're too stubborn to realize how right I am, your baby will be thanking me the minute it comes out of the womb. '*Thank you, MacDaddy Gus, thank you for saving me from that crazy lady's food addiction*'."

I snorted. "My baby's going to kick your ass for depriving her of chocolate. Did you feed the dogs? Or did you toss their food out too?"

"Of course I fed the monsters. I'm all about self-preservation. Last thing I need is them gnawing on my arm because they're feeling peckish. Is that all you wanted?"

"No." I poured myself a glass of milk, liberated a giant wedge of Jarlsberg Swiss cheese and filled Gus in on the argument with Paul.

"Screw him," Gus said, wiping his hands on a kitchen towel. "Put me down on the birth certificate, instead."

Chapter 18

"What? Really? Wow." Gus wanted to be my kid's dad? That totally took me by surprise.

"Why not?" he asked. "Unlike wuss-boy, I've always wanted a demon witch baby. And if it's born with horns, that's a bonus. Paul can go fuck himself."

I nodded. "Let me think about it."

And I did. And I realized that actually, I was okay with Gus being my baby's MacDaddy. Even if Aunt Tillie was on the fence about him. Which reminded me…

"Aunt Tillie says put the weather back where it belongs or else. And she's not too happy about the toad ritual either. She was all, *'there are fates worse than death'-y* about it."

Gus stopped stirring and gave me an annoyed look.

"Don't blame me. She's the one who's freaking out. She says the weather thing's going to bite us, and your plan for Grundleshanks will bring madness or death—at some point. She wasn't clear on the timetable. But she sounded pretty pissed off. And a pissed-off Aunt Tillie is never a good thing."

"Sometimes I wonder," he said, narrowing his eyes.

"What does that mean?!" I asked, indignant.

"Nothing." He went back to stirring. Then he stopped. "I just think it's odd that you're the only one who can see her anymore."

"I know. It's totally odd." I shrugged. "And she's not being all poltergeisty either. She's using her words instead of flying knives. Maybe she used up her mojo."

Suddenly, it dawned on me what he was really saying.

"Wait, just one gosh-darned minute, mister," I snapped. "Are you trying to say that I'm making her up?!"

He shrugged. "Maybe. Maybe not."

I stared at him. "I'm about three seconds away from throwing your clothes into a wood chipper."

"Oh, relax. Of course, I believe you—at least, I believe that *you* think you're talking to your Aunt Tillie."

"Excuse me?" I asked, icily.

"I just think you may be being unduly influenced by your own fears."

"It's not *me*. Personally, I don't care what you do with Grundleshanks's bones. It's between you and the toad. I'm staying out of it."

"Tell it to your subconscious."

"It's not my subconscious! It's Aunt Tillie. You're pissing her off royally. She wants you to undo the weather and forget about the toad, before it's too late."

"Uh-huh. So, did good ol' meddlesome Aunt Tillie tell us how?"

I rubbed my forehead. This conversation was starting to give me a headache. "Seriously? You cranked up the sun and you don't know how to undo it?"

Gus snorted. "I meant about our dire *worse-than-death* fate?"

"She never elaborates on that. Just drops those D-bombs and vanishes." I shrugged. "Knowing Aunt Tillie, it'll probably be at her hands. Maybe she'll run us over with a car, or shove us into the lake."

Gus snorted. "I'd like to see her try."

"Don't tempt her. She's grown quite a homicidal streak since she died. Did you seriously not have a plan to restore winter? That *had* to be part of your negotiation."

He sighed. "I barely had time to ask for summer to return until I could do the toad bone ritual, before you pulled me back."

I could feel the air rushing out of my lungs, like I had just gotten punched in the gut. "Did you say *until* you can do the ritual?"

"Yes. So, if I don't do it, summer's here permanently and that's going to suck for a whole lot of people. If I do the ritual, according to your Aunt Tillie, we may be looking at a dire *worse-than-death* fate. So, tell me, what am I supposed to do?"

Fuck. No wonder she thinks Gus and I are witchy menaces. We pretty much are.

"What happens if Aunt Tillie kills you before you can do the ritual?" I asked.

"We'll have one hell of a drought."

"I'm being serious."

He shrugged. "I'm sure the weather will undo itself, eventually. Nature will always right the balance. Even if she has to flip the poles to accommodate the reversal in seasons."

"We are so totally screwed," I said.

"Damned if I do, damned if I don't," he agreed. "Caught between the Devil and the deep blue sea."

"Well, it's been nice knowing you. So… do we have anything around here for dessert? If you're going to kill us, I want chocolate first."

He pointed a wooden stirring spoon at me. "See the fruit bowl on the counter? Take a banana and get out. *Now*. Before I feed your portion of tonight's dinner to the dogs."

Aramis and Apollo wagged their stumpy tails. They were completely on board with that outcome.

* * *

I put one of Gus's classical music CDs in the player, plopped down on a chair and tried to focus on something else—anything else—other than weather and toads.

The baby stretched and I patted my tummy. "Sorry about yesterday, kiddo. I know your dad sounds like a jerk, but he's been going through a hard time. I'm sure he'll love you just as much as I do, once you're born."

I had to snort. Even I didn't believe that one. I'd have to pull the tarot cards and see what they had to say about Paul and the baby—assuming they were still talking to me. They got touchy about being ignored, and since I hadn't used them in awhile, it was a bit of a toss-up about how responsive they were going to be.

"Well, okay, even if he doesn't love you as much, it doesn't matter. With Gus around, you're going to get a lot of daddy love."

The more I thought about it, the more pulling the cards sounded like a great idea. Maybe I could get some insight into the corner Gus had backed himself into. I went to the shelves to get my velvet card bag, but it wasn't there. I searched the room. Nothing. I expanded the search to the cottage, but I couldn't find it anywhere.

I went back downstairs, and plopped down on the couch, seriously disturbed. It's not like cards can go off on their own. Where could they possibly be?

The ghost of Grundleshanks appeared on the side table and stared at me.

"Hey, Grundle. Have you seen my cards? They were in a blue velvet bag?"

He made a croaking sound. In my belly, I felt the baby turn to look at him.

Wait a minute...

The baby could sense Grundleshanks's spirit.

Chapter 19

"Well. That's an interesting turn of events." I muttered.

Gus was going to hate being out-numbered in the *Seeing Dead People* department.

"What are you doing here anyway, Grundleshanks?" I asked.

"Bored," popped into my head.

"I can understand that. You were definitely more fun when you were alive," I said.

The doorbell rang. The Dobies raced out of the kitchen to hurl themselves against the front door.

"Can you get that?!" Gus hollered. "I have my hands full!"

* * *

I pushed past the barking, snarling fiends and opened the door to find Paul standing there. Once the Dobies realized he wasn't a serial killer, they quieted down.

"I thought you'd be awake by now. It's after noon," he said, pointedly looking at my pajamas and mussed up hair.

"Since when did you become the sleep police?" I replied, testily.

"Who is that?" Gus hollered from the kitchen.

"It's for me," I hollered back. "It's Paul."

I heard a muffled curse, before Gus closed the kitchen door.

I stood in the doorway and contemplated Paul. "I thought you weren't talking to me."

He sighed. "You dropped a bomb on me, Mara. What kind of reaction did you expect?"

"I don't know. But I'm feeling kind of nauseous and I have to pee, so whatever you want, make it snappy." I didn't really, but I figured it would encourage him to leave.

He looked a bit taken aback.

I cleared my throat. "What do you want, Paul?"

He shifted from one foot to the other and stared down at his hiking boots. "To apologize."

"Really?" That was totally unexpected.

"Can we go somewhere and talk?" He looked up and gave me a lopsided smile.

I opened the door wider. "Come in."

He hesitated and nervously licked his lips. I got a sudden flash of what was going on in his head.

He was afraid.

I couldn't blame him. Last time he had walked into my cottage, his life had been blown apart.

Apollo, the red Dobie, slid past me, out the front door, and leaned against Paul's legs. Paul bent to pet him and I watched, fascinated, as calmness and strength flowed out of Apollo and into Paul.

That was new and different. I didn't know the Dobes could do that.

Finally, taking a deep breath, Paul came inside, Apollo leaning against him the entire way. I led them into the living room. Paul tentatively sat down on the couch. Apollo jumped up next to him and rested his head on Paul's leg.

I sat down in the armchair, Aramis sat next to me, and we both watched Paul relax as he continued to pet Apollo.

"I've been thinking about what you said. I called a high-risk pregnancy O.B. in Trinity Harbor and he told me about a Center that specializes in genetic testing."

I took a breath to protest.

He raised his hand to stop me. "Hear me out. The Center uses 3D ultrasounds to detect Down's syndrome in fetuses. It's non-invasive, and we'd get a clear picture of the baby. We'd actually be able to see the baby's face."

That sounded interesting. I really wanted to see what my baby looked like and whether or not I was right about the gender. While I didn't think there would be any birth defects, a non-invasive way to make sure would be great. But Trinity Harbor was so far away and it sounded like a hugely expensive proposition.

"If you can see for yourself that the baby doesn't have horns, or an extra head or hooves for feet, do you think you could not treat it like a sideshow freak when it's born?"

Silence from him as he petted Apollo.

Then: "I'll still want a paternity test."

I sighed. "Of course you will. Okay, let's say I'm on board. How much is it going to cost?"

"Insurance covers it."

"And if you don't have insurance?"

Paul gave me a look. "They only accept insurance. They don't take checks."

"That's us out, then."

"Are you kidding me? You don't have health insurance?" Paul tensed up again, the veins in his neck bulging.

Apollo edged forward on top of his lap, until his front legs and chest were on Paul, effectively pinning him down.

Paul took a deep breath. "Mara. Do you have any idea what hospitals and doctors and anesthesiologists cost? How are you going to afford to have the baby?"

I shrugged. That question had been keeping me up nights. "I don't know. I'm still working out the details."

Paul looked completely flabbergasted. "That's not acceptable."

"Women used to have babies in fields."

"They used to die in childbirth, too. But now we have modern medicine."

"I have to work with what I've got," I said, exasperated.

"This whole thing is completely unacceptable."

"What do you want me to do? Sales in our online store have been non-existent and no one wants to hire a preggie. I've been looking. My options are kind of limited."

"Are you taking prenatal vitamins at least?"

"Of course I am," I snapped. "And I'm seeing Doc Brady for check-ups." Thankfully, the doc was willing to trade well-visits for spellcrafting candles, incense and mojo bags, or I'd be in even worse shape.

Paul gave me an annoyed look. "Don't get snippy with me. I'm just trying to figure out what's going on."

"I'm sorry," I said. "I don't mean to. It's not like I don't want health insurance."

He sighed. "Then I'll have to figure out a way to get you insured, won't I?"

"Really?" I asked, surprised.

"Yes."

I hoped he had a good game plan up his sleeve. "You know, it's times like this I remember why I wanted to have sex with you to begin with." I quipped.

He moved Apollo off his lap and stood up, barely cracking a smile. "I'll text you the info about the Center."

As I walked him to the door, I asked how his therapy sessions were going.

"They suck."

That surprised me. "Why?"

"Because every time I make any forward progress, you hit me with something new."

"Oh," I could feel my face flush. "Sorry."

"It's okay," he muttered, clearly not meaning it.

He bent and petted Apollo's head again.

The dog was sticking to him like Velcro.

"He really likes you. Why don't you take him home and work with him for a bit?"

Paul looked at me, quizzically. "What are you talking about?"

"I read about Dobermans being used as therapy dogs. And the two of you seem to really get along well." I stopped, as a cloud passed across Paul's face.

I had to tread lightly. If I made it seem like I was doing him a favor, he might nix the whole thing. But if I could turn it around...

"Taking care of two big dogs, Gus, and soon a baby... it's just too much for me. If you could help me out, by taking Apollo for a little bit—just until I get my groove going—that would really be awesome."

He paused and thought about it. "I do too much traveling to have a full-time dog."

"It wouldn't be a permanent thing. Just for a little while. I'm good with joint custody," I said. "It'll be good practice for when the baby gets here."

"Let me think about it." Apollo licked his hand and Paul cracked the first genuine smile I had seen on him, in a long time.

*   *   *

After Paul left, I went to take a shower and change. Apollo trotted over to the kitchen to see about scraps, but Aramis glued himself to me so tightly, he got soaking wet from the shower. So I bathed him and clipped his nails. When Apollo came in to check on us, I bathed him as well.

Gus had propped the kitchen door open, and a delectable heat was slowly filling the cottage. By late afternoon there were so many yummy smells coming from the kitchen, I was having a foodgasm.

I checked to see if anything was ready to be carried out, but Gus was being all "you sit your pregnant butt down, little lady, and let the man do the work."

With Apollo following him, he hiked supplies down to our little cemetery in the woods. I was hungry again, so I went into the kitchen and grabbed a plum to tide me over. I was just washing it when the doorbell rang, startling me.

The plum dropped out of my hand, into the garbage disposal. I fished it out and tossed it where the garbage can used to be. To my surprise, it dropped and rolled on the floor.

I looked around. *Where the heck was the garbage can?*

Unless he hid it for some reason, Gus must have taken it to the cemetery.

The doorbell rang again, insistent.

"Hold on! I'm coming!"

Geez, it was like Union Station around here. After weeks of having no visitors, I was suddenly inundated with people.

I picked up the plum and tossed it in the sink, to throw out later. Maybe I could leave it outside for woodland creatures. It would probably be okay for them, right?

I opened the door, expecting to find Paul, but instead, I found the suave older guy, with the dazzling blue eyes, from the diner.

Chapter 20

He had a large box at his side. He smiled at me and nodded, as if I should be expecting him—as if we were old friends.

"What are you doing here?" I asked, alarmed.

The wards hadn't gone off, so the guy must not be a danger to the cottage, but that didn't mean he wasn't a danger to me. What kind of nut tracks you down at your home address?

Aramis growled at him from behind the safety of my legs. That was unusual. Normally, he'd be in front of me, snapping his teeth in the famous Dobie smile that terrified strangers.

"Aren't you going to invite me in?" the man asked, politely smiling.

"No. How did you find out where I lived, anyway?"

He shrugged. "It's a small town."

"It still has a police force."

"Are you always this rude to your guests?" he asked. And he smiled again. He had perfect, almost sparkling, white teeth with sharp incisors.

"What are you talking about? You're no guest of mine."

"Are you sure about that?"

"I think I would know. What do you want?"

"What do you think I want?"

I peeked out at the street. A bright red luxury sports car with dealer plates was parked by the curb. "Did you get lost on your way to the gas station?"

"No."

"I give up. Are you selling Girl Scout Cookies?"

"Do I look like a Girl Scout?" he said, grinning.

"Avon?"

"No. Not Mary Kay, either. Try again."

"Census taker?"

"Nada."

I was starting to get exasperated. I always hated being put on the spot to cough up *fill-in-the-blank* answers when I was a kid, and this was feeling a lot like a *fill-in-the-blank* conversation.

"Are you a Jehovah's Witness? Because I'll tell you right now, if you are, Gus will want to talk to you. In fact, he may want to sacrifice you to Cthulu. So you should probably run while you can."

The man laughed, a deep baritone laugh, his cheeks creasing into dimples. "I take it Gus is an H.P. Lovecraft fan?"

"On alternate Fridays. Okay... Well, it was nice talking to you. Goodbye." I tried to close the door, but he blocked it.

"Is this an appropriate way to treat a gentleman caller?" He asked, raising an eyebrow.

"I told you at the diner, I wasn't entertaining any gentlemen callers."

"I'm not here for you. I'm here for Gus. I never turn down an invite to a night of Misrule." He held out his cell phone, so I could see Gus's text message.

"You're... Forrest?!" I asked, incredulous. I felt my cheeks get hot.

"Nice to officially meet you," he said.

I tried not to let the disappointment show on my face. He wasn't supposed to be here. Tonight was just supposed to be me and Gus.

And then I realized that I must have looked like an idiot at the diner, assuming his interest had been in me.

"Are you going to let me in?"

"Sure. I guess so. Come on in. Welcome to Gus's Rule. Formerly known as Misrule." I stepped aside, so he and his box would have room to enter.

"Gus's Rule?"

"He can explain it."

Once Forrest was inside, Aramis calmed down and sniffed at the box.

"You don't have any livestock in there, do you? Or more vegetables?"

"It's a surprise for Gus." He sniffed the dinner aromas appreciatively. "I take it he's in the kitchen?"

"Why would you assume that?" I asked. "I know how to cook."

"Not like that, you don't." He laughed. "Gus is a *gourmand*. I just hope he's made enough. I know how you pregnant women get about your food. I would rather not have you gnawing on my arm."

I rolled my eyes. At least I could hear movement in the kitchen, so Gus must have returned.

*   *   *

"Forrest!" Gus said, obviously thrilled. "Sexy shirt. It brings out the blue in your eyes."

Forrest put his box down on the floor next to the kitchen counter, and Gus embraced him.

I remembered about the plum I had left in the sink and went to toss it outside, but it was gone.

When they broke their clinch, I pulled Gus aside.

"Gus? Where's the plum?" I asked. "It was in the sink."

Gus looked at me like I was an idiot. "I ate it."

I gasped.

"I know. It was the last one. I'll get you more tomorrow."

"It's not that." I said.

I looked over at Forrest. He was busy opening the box and ignoring us.

I turned back to Gus and lowered my voice. "That plum fell in the garbage disposal."

"Ewww. I thought it tasted weird. Why didn't you throw it out?"

"Because you vanished the garbage can!"

"I didn't vanish it, I relocated it."

"Why would you eat something that's sitting in the sink,

anyway? It's not like I had left it on the counter."

"I was craving the firm, tart sweetness that only a plum can supply. And it was the last one."

"Fruit addiction is an ugly thing." I snapped, using his own accusation against him. "Do you know what kind of nasty, moldy, bacteria-laden stuff gets tossed down the disposal?"

"I'm sure it'll be fine. I rinsed it first."

I looked at him, darkly. "Right. Tell me if your insides feel like they're going to explode."

Forrest cleared his throat, interrupting us. "Ta-da!"

He stepped aside, doing the big reveal, and I yelped in surprise. There, sitting on the counter, was a lit-up aquarium that contained small trees, a miniature pond and a Grundleshanks replica.

As I got closer, I realized it wasn't a replica. It was actually Grundleshanks, stuffed and motionless. "What the hell?"

Gus was pleased as punch. "Grundleshanks lives!" he said, cackling an evil witch laugh. "That's totally brilliant."

"Disturbing is more like it." I looked over at Grundleshank's spirit, who was curiously checking out his body double in the tank.

"I tried to get the rest of the remains, but the taxidermist said he didn't have them." Forrest frowned.

"Of course not. You think I'd let those bones out of my sight? He just needed the skin. I have the rest safely tucked away."

I quickly looked around the kitchen, in case anything caught my attention. The last time Gus had safely tucked away any remains, it was in my freezer back in Los Angeles. But nothing jumped out at me.

I sat down on the kitchen chair and Aramis jumped on my lap. I petted him while Apollo kept trying to jump up on the counter to check out the aquarium. Thankfully, he was still too little to quite manage it.

With a croak, the spirit of Grundleshanks drifted through the tank and settled into the body. Then he sighed and seemed to drift off to sleep. Or whatever it is dead toads do when they want to tune out the world.

Forrest looked around. "Do you hear something?"

Gus listened. "Mara, I think your radio is playing."

"What? No way. It's not plugged in. That would just be weird."

"Can't you hear it?" Gus said.

I tried to listen.

Very faintly, I thought I caught a few notes.

* * *

As I took the steps upstairs, the song got louder. By the time I walked into the bedroom, the radio was rocking *Devil Went Down To Georgia* at full blast.

I could have sworn I unplugged it. I turned the radio off, then followed the cord to the wall socket. *Ha!* I *had* unplugged it. I knew it.

"Well, that's just odd." I wondered if Aunt Tillie had been running the radio, but Charlie Daniels Band was not her cup of tea. Maybe if it had been classical music…

I looked at the plug. Was it possible that I had left it half-in and half-out of the socket and when I followed the cord just now, was when I'd actually unplugged it? Or maybe Gus had plugged it back in when he came upstairs? I curled the plug up on the dresser, so there'd be no doubt. Just in case it happened again.

On my bed was a neatly-placed pair of trousers with suspenders, a vest, an old-fashioned suit jacket, a derby bowler hat with a feather in the band, and instructions on how to use fake hair, glue and an eyebrow pencil, courtesy of Gus.

Since Gus and Forrest were putting the finishing touches on dinner, I put on the outfit, complete with makeup and ritual jewelry—especially my pentacle. I wanted to be prepared and warded since we were going to spend the evening in the cemetery.

* * *

I returned downstairs, just as Forrest was saying, "Come on, show me. You know you want to."

"No way. Mara will freak. Trust me, you don't want to see her in full freak-out mode. It's Stephen King-style mayhem."

"Are you talking about your penis again? Been there, seen it, got the postcard. I'm pretty sure it's internationally famous by now." I said, stepping into the kitchen. "What am I going to freak about?

Gus snorted as he drizzled olive oil on a Greek salad (cut-up tomatoes, feta cheese and cucumber slices seasoned with oregano). "We're talking about Grundleshanks's remains."

My face must have turned green, because Gus smacked Forrest's arm and pointed at me.

"See? That's what I mean. Right there. Her head's going to start spinning at any moment."

"Shut it," I glared at him, pressing down on my wrist, until the wave of nausea ceased.

Chapter 21

"**I** like the new look," Gus said, winking at me.

"You would," I replied, still concentrating on getting my nausea under control.

Since it was Misrule, everything had to be turned on its head, including gender. So I currently looked like some middle-aged man out of the last century, sporting a beer belly.

Once my stomach settled down, I took the platters of Greek salad and warm pita bread from Gus and headed out with the Dobes. I'd rather be outdoors at the cemetery, than in a kitchen that seemed to be growing smaller by the second, with Gus and Forrest talking about stuff I didn't want to think about.

What was it with boys and gross things? Although since Gus hadn't brought out Grundleshanks's remains, my guess was he probably didn't have them in the house (thank the Goddess). Or maybe there was some kind of magickal reason why he had to keep them hidden until the next full moon.

Once Gus told me what he was planning for Grundleshanks, I looked up the ritual. I found some stuff online, but most of the details were in Gus's esoteric lore books.

The toad was a shamanic creature, that dwelt on both land and water, a totemic guide for a witch who dwelt both on Earth and in the Otherworld. So I could see why Gus was a huge toad fan. And

Grundleshanks had been the coolest toad ever.

The toad bone ritual was part of the Horseman's lore. They used the bone to exert almost preternatural control over a horse, commanding it to become gentle or go wild at a whisper. And while I could understand that would have been super-important in an era when we relied on horses for everything, we were living in the era of the automobile.

Besides, the last time I suggested we go trail riding, Gus adamantly refused. He didn't want anything to do with an object of transportation that didn't have drink holders, seat belts or a GPS.

* * *

When I arrived at the cemetery, I found the missing garbage can, a long table and chairs, boxes of decorations, and coolers filled with appetizers and drinks. For the guys, there were two sweet wines: the red Mavrodaphne and white Samos of Muscat, and a bottle of the turpentiny-tasting Retsina. And for me, a giant bottle of coconut water. There was even a large can of dog food for the Dobes.

Since I had nothing else to do, while the dogs ran around sniffing everything, I started transforming the cemetery. I covered the table with a few large Celtic sarongs. Then I put our skull, whom we had started calling Bertha, on top of a hearthstone that Gus had carved with sigils. I set the skull and the stone at the head of the table, laid a silver bell on one side and priapic wand on the other, and then circled the hearthstone with candles.

I don't know what got into me. But as the sun started to set, everything looked so perfect and magickal, I couldn't help myself. I lit the candles and did a small calling to the spirits of the ancestors, the spirits of the dead who surrounded us.

I told myself that I was just trying to prime the space, to acknowledge the spirits and let them know we were here, so that when Gus called them in—since it was *his* dinner after all—they'd come in like gangbusters.

Instead, I got a response I wasn't expecting. White wraiths rose up from the ground, spirits passing through coffins and dirt, so thick in their manifestation, it was like standing in fog.

The dogs whimpered and pressed closer to me.

My heart pounded faster and I stopped breathing, wondering what in the world I had just done.

The fog rolled out, stretching, before forming separate shapes.

Finally, I recognized my Aunt Tillie and my mom, and a whole bunch of people who I didn't know, but who felt familiar.

I started breathing again. Aramis growled, while Apollo started barking. I petted them and told them to hush. They quieted down, but the hair on their necks still bristled.

"It's bad form to call us in girl, when there's no food on the table," Aunt Tillie said, sidling up to me.

"I'm sorry. I didn't mean to actually call you in yet. I don't know what came over me."

I quickly took a little of each of the cut-up veggies, fruit, and Greek cheeses—kasseri and feta—from the cooler and put them on a plate for the dead, adding a spoonful of Greek salad and a torn off piece of pita bread. Then I opened the container of tiropitakia (Greek cheese triangles) and spanakopitakia (Greek spinach triangles)—which Gus had made from scratch—and added one of each to the platter.

"I know what it was," my mom said, winking at me, as she sat down. "You missed us."

"That must be it," I agreed.

"You look ridiculous," Aunt Tillie sniffed.

"When it comes to missing people, I wasn't talking about *you*," I told my great-aunt.

"Ignore your Aunt Tillie," my mom said. "You look adorable. Just like your brother."

Aunt Tillie hissed and the whole world came crashing down around me.

I heard a faint roaring in my ears.

"My *what*?!" I asked.

"I meant, if I had had another child."

"That's *not* what you said," I glared at her. "What brother?"

"You never did know when to shut up, Adele," Aunt Tillie said.

"*What* brother?" I repeated.

My mom sighed. "Before I met your father, I fell in love with a boy in my school. Things went a little too far. I was young and back then, babies didn't raise babies."

I set out the bottles of wine while I mulled that over. From what I had gotten to know of my mother, I didn't think she would have terminated the pregnancy. And if she did, she wouldn't be talking about him in the present tense.

"So, somewhere in the world, I have a brother?" I asked, trying to gauge the answer by their reactions.

"And you'll shut the *h-e-double-toothpicks* up about it," Aunt Tillie snapped. "Unless you want him to go through the same hell you went through, with that she-devil ancestress of yours."

I looked around, to see if Lisette, the witch whose spirit had possessed my body and who had wreaked havoc on my life, had shown up.

"Lisette's not here," my mom said. "She's still being pursued by the Wild Hunt."

Aunt Tillie cackled. "Serves her right. Now, can we get off this entire topic? Before we draw unwanted attention to it?"

"Please," my mom begged, looking at me.

"This isn't the end of it," I said. "We will be talking about this again. I have way too many questions to let this go."

I couldn't quite wrap my head around it. Somewhere in the world, I might have a brother.

"Fine. Later. Not Now." Aunt Tillie said, shooting my mom a dirty look. Then she turned to me. "Did you talk to Gus?"

I sighed. "He tied the seasonal ritual into the toad ritual. He can't break the one without doing the other."

Aunt Tillie gasped, horrified. I could tell she was gearing up to go into full-out nag mode and give me an earful, so I tried to cut her off at the pass. "It's not that big a deal. So he'll wind up with a bone that controls horses. Who even has horses anymore? Besides, I think Gus is scared of them anyway. I doubt he's going to turn into the next Monty Roberts."

Monty Roberts was the only real-life horse whisperer I had heard of. I wondered if he had a toad bone in his mojo bag.

"There should be some kind of licensing or regulation of witches. Before you're given your powers, you need to be intelligent enough to know when not to use them," Aunt Tillie snapped. "I've never seen two people who deserve to be completely mortal more than the two of you."

My mom frowned. "What Gus is planning to do, is forbidden."

Aunt Tillie shook her head. "The fool is going to hand himself over to—"

"Don't say it," my mom warned her.

"And there's nothing we can do about it," Aunt Tillie finished.

I felt like screaming. "Can we drop the melodrama? Come on. It's Gus. He just wants to do the ritual, to prove that he can. To have a magickal remembrance of Grundleshanks. It's not that big a deal. The bone will probably never leave his altar. And even if it does, it's freaking horses, for cripe's sake."

"It's a very big deal," my mom said. "Have him find another toad. He must release that one."

"There is no way he's going to do that. Grundleshanks is the whole reason he wants to do the ritual. What's the problem with Grundleshanks, anyway?!" I asked, exasperated. "You two are being impossible."

Aunt Tillie grabbed my arm and an image of Gus popped into my head, his flesh dripping off of him, until he was nothing but bones.

A wave of sadness, regret and guilt punched me in the gut.

Angry, I pulled away.

"Why can't you leave me alone?!" I yelled. "Stop putting things in my head. Gus will be fine. He's a big boy."

Responding to my emotions, both Dobes softly growled in Aunt Tillie's direction. I didn't know if they could see her as clearly as I could, but they could definitely sense her.

"Leave the child be," my mom said, softly. "It's too late. The process has already begun. The dominoes are starting to fall."

"What exactly does that mean? No dominoes," I said. "Forget

the dominoes. Life is *not* a game of dominoes. It's *never* too late."

Aunt Tillie looked at my mom. "I would have expected something more intelligent out of your side, Adele. She must take after her father. I warned you adding human blood into the mix was a bad idea."

"Hey!" I protested. "I'm sitting right here."

"Hush," Aunt Tillie hissed.

From the edges of the forest, I could see wraith-like figures closing in on the gathering. They were extremely tall, with long hooded cloaks.

Inside me, I could feel the baby turning to look at them.

"What in the world...?"

As the cloaked figures got closer, the spirits in the cemetery vanished, one by one.

Chapter 22

"Well, that was interesting," I muttered.

"Hope you're hungry!" Gus hollered, interrupting my thoughts.

I looked over and laughed.

Gus looked like a ridiculously sexy, gender-bending escapee from *Rocky Horror Picture Show*. He was all decked out, from a black leather corset, bright blue mini-skirt and fishnet stockings to a pearl necklace, blue feather boa and platform glitter heels. The look was finished off with heavy Goth make-up and a black cape with a brilliant blue lining.

Forrest, on the other hand, looked scary and kind of awesome. His face was painted like a harlequin skull, and he was wearing a court jester's outfit, a crown-like hat with bells on the points, and a crooked sign around his neck proclaiming him the Lord of Misrule, but *Misrule* had been crossed out and replaced with *Gus's Rule* in blue marker. Strapped to his waist was a black, white and red pole with a skull at the top wearing a mini-jester's hat.

They were both loaded down with food, carrying a platter in each hand. With the way Gus was teetering on his heels, I wasn't sure he'd actually make it to the table before he lost his balance.

Aramis and Apollo ran towards them, joyful at the prospect of up-ending Gus and enjoying a free meal.

"Starved," I called back. I could feel the baby settling back down, now that all the wraiths were gone. I clapped my hands. "Hallelujah, the victuals have arrived. Thank the Gods."

"I always love being the answer to people's prayers," Forest said, grinning, giving his skeletal make-up an even eerier appearance.

They both navigated the Doberman crew and made it to the table, platters intact, where I helped them lay out the main feast: Slow-cooked leg of lamb with fresh oregano and rosemary, roasted potatoes sprinkled with dill, finished off with a side of spinach and rice in a tomato sauce base. There was also Greek Spaghetti baked in tomato sauce, with freshly-ground black pepper and myzhithra cheese, since I was having a hard time dealing with meat these days.

It was an embarrassment of riches, and easily, a three thousand calorie dinner.

Once all the food was on the table, Gus did an elaborate invocation of spirit. He quoted Shakespeare, lit more candles, rang the bell and pounded on the hearthstone with the wand.
"I call on all our ancestors,
Kith and kin to join us, in this time of Gus's Rule.
Red threads and black, white threads and grey.
Mingle, mingle, mingle who may.
Round and about, thout a tout tout,
The good stay in and the bad stay out!"
I looked around, expecting to see a repeat rolling in of the wraiths.

But there was nothing.

I tried to open a mental door to the other side, and it was swiftly closed in my face.

"Fantastic calling. Let's eat." Forest said, sitting down.

"That was one of my better ones." Gus seemed pleased with himself as he added food to the plate I had started for the dead. He poured a glass of each of the wines and set them in front of the skull. I looked to see if Forrest wanted to add anything to the plate, but he was already eating.

How could Gus not sense that we were alone? Even the baby seemed to be taking a nap. Had the cadre of cloaked figures that had shown up earlier been some kind of ghostly police force? Is that why the spirits had vacated so quickly? And why they weren't returning?

And why couldn't Gus sense anything? He was arguably the strongest witch I knew. Were his internal sensors out of whack? Or was it mine? Were they actually here and I was blocked from seeing them somehow?

But why would that be? Would my abilities have gone on walk-about because I had pissed Aunt Tillie off?

I thought about it, and dismissed that last scenario. If Aunt Tillie had the power to render me a mundane human, she would have done it months ago. Which meant, the spirits hadn't returned. But why couldn't Gus sense that?

And what was the deal with the whole brother thing? Would I ever find him? Was it possible that I met him already, and didn't know it?

Gus has always felt like my brother. We called each other siblings of the soul. But what if there was more to it than that? Wouldn't it be the coolest thing ever if Gus turned out to actually be my brother?

But I had met his family before, and no one had ever said a word about Gus being adopted. Although, it's not something that normally comes up in conversation. *"Pass the potatoes, and by the way, Gus is adopted."* I think I would have remembered that.

Besides, he looked an awful lot like his *yaya*, his grandmother. This whole thing was just wishful thinking. What I needed was some kind of compulsion spell. Damn spirits were never as forthcoming with information as I wanted them to be.

Apollo nudged me, to remind me that they were under the table, watching for scraps. I dropped a piece of cheese on the ground for each of them, along with some carrots

By the time I looked back up, the sun had set, the dinner was lit completely by candle and moonlight, and Forrest and Gus were in mid-conversation.

"Brilliant plan. The taxidermist was a stroke of genius. So, when are you going to let me hold the bones in my hot little hands?"

Forrest asked, his eyes twinkling in the candlelight.

"When I'm ready," Gus said.

"Why do you even care?" I asked.

"Because I'm a guy. We're all about experiential learning. Ask Gus. He understands. Hey, we could bind some of those bones together, and make a miniature bone knife."

I made a face. I used to have a bone knife once. It was also known as a fairy knife, since it had no metal, just a bone handle with an obsidian blade. My dad had bought it for me, two birthdays before he died. But holding it, I could see and feel the hunt, and the deer's death, and it was just the saddest thing. I had to give the knife to Gus, because I couldn't hold it without crying. Gus said it was because the bone hadn't been obtained properly. And then he went out and bought me a bone knife that looked the same, but didn't make me cry. So he was probably right.

Gus teased me about having the ability to be a great witch but being too sappy to ever fulfill my potential, and he was probably right. While I had made peace with him bouncing in and out of gray magic realms, I preferred to stay firmly in the light—when I had a choice. Even though Gus says my talents as a necromancer automatically puts me on the same path as him.

I have to admit, there are days when I talk far more to the dead, than I do to anyone who's alive. But it's not like I go out and intentionally perform magickal rites with the dead, which is what I think of, when I hear the word *necromancer*.

It's more like the spirit world keeps seeking me out and sometimes, (like with my Aunt Tillie, when I first moved out here), I have to defend myself. So I don't think that should count.

Gus, of course, thinks I'm ridiculous. Before he left for Chicago, he got me a tee-shirt that said *Mara Stephens: FortuneTeller, Witch, Reluctant Necromancer*. I only wear it though, when I'm cleaning house or doing laundry. I wondered if my brother had the same aversions and talents that I did, or if he'd be completely different than me—assuming I was ever able to find him at all.

I was so deep in thought, I totally missed the conversation going on around me, until Forrest asked my opinion.

"Sorry, I wasn't listening."

"I could tell. Are we boring you?" He asked, one eyebrow arched. "Do we need to pair our scintillating dialogue with common circus tricks, to hold your attention? Should I start punctuating my questions with backflips?"

I could feel my nostrils flare and the edge of my upper lip start to pull up into a snarl as I stared at him. I quickly clamped down on my reaction and rearranged my face into a neutral expression. All sorts of responses were running through my head, but with a baby on the way, I was trying really hard not to swear so much.

"Could you?" I asked sweetly, baring my teeth in a semblance of a smile. "After all, you're wearing the right costume for it. And I would really appreciate the added entertainment. Watch out for the gravestones though. I would hate for you to hit your head."

Unless you whacked yourself hard enough to do permanent damage, I added in my thoughts.

I smiled and Forrest narrowed his eyes at me. *Crap.* I really hoped reading thoughts wasn't one of his talents.

Chapter 23

"She hasn't been ignoring us on purpose," Gus said, interrupting our staredown. "It's just what she does. She gets hyper-focused on something, and it's like nothing else exists."

"What are you talking about?!" I asked, offended. "I don't do that."

"Are you kidding me? When you're reading a book, I can walk up to you, yell directly in your face, and you won't hear a word I'm saying. You won't even know I'm standing there, unless I take the book away."

"That's because I'm *reading*. When I'm reading, I'm totally immersed in the world of the book. Doesn't everyone do that?" I asked, looking from one to the other.

Both of them were shaking their heads.

"How can you *not* read like that? That would be so totally boring."

"It's not just reading," Gus said. "You do it when you're writing, when you're spellcrafting, when you're in ritual, when you're painting, when you're thinking. Everyone does it a little bit, but you take it to an extreme."

"I'm pretty sure we could have set one of the serving platters on your head, and you'd have no idea," Forrest said. "Hell, we could have probably lit your shirt on fire, and you'd be clueless."

"I'm sure she would have figured it out, once third-degree burns set in."

"Shut up! You guys are totally exaggerating." I said.

Gus looked at Forrest and raised an eyebrow. "The only time you don't do it, is when you're watching TV. And that's only because you fall asleep during the first commercial break and don't wake up until the show's over."

"I do not! Well, maybe now, but only because I'm pregnant. I'm a woman. We multi-task. I may not look like I'm paying attention, but I totally am. I'm not sleeping. I'm resting my eyes. But I'm listening and following every plot twist."

"Bullshit," Forrest snorted.

"I don't think multi-tasking actually exists," Gus said. "I think it's something women invented to give men an inferiority complex. Because I haven't seen anyone do it well."

"I can totally multi-task," I protested.

"Prove it. What were we talking about? You don't even have to give me an entire sentence. A sentence fragment will do," Gus said, calling my bluff.

"You are so mean. You were talking about... Grundleshanks's bones."

Gus made the sound of a buzzer. "Nope. Sorry. That was two conversations ago. Try again?"

I tried to think back to what they had been saying, but I had been so busy listening to the thoughts inside my head, I hadn't heard anything going on outside of it.

"Well, I can normally multi-task. I was just... distracted, that's all."

"Uh-huh. We were talking about the three strikes law. I think it should be done away with," Gus said.

"And I think it should be strengthened. Three strikes, automatic execution, go sort things out with your Maker." Forrest said.

"What about wrongful convictions? Or petty crimes?" Gus asked. "That doesn't seem fair, to be executed for shoplifting."

Forrest shrugged. "Collateral damage." Then he grinned at me—at least, it resembled a grin. Although what it reminded me most of was a wolf about to eat its prey.

"This is why I couldn't remember the conversation. It was dumb. Besides, I thought Suppers for the Dead were supposed to be silent."

"Not necessarily," Gus shrugged.

"We had a moment of silence. That's enough." Forrest said.

"So, what do you think?" Gus asked.

I paused. I hadn't actually given it a lot of thought before.

"A woman who doesn't have an opinion on everything?" Forrest asked. "Stop my heart."

"I think… it should be limited to violent crimes only," I said.

"Fascist," said Gus.

"Commie pinko liberal," said Forrest.

"Are you two sure you're dating?" said I.

"You're a hoot," Forrest laughed. "But c'mon, you can't tell me you wouldn't like to see all the criminals in the world magickally vanish? A Rapture of evil instead of good. Think of how under-populated this planet would become."

I shot him a dirty look. "Vanishing isn't the same as being executed."

"Oh, I'm sorry. Am I not being namby-pamby enough for your delicate Wiccan sensibilities?" Forrest snorted.

"I'm not Wiccan," I said.

Which was true. While I appreciated Wicca and was grateful it had become a more widely accepted religion, I wasn't actually Wiccan. And anyone who watched me work, especially when it came to circle and ritual construction, would know that.

While I tried (usually not very successfully, if you asked my Aunt Tillie) to follow the Wiccan *'Harm None'* rede, Traditional Witchcraft seemed to be closer to what Gus and I practiced. Although neither one of us were big on rules and dogma. Gus once told me we were *gnostic, heretical witches*, and that seems like an excellent description to me.

"I just happen to think that most people, at heart, are good. So, I fundamentally disagree with your premise." I said. "And I don't appreciate patronizing asshats like you taking pot shots at Wiccans."

"Awww," Forrest said, making a face. "That's so cute. You're getting that mother bear instinct down pat."

He patted my hand and I quickly moved it off the table, glaring at him.

"Lay off her," Gus said.

"I'm just yanking her chain," Forrest said, his eyes twinkling. "It's fun."

"For you," I snorted.

"Oh, come on now, don't tell me you can't deal with a little friendly joshing. Time to put big girl panties on, sweetheart."

I frowned and helped myself to more spinach and cheese triangles.

"Why aren't you eating any lamb? Have a problem with slaughterhouses?" Forrest chuckled.

"What business is it of yours?"

"Guess I'm a traditional type of guy." Forrest smiled. "It's not a meal if you're not chasing bloody meat around on your plate."

I made a face.

Gus kicked me under the table, earning low growls from Aramis and Apollo. "Mara's stomach can't deal with red meat. Although she's okay with fish and eggs. Seems our baby is leaning towards Pescetarianism."

Forrest coughed on his drink. "*Our* baby? I thought you two weren't involved?"

He seemed flustered for the first time since I had met him and it may be bad of me, but the sight brought joy to my heart.

"Of course, we're involved," I said, savoring the moment. "We live together."

"We're just not involved sexually," Gus clarified.

"But Gus is the honorary daddy, so he's *very* involved."

"Oh," Forrest said, nodding. "I take it the real dad is a deadbeat?"

"No." I suddenly felt defensive of Paul. "He's just... confused."

"It takes a village," Gus said.

"Not for most people," Forrest replied. "There's a lot of single parents in the world."

And pretty much, that's how the rest of dinner went. Forrest yanking my chain, Gus (sometimes) rising to my defense, and me really wanting to slap Forrest but making do, instead, with quietly dropping a few table scraps to the dogs. Gus caught me a few times and frowned, but they didn't get scraps often, so I figured this was a special treat for them.

During dessert, (*galaktoburiko,* a Greek honey-soaked custard with *phyllo,* which the baby seemed to enjoy as well), after repeated nudges from Gus, I forced myself to try and make small talk with Forrest. I got to hear all about his perfect life, his perfect upbringing, and his unabashed view of himself as a male Adonis.

At least, Forrest and Gus had that supreme type of self-confidence in common. The difference was, it didn't annoy me when Gus said over-the-top stuff. I was used to him proclaiming he was the frosting on the cake of life. But wow, did I have a hard time tolerating it from an asshat like Forrest.

And it didn't help that Gus couldn't say anything without Forrest either correcting him or one-upping him or laughing at him indulgently, like Gus was a precocious child or a favorite pet.

Normally, that type of behavior would drive both of us crazy. But Gus was so stupidly besotted with the guy, he couldn't see past his own penis. And if I said anything, Forrest turned it around on me, so it looked like he was the reasonable, magnanimous, witty dinner companion, and I was the stick-in-the-mud, irrational grump.

By the time dinner was winding to a close, I was ready to beat Forrest to death with the gnawed-on remains of the roasted leg bone.

Chapter 24

Once we were done, Forrest folded his hands, like he was going to lead us in a closing prayer, so I hurriedly jumped in instead.

Sure, Forrest could be charming—when he wanted to be—but he was a jackass. And even when he was on his best behavior, there was something about him that made my skin prickle. For him to lead any kind of prayer felt like blasphemy.

"Dear Goddesses and Gods, thank you for having granted us this bountiful feast. May all which sustains us, whether it's food or friendship or love, have your blessings upon it." I said.

Then Gus took over and released the spirits (which still hadn't shown up). I looked over at Forrest and I could have sworn he was grinning to himself like he knew what had really been—or not been—going on at that dinner, and he wasn't about to clue Gus in.

*   *   *

Shortly afterwards, Forrest got a text message and made an excuse about why he had to immediately leave—something about cats, a crazed breeder and his stepsister. He went ahead of us to the house, to change into his street clothes, leaving Gus and me to bring everything back ourselves.

Since it was so late, Gus was all for leaving it and putting things away tomorrow, but I was worried the food would attract raccoons and bears and who all knew what else was living in the woods of

Northern Wisconsin.

Having the Dobes race around us, trying to get at the plate for the dead, made things even more challenging. I took them back to the house and locked them in the run.

Forrest must have been the fastest clothes-changer in history, because his outfit was draped over a kitchen chair, and when I checked the front, his car was nowhere to be seen.

Walking through the house again, I could hear Mitch Ryder and the Detroit Wheels singing *Devil With A Blue Dress On*. I thought about going upstairs and checking on the clock radio again, but I wasn't sure what else I could do with it. It was completely unplugged. *Stupid electronics.* I made a mental note to tell Gus about the song though, since he had blue in his outfit. He'd definitely get a kick out of it.

* * *

I trekked back to the cemetery, where Gus was setting the plate for the dead out on one of the graves. Since it was just a plate, rather than the entire buffet, I swallowed my worries about visiting critters and tried to think of them as messengers of the Underworld, ferrying food to the dead, rather than rampaging and possibly rabid raccoons.

It took a bunch of trips to get everything back to the house. Trying to move it all with nothing but the moon and the flashlight app on our phones to light the way, made things extra difficult. No wonder Gus had spent all day getting everything down to the cemetery, when he was doing it on his own. Thankfully, the table—which was the last thing we were moving—was collapsible and more awkward than heavy.

Once we got everything back to where it belonged—all the leftovers put away, the dishes stacked in the dishwasher and the pans soaking in the sink—I went upstairs, changed out of my suit, into pajamas and took a last look at my face before I removed the false hair.

Huh. So that was what my brother—whoever he was—might look like. I took a photo on my smart phone and saved it. Maybe I could upload it to Google and do an image search. I thought about telling Gus about this previously unknown member of my family tree, but he'd have a ton of questions and I had no answers—not yet, at least. Although, I was planning to rectify that, as soon as I could. I decided to keep it to myself for now and tell Gus later.

When I was done, I helped Gus out of his fancy get-up and into shorts and a tank top. It took me a few tries to get all of the make-up off of him though. I swear, he had shellacked it onto his face.

Once I got him looking like his normal self again, we let the dogs in and Gus made us two mugs of hot cocoa, spicing his up with Kahlua and Baileys, and mine with extra whipped cream.

Real whipped cream, that he whipped himself. Mainly because he had thrown my canned whip cream out, grumbling about how all the canned whip creams have either high fructose corn syrup or carrageenan, and how carrageenan was stripped out with industrial solvents and why did anyone think that would qualify as an organic ingredient.

Then we curled up on the couch and with the puppies snoozing by the fireplace, we talked about boyfriends.

*   *   *

I wanted to learn more about Forrest, but Gus had Paul on his mind.

"I don't know what you see in him. He's an ass."

"Funny, I was just thinking the exact same thing about Forrest."

"The difference is," Gus explained, "Forrest is an ass to *you*, not me. Paul is an ass across the board."

"He's just overwhelmed. He's gone through a lot since he's met me. Even though I didn't mean to, I've put him through a supernatural wringer."

"Oh, please. He's a typical straight man."

"What's that supposed to mean?" I asked.

"He's got no fashion sense and no sense of how to treat a woman. He's stupidly obstinate and scared of responsibility. He wants everything his own way and he wants it now."

"I don't think you can blame that on gender or sexual orientation," I said, thinking of how stubborn Gus could be when he wanted something.

He set his mug on the coffee table with a bang. "I can if I want. I'm entitled to my opinions."

"Of course you are, honey," I said, soothingly, patting his arm. "Even when they're wrong. Heaven forbid, I try to affect them in any way."

Gus made a face at me. "You know what the problem with you is? You have lousy taste in men."

I laughed. "And you don't? Sure, Forrest may be charming and handsome, but he's a self-centered, self-righteous windbag, with the type of Machiavellian black-and-white view of the world that used to drive you nuts."

"He just needs more Gus time. Just you wait. Give me a year and he'll be a changed man."

"Right. I'll bet when he finds injured animals on the road, instead of taking them to a vet, he runs them over, to put them out of their misery. And then he puts the car in reverse, and does it again. Just because he enjoys it."

"Take that back!" Gus howled.

"Will not!"

Gus made a face at me. I made a face at him.

Finally, he smiled and said: "You just don't want to share me."

"Damned right, I don't." I frowned. "And if I do have to share you, it had better be with someone who's head over heels in love with you. Not some half-assed, hard-nosed, hard work-avoiding, sugar daddy."

"I feel the same way about you, Miss Thing. I want you to find true love. Not settle for the first guy who unintentionally knocks you up. Biology isn't everything."

"I know," I sighed. "I thought we were heading towards a happily ever after, when everything blew apart. You gotta admit, this is a weird situation. Paul's trying to step up as much as he can. He just has a lot of... uncertainties. I knew, when I made the decision to keep the baby, I might be raising it on my own."

"Fuck Paul and his uncertainties. You'll always have me. I'll help you raise the baby. DNA doesn't count for everything. Family is what you make it. And if Paul wants to miss out on a family this amazing, it's his loss."

I smiled at him, and wiped away a stray tear. "Paul said he found a place that does non-invasive 3-D ultrasound. So, we'll be able to see the baby soon."

Gus perked up. "Can I come? I'd love to see that!"

"You and Paul in the same car for the entire drive to Trinity Harbor? I don't think so."

"I'll only hurt him a little. Break some non-essential bones."

"Exactly." I said. "I'll bring you back a picture."

"So let's assume the worst. What if the kid is born with horns and hooves. What are you gonna do?"

"Raise it, of course. Buy it a cool collection of hats and boots. Although, if it's up to Paul…" I shuddered to think of what would happen.

Gus frowned. "I'll break his arm first."

"That's gonna be hard to do from the lobby. Unless you want to be in the delivery room?" I asked, hopeful. We hadn't actually talked about it before, and I suddenly realized how much I wanted Gus to be there with me.

"Are you kidding? Of course I'm gonna be there. I'll bring hoof polish—and a Taser, just in case that dirt bag looks at the baby cross-eyed."

I laughed. "Really?"

"Really." He said, winking at me. "I don't think you have anything to worry about. After all, that baby is half you. Hell, you're a witch—it's probably mostly you. Which means it's going to be spectacular."

He got up and took our mugs to the sink.

I sighed and a whole bunch of tension I didn't even know I was holding onto, rushed out of my body.

"I love you," I said, walking into the kitchen and hugging him.

"You'd better," he replied.

We stood there, forehead to forehead, basking in the love and energy that surrounded us like a giant bubble.

Just as Gus was about to say something, his gut made a horrible noise and a wicked stream of burps came out of him, smelling like brimstone and hellfire, breaking the spell.

Chapter 25

Gus looked at me, panicked. "Ugh, ugh, ugh," he repeated
"What the hell?!" I quickly backed away, turning my head,
trying not to breathe. "That's just nasty."

Gus made a face. "It's nastier on my end. How it smells is exactly
how it tastes. Don't light a match. It's like I'm farting sulphur out of
my mouth."

"Please, stop. My stomach can't take the visuals."

"On second thought, maybe we should get the matches. That
could be cool."

Another burp rumbled up, sending me to the other side of the
room, while Gus opened his mouth as wide as he could, to let out the
smell.

"Oh, that's horrible," he gasped.

"Are you done?"

"I sure as hell hope so. But just in case... where's the fireplace
lighter? And your cell phone? You start filming and next time I burp,
I'll light it up and it'll be like I'm breathing fire. How cool will that
look? I'll be a YouTube sensation!"

"I'm not filming you lighting your face on fire. Forget it."

"Wuss. Go on, get your phone." He geared up for another burp.

"Stop! Please!"

"I'm trying! This isn't exactly fun for me, either. Where are the antacids?"

I got a bottle of Tums out of the cabinet and tossed them over.

His gut started growling again before he could open the container.

"Maybe if you think about something else. What were you about to say?"

"When?"

"Before your gut became a volcano of *ick*."

"I have no idea."

"Something about Grundleshanks?" I suggested.

He thought about it. "Maybe. I was probably going to do an '*I told you so*' dance. I hadn't exactly formulated the sentence before my gut attacked." Another burp hit, making him grimace. He started pawing through our junk drawer. "Where the hell's a lighter when you need one?"

"*Told me so* about what?"

"The toad bones are almost ready," he said, his face lighting up with joy. He closed the drawer and pointed at me. "Oh, ye of little faith. I told you the weather magic was absolutely the right call."

My blood ran cold.

The process has already begun. The dominoes are starting to fall.

Was Gus's gut distress part of it?

"Don't do it, Gus. Please."

"Why not?" He asked, mystified. "Because of your Aunt Tillie? You know what I think about her cockamamie warnings."

Another growl and a massive burp ripped out of him, sending Gus into a spasm of "Icks!"

"No! Because I'm not ready to lose you!" I said, covering my mouth and nose with the top of my shirt.

*   *   *

Gus spent most of the night in the upstairs bathroom. I tried to go to bed, but the smell on the second floor was so bad, I gave up. I opened all the windows, but there was barely a breeze to shift the cloud of stink.

Since Gus was still awake, I texted him on my phone: *It had to have been the plum. I told you, you'd regret eating that plum.*

Gus texted back: *Shut up. I know.*

Me: *I'm sleeping downstairs. We may need a hazmat team to come in and clean up the second floor, when you're done.*

Gus: *Very funny. I hate u.*

Me: *You love me. You just can't handle the truth. Feel better.*

Gus: *Trying.*

Me: *Will check on you in a.m., make sure you're not dead.*

Gus: *You're 2 kind. With this much compassion, you could be next Mother Theresa. Ugh. Worst food poisoning ever.*

Me: *Want me 2 take u 2 hospital?*

Gus: *No. Now leave me alone, so I can rot away in peace.*

I spent the night downstairs, on the couch. My brain must have been working overtime because, in the middle of the night, I woke up with a brilliant idea.

The Internet.

Everything's available on the Internet, right? And since, according to my mom and Aunt Tillie, the problem seemed to be that it was Grundleshanks's bones, I could just order some anonymous toad bones and swap them out for Grundleshanks.

I jumped on the computer. Amazon had a toad skeleton, but it was glued to a base. After another hour of clicking around, I finally found a loose skeleton from a toad farm in China. I hit 'buy' and went back to sleep, pleased with myself.

Now all I needed to do was find Grundleshanks's bones, get rid of them, and distract Gus from doing the ritual until the new bones got here. I wondered how long shipping from China was going to take.

*　　*　　*

In the morning, I fed the puppies and let them out for their morning run in the back yard. When they were done, I brought them in, poured myself a cup of decaf and looked at the stuffed toad in the aquarium.

"Where are your bones, Grundleshanks? Did Gus put your remains back under the dolman?"

Grundleshanks, very slightly, tilted his head—at least, that's what it looked like.

"What the heck?!" I tilted my own head and looked at the toad.

It wasn't even real—not in any actual sense of the word. It was stuffed. The skin was real, but that was all. The inside was some kind of plastic form. How could it possibly have moved?

Was it Grundleshanks's spirit I was seeing?

Or was I hallucinating?

The process has already begun.

Remembering those words caused a chill to run down my spine.

I rinsed the cup out and put it in the dishwasher. Time to go check on my roomie, and make sure he had survived the night.

I went over to the stairway and hollered Gus's name.

There was no answer.

I cautiously walked up the stairs, expecting to be incapacitated by stink, but the smell had dissipated.

I walked down the hall and knocked on his bedroom door.

Nothing but silence.

I slowly opened the door.

There was no sign that Gus had been there at all. The bed was neatly made, and everything looked untouched.

I checked my bedroom and both bathrooms, halfway expecting to find Gus dead on the floor, but they were also devoid of human occupants.

Where could Gus have gone?

*   *   *

I quickly looked through the rest of the cottage. He was nowhere to be found. I was torn between worrying about him and rejoicing at the unexpected opportunity.

But I figured he would have woken me, if there was anything to worry about—if he had gotten worse or needed a ride to the hospital.

So, opportunism won.

With Gus away, I could find those bones, conveniently lose them and blame the dogs. The puppies were always getting into stuff.

I gave his room a quick once-over, eyeballing it. It didn't count as actually searching, unless physical touch was involved, right?

But there were no bones conveniently sitting out for me to find.

Not on his personal altar.

Not on his dresser.

Not on his nightstand.

Damn it.

*　　*　　*

I took the Dobies with me to the cemetery. I decided to start there, just in case Gus had returned to his original plan and the remains were at the cairn.

When we got there, I found the plate for the dead had been licked clean by whatever animals had been out roaming last night. I looked around until I spotted the small stone cairn and dolmen Gus had erected for Grundleshanks's remains.

I lifted the stones, but other than some smears on the ground and a bunch of ants, there was nothing. Since the stones had been undisturbed before I got there, I didn't think an animal made off with the bones. Gus must have stashed them somewhere else.

I ordered the Dobes to look around and find the bones, but they just tilted their heads and looked at me, tongues hanging out, panting. Their grasp of English seemed to be limited to commands like, *outside, treat, come, sit, stay, walk.* Too bad. I could really have used *find* in their vocabulary right about now. I made a mental note to start training them on it.

I picked up the plate from the grave and headed back to the house. I put the dogs in the run, where they made a beeline for their water bowl and then flopped down in the shade.

If I was Gus, what would I have done with the bones?

Maybe they were inside one of the many decorative containers on his personal altar? Or tucked away in one of his drawers? I sighed. Normally, I would never snoop through Gus's stuff without asking. But this was an emergency.

Chapter 26

In the kitchen, I called out Gus's name, just in case he had returned. But the cottage was as silent as a tomb. I walked upstairs, down the hall and knocked on his bedroom door.

Nothing.

I slowly opened the door and slipped into Gus's room.

I was starting to feel guilty about my plan to trash the bones. Maybe trash was too harsh a fate. If I could find them and stash them somewhere, Gus still wouldn't be able to do the ritual—at least, not until the new bones arrived. And I could give Grundleshanks's bones back to him when he was an old man and no longer obsessed with toad bone lore.

Hating myself a little, I searched through the drawer in his nightstand and then went through all the drawers in his dresser. I was worried about putting the contents back in order but, unlike the room's neat facade, the inside of the drawers were such a mess, I didn't think he had any idea what order his stuff was in.

Which was good, because I was going to have to dig through everything. So much for trying to pass off finding the bones as anything other than me snooping.

Once I started digging, I couldn't stop. I looked in every drawer, through his pants pockets, through his collection of man bags, under the bed, in the back of his closet, on top of shelving units. I found a key in the bottom of his sock drawer that unlocked a trunk stashed under his bed, and I even looked in there. But all I found was sex toys that made me shudder.

On top of his dresser, there was a framed picture of Gus and the dapper, grinning Forrest (which also made me shudder), a dollar eighty-five in change, fifty-eight dollars in bills, and a handful of receipts.

No bones.

Damn it.

I put everything back, but as I was about to leave, Aunt Tillie appeared, scaring the bejeezus out of me.

I jumped, knocking over the picture of Gus and Forrest.

"Geez, Aunt Tillie. Can you wear a bell or something?" I asked, clutching at my chest and focusing on slowing down my heart.

"Did you stop him?"

"I'm trying." I snapped, as soon as I could breathe normally. "He's more stubborn than you are."

"That's unfortunate."

I picked the picture up. The glass had a long, jagged crack. *Damn*, how was I going to explain that to Gus? Earthquake? Train? Poltergeist? The vibrations from a semi-tractor-trailer driving down the road?

I left the picture facedown, hoping he would think he knocked it over without realizing it.

I turned to Aunt Tillie. "I still don't understand what's so bad about Grundle—"

"—Hush. Words have power. If you don't want an entity to become aware of you, don't go around speaking its business," Aunt Tillie said, frowning.

"What entity?" I asked, mystified. "The toad? Or Gus?"

"Think with your head, not with your mouth, girl." She snapped at me. "Or is the baby sapping your brain power?"

"Would you stop? I don't have the patience to spar with you today. Gus was sick most of the night, so we didn't get a lot of sleep."

Aunt Tillie shook her head. "Adele was right. It's already started. It's too late."

"What are you talking about?" Suddenly, I had an epiphany. I narrowed my eyes. "Death doesn't confer omniscience, does it, Aunt Tillie?"

"That's not what I said," she snapped.

I continued to stare at her, starting to get pissed off. "Right. It's all code for *You Don't Know.* You're freaking me out and making me jump through hoops and you don't even know what, if *anything,* is going to happen. You're making educated guesses like the rest of us. If you *knew,* you and mom would be on the same page. But you're not."

She glared at me. "Trust me, we have more information than you have guesses."

"Then give me something concrete to work with. You keep saying this ritual is anathema, and using Grundleshanks is forbidden, but *why?* All I'm asking for is a clue. Something I can use to get through to Gus. Give me something quantifiable or if anything goes wrong, it's going to be on you. Not me. I'm trying. You're the one holding out."

But if anything, she got even tighter-lipped.

"You keep making that face, it's going to freeze that way," I snapped.

"You stupid, obstinate child," she said, giving me a look like I was the dumbest person alive. "There are rules against willy-nilly telling Breathers what's going on in the Otherworld."

"No, there isn't. Witches look into the future all the time."

"There is a significant difference between you getting visions of the future—or potential futures—and me waltzing in here and laying it out, exactly."

I growled. I *so* needed my tarot deck. I put it in a time-out after my adventure with Lisette. I had been counting on it coming back when I needed it to, but it was still nowhere to be found.

Gus! Gus had a tarot deck. I had seen it, in one of the cubbies on his headboard. I quickly pulled out the black velvet bag with the silver pentagram, and dumped out the cards. They all seemed to be there.

"Fine. I need to see it for myself? Then that's exactly what I'm going to do. You can go back to wherever it is you vanish to." I told Aunt Tillie. "Hell, Purgatory, Summerlands, Heaven, wherever. Bye."

She ignored me. As usual.

I shuffled the deck and laid out three cards on the bed.

Devil, Devil, Devil.

"That's impossible," I muttered.

Aunt Tillie stood there, looking smug.

"Stop it!" I told the cards. "Show me something else."

Death. Three of Swords. The Tower.

Transformation. Sorrow. Change through destruction. Boy, those cards sure as hell were familiar.

"Seriously? We are *not* going through that again. That was so four months ago," I said. "Show me what's going on *now*."

I laid out three more cards.

Devil, Devil, Devil.

I flipped over the entire deck and spread it out.

All the cards were Devil cards.

"Now do you understand?" asked Aunt Tillie. "Gus is courting one powerful enemy."

"But what does the D—"

She shot me a look

"—bag," I hastily amended, "have to do with our toad?!"

"I can't tell you. I didn't even tell you this much. You figured it out on your own."

Ugh. I felt like I was beating my head against the wall.

"I tried warning him," I said, exasperated. "Gus doesn't buy it. He doesn't even see you anymore—or any spirit for that matter. He thinks I'm lying to him. Why can't you make him see you?"

"Knows everything, does he?" Her eyes glittered. "He's going to bring trouble you don't need."

"That may be, but we're stuck. He's tied the rituals together, so he has to go through with it. If he doesn't, we're looking at permanent summer. Talk about a global warming nightmare."

"You have to find another option."

"I'm trying to swap toads on him, but I have to find Grundle's bones, or the jig is up. Help me at least find the bones. I don't know where they are."

"I cannot continue to put myself at risk, to cure the two of you of your case of the stupids," she said. "I'm already pushing the boundaries."

"Are you kidding me?! You've barely been any help at all!"

She pointed at me. "Gus is only my concern insofar as he affects *you*. You stay out of it, you hear me? If you can't stop him, then leave him to his fate and step away. Don't try to save him."

As she vanished, I heard a floorboard creak downstairs. I quickly put the tarot cards back in their bag, returned it to its cubby and slipped out of Gus's bedroom, hoping he wouldn't realize I had been snooping through his stuff.

But when I turned around, he was standing right there, holding an enormous carrier bag and glaring at me.

Crap.

Chapter 27

"Gus! You look better. Are you feeling better? I was worried about you."

"Is that why you were in my room?" Gus asked, his eyes so cold, I involuntarily took a step back.

"Yes… and no. I was talking to Aunt Tillie," I said. And then mentally kicked myself for not just going with *yes*. After all, it was true. Just not all the way true.

"In my room?" he repeated.

"We were talking about you. She still wants you to call off the ritual."

"Not a chance." Gus snorted. "What were you really doing?"

The enormous carrier bag started moving.

"What's in the bag?" I asked. And promptly sneezed.

"I asked you first."

"I answered you. I was talking to Aunt Tillie." I sneezed again. "Are you going to tell me what's in the bag or not?"

"A fur-covered favor. You can talk to your Aunt Tillie anywhere you happen to be. Care to elaborate on why that had to be in my room?"

The bag started meowing.

"Are those… cats?" I kept my eyes fixed on the carrier—it was better than looking at Gus. That must be why I was sneezing.

"Two sweet, innocent kittens. Barely a few months old."

"Two kittens, my ass," I said and sneezed. "That bag's big enough to fit an entire litter of Dobe puppies."

"They're big kittens." They moved around again, the bag sagging under their weight.

"Where'd you get them from? Chernobyl? Three-mile island?"

"You exaggerate, Miss Thing."

"Look, I don't care if they're giant, genetically-modified cats, a gang of hairless Chihuahuas or two small miniature ponies, they can't stay here. I'm pregnant and I think I'm allergic to them."

"What the hell kind of witch are you?" Gus frowned. "You can't be allergic to *cats*. Witches are *simpatico* with cats. Besides, you've never been allergic to cats before."

I sneezed again. "Guess there's a first time for everything. Why are they here at all? You can't just unilaterally decide to bring home giant mutant cats."

"They're not mutants. They're sick and Forrest can't have pets at his place. I'm taking care of them until his stepsister can take them."

"You know pregnant women are not supposed to go near litter boxes, right?"

"I do, now," he said, sighing. "So much for asking you to help me."

"And we have two Dobermans who have never seen cats. I have no idea what's going to happen when they meet."

"It's temporary. They don't have anywhere else to go. I'll keep them, and their allergens, and their litter box, in my room. You'll never even know they're here. Assuming *you* can stay out of my room."

"What about boarding them?"

"Forrest tried. It didn't work out."

The yowls and growls coming out of the bag didn't sound very kittenish. I tried to use my 'sight' to poke around, but all I could see were two, large spotted stomachs—one white, one bronze.

The cats screeched in protest at my intrusion, and I felt goosebumps rise on my arms. "Those aren't normal cats."

Gus looked down at the bag, and thought about how to answer.

"You may as well tell me. I'll find out, sooner or later."

He sighed and looked past me, at some point down the hall. "They're... kind of..."

"What? They're kind of what?!"

"They're... Asian leopards," he said, looking guilty. "Forrest's stepsister wants to start a breeding colony. They're a little... feral."

Was *that* what I was feeling?

"Are you fucking insane?!" I yelled at him. "You brought home two baby leopards? Are you crazy? What if they eat the Dobes? What if they eat us?"

He thought about it. "They probably won't. They're still young."

"Have you ever even owned a normal cat before? Do you have any idea how to care for one?"

"I'm sure it's not difficult. Witches have a natural affinity for cats. Besides, they're only visiting. They're not staying." Gus said.

"They've already been here too long." I sneezed.

"In case you forgot, we're sharing this house, Miss Thing. You're not the only one making decisions. Now, why don't we get back to why you were in my room."

I shuffled through one lie after another in my head—*I was looking for the remote, I thought I'd do your laundry, the door flew open on its own*—and discarded them all. The problem with talking to another witch, is that they can always tell when you're lying. It gets annoying.

I sneezed again and finally said: "I was looking for the toad bones."

"They're not in my room."

"I noticed. They're not outside either."

"No, they're not."

"Where are they?" I asked.

"None of your business, Ms. Nosy Parker."

I tried to tune into the images in his head, to get the answer he wasn't willing to tell me.

"What the fuck do you think you're doing? Do you think I'm a neophyte?" He snapped, and blocked me from his thoughts before I saw much of anything.

Damn it. That was stupid of me.

"If I have to guard my thoughts from you, then maybe it's time we re-think this arrangement. Because I will *not* live like that."

"I'm sorry." I said, my cheeks flushing red. "It won't happen again."

"You're damned right it won't."

Gus pushed past me, then turned back around. "What's with you, anyway? We both agreed that the Toad Bone Ritual was a fitting tribute to Grundleshanks, rather than just letting him rot. Besides, we don't have a choice. That ritual needs to happen. So I don't understand why you're so hell-bent on stopping me. And don't tell me it's your Aunt Tillie. She hasn't been around since she crossed over. I would know."

My mouth opened and closed a few times. What could I say? It totally was Aunt Tillie. She didn't just push my fear buttons, she danced a jig on them.

But why couldn't Gus see her? How could I convince him that his sight was on the blink? Unless he was right, and my imagination was on overdrive? I didn't think I was imagining her though—or what had happened at the cemetery supper, or in Gus's room.

"I'm afraid," I finally said. "You saw how sick you got last night. What if this ritual actually is capable of destroying you? Even if you don't think Aunt Tillie is really here, what if there's a reason that thought keeps popping up in my head, dressed in Aunt Tillie's skin? I like what we have. I don't want anything to change."

"Then you'd better take a snapshot, Miss Thing. The only thing the future is guaranteed to bring is change. The cauldron is always bubbling. Change is the very essence of life."

And with that, he stomped into his room and slammed the door in my face.

Chapter 28

I stood there for a few minutes, shocked. I hated being at odds with Gus. I'd never seen that coldness in his eyes before, and it creeped me out.

Then I heard a screech and a yowl from Gus's room, followed by a string of cuss words. So, I hustled my butt out of there. Last thing I needed was Gus thinking I had been standing there, eavesdropping on him and his feline monsters.

* * *

I grabbed my car keys and was about to leave to pick up my prenatal vitamins, when I got the oddest sensation from the cottage. It was wary about something.

I quieted my breathing and tried to sense what was causing the wards to get prickly. It was coming from the front yard.

I looked out the window and saw J.J., the stoner clerk from the Trading Post, walking up the front stairs, then back down and out to the street. Then he took a running start back up the stairs, his black Doc Marten boots thumping on the wood, only to stop before he hit the door, and run back down to the street.

I figured I'd better stop whatever he was doing, before the cottage decided he was a two-footed missile and turned him into a rhododendron.

I opened the door. "J.J., what in the world are you up to?"

He screeched to a halt and whirled around, whipping his stringy hair out of his eyes. "Oh, Dudette. You are here. I need you to do me a solid, but like, I'm scared shitless of your house."

I could understand that. The cottage had turned J.J.'s great-great-grandfather into a rowan tree, when he tried to set fire to the place.

"Then stop poking the wards. Come in and act like a normal person."

J.J. cautiously sidled up to the door, like he was worried the cottage would grow arms and grab him.

I yanked him inside. "Would you stop annoying my house," I said. "Before it turns you into an end table?"

His eyes got big and the blood rushed from his face. "Maybe we could talk later. Like, maybe you can come by the Trading Post?"

"You're here now," I said. "The cottage has let you in. Talk to me before it changes its mind."

He looked around, nervous, and edged closer to me. The smell of cigarettes, stale sweat and body odor was suddenly overwhelming. I ran for the bathroom.

*   *   *

When I came back out, J.J. looked like he was on the verge of passing out from fear.

"Sorry," I said, pulling my hair back into a pony tail. "The perils of pregnancy. What can I help you with?"

"Nothing. I'm good. See you later." He took off, running out the front door, down the stairs, down the walk and into the street.

I sighed. What a weird kid. I looked out the window, but he was long gone. So, I went out back to check on the puppies. They were ready to come in.

I lured them into my bedroom with puppy treats, and they promptly settled down on top of my bed. I petted them and left, locking the bedroom door behind me, to make sure it wouldn't accidentally open. I wasn't worried about Gus going in my room, I was worried about his baby leopards escaping and going on the prowl for a snack-sized canine.

Then I went down to the kitchen to grab a bottle of water.

That's when I noticed J.J. sneaking around in the back yard. It looked like he was trying to be stealthy. He had pulled his hood up over his head, to make himself less noticeable. But the huge KISS logo on the back, and the stained cargo pants with bulging pockets, gave him away.

I slipped on my gym shoes, then grabbed my shoulder bag and car keys. He was up to something, and I was going to find out what.

*   *   *

J.J. walked bent over, a magnifying glass to his eye, looking for something. He was so focused on what he was doing, he didn't notice me standing on the back porch, watching him.

He wasn't really going all that fast, mainly because he wasn't moving in a straight line. He was meandering in a serpentine. More than a few times, he came dangerously close to walking into a tree. When he moseyed on down the path, I followed.

I was able to track him pretty easily. He was so totally immersed in whatever it was he was doing, he had no idea I was behind him.

When he cautiously entered the family cemetery, searching around the tombstones, I couldn't keep quiet any longer.

"Did you lose something?" I asked.

J.J. screamed and fell backwards over a tombstone, landing on top of my Great-Uncle Bertram's grave. Then he screamed again.

"Would you stop that? It's just me."

J.J. kept screaming, until he was able to locate me, standing next to the angel statue at Lisette's grave.

"Snap out of it before I slap you. I'm not a ghost. If you don't believe me, I'll be happy to kick you in your goonies."

His hands crossed over his crotch and he sniffled. "Dudette. It really is you. I thought I was hallucinating. I hate this place. Who the hell has their own cemetery?"

"Then what are you doing here?" I asked, as I walked over and gave him a hand up. "I thought you were leaving."

"Yeah… I thought I'd pay my respects to your Aunt Tillie before I go." He said, brushing dirt off his pants and trying hard to look bashful and earnest.

139

"Did you think I buried her in the back yard?" I asked. "Is that why you were snooping there first? Or that I had chopped her into pieces and you needed a magnifying glass to find all of her?"

He looked at me blankly for a second, before he caught on. "Oh, right. Probably not so much."

"So why don't you knock it off and tell me what you're looking for."

"No disrespect, Dudette. But I would really rather not." He shoved the magnifying glass into one of his pants pockets.

"Have you ever wondered why this place and I get along so well?" I asked. "It's because we're cut from the same cloth."

"What does that mean?" he asked, his voice a low whisper.

"It means the cottage isn't the only one who can turn you into a tree."

J.J.'s eyes widened.

You had to love J.J. He was so gullible and sweet. I figured it was due to random brain cells being atomized by his on-going love affair with all things marijuana. If he wasn't human, he'd be a stuffed toy—albeit a dirty, slobbered-on, stinky one that was more than ready for the washing machine.

"So, cough it up. What are you looking for?"

He sighed, made a face and stared down at his dirt-covered sneakers. "It's kind of embarrassing."

I looked at my watch. "Great. Then you can tell me in the car."

Chapter 29

I grabbed his arm and dragged him with me—willing or not—over to Zed, my SUV. Zed had been Gus's SUV, but I had traded him my red Mustang convertible when I moved out here, never expecting that Gus would soon be following me out.

"Dudette! Where are we going?!"

"I need to get to the pharmacy," I said. "I can't waste the day out here with you, while you debate whether or not to tell me the truth."

*   *   *

Thankfully, it was warm enough that I could keep Zed's windows rolled down as we drove into town. Because the smell from the kid was killing me.

"J.J., you know soap is supposed to be practical, not a decorative accent, right?"

"What are you getting at, Dudette?" He frowned at me. "I use soap."

"Really?" I raised an eyebrow. "You shower every day with soap?"

"Well, no. It's like bad for your skin. So I only use it once a week or so."

"Seriously?" I glanced over at him, but he wasn't laughing. "Not using soap is bad for your social life."

"My buds don't complain."

"Between the cigarettes and the joints, your buds no longer have a sense of smell." I turned the radio on, but the only station I could tune in was playing country, so I turned it off.

"You know what your problem is? You are a smell snob."

"Just because I have a functioning nose, doesn't make me a snob." I tried to cast my mind out to J.J.'s apartment. The image I saw was dark. I could barely make out a rank-looking maroon-colored towel hanging on a bar by the shower.

"How often do you wash your towel?" I asked, then amended, "With detergent."

He looked at me blankly. "I don't know. Like… every month or two, I think. I mean, it's not like I wear my towel."

"That's the problem. You're taking a shower and then rubbing the stink back on when you dry off. You know what's a good rule of thumb? When you wash your clothes, wash your towels. Pick one day a week and make it laundry day."

"Seriously? Doing laundry that often would suck. I'll just buy more towels." He reached forward to turn the radio on, and the movement along with his sudden nearness, made me cringe.

I tried not to breathe as I turned the radio back off. "And if you forget the laundry in the wash, for like, a day or two—"

"—How'd you know that?" he asked. "Do you do that too?"

The smell was starting to make sense. "You need to re-wash it."

"Why should I? I washed it once already. I just toss it in the dryer."

I rolled my eyes, wondering how he ever got to his early twenties without learning the basics of hygiene.

"Besides, too much detergent is bad for you and the environment," he said. "I try to be green and limit my use of chemicals."

"But you smoke cigarettes? That's worse than all the detergent boxes put together."

"Nah, Dudette. I got righteous. I quit those ciggies from The Man. I don't need to make some fat, old, white men rich by ingesting their toxic chemicals. I roll my own. Pure, homegrown tobacco leaf. The Marlboro Man can suck my—."

"—Hey! What about soap nuts?" I interrupted. "They're actually berries, so they're totally natural, and they work on laundry. I think MyLife has them." MyLife was the local organic store.

"Seriously? The Crunchy Granola Store has berries that can wash clothes? Berries?! That's so totally fucked up. Do they work? What if you get wasted and try to eat them? Does your mouth soap up? Or do they kill you?"

"I don't know. Why don't we stop there and you can ask them. I'll bet they even have some natural, gentle-to-the-earth organic soap for your showers, too. Maybe even some organic toothpaste."

"Nah, I'm good for that. I use baking soda. If you've got baking soda, apple cider vinegar, tomato juice, coconut oil, aloe and mayonnaise, you can pretty much make everything you need. I make a killer hair conditioner with mayonnaise and coconut oil."

"How long are you leaving that in, before you rinse it? Minutes? Or hours?"

"I get distracted sometimes," he admitted.

That explained the stringy hair.

"J.J.!" I rolled my eyes. "Do you ever want to get laid?"

"Dudette! Are you propositioning me? I'd be totally into that."

"No!" I said, laughing. "I'm just trying to point out to you, I'm all for being green, but you have to do it right. You can't just slop food on your head and hope for the best."

"The Jayster doesn't believe in rules and recipes. I am all about experimentation."

"The 'Jayster' seriously needs to decide what's worse. Giving in to personal hygiene? Or dying a virgin?"

"Ouch. Harsh." He scratched his head, reminding me of the puppies when they had fleas. "Let me mull it over."

*   *   *

I pulled up to the green loading zone, by the old-fashioned soda fountain/pharmacy on the corner of Main. It was a busy shopping day for the little town. Even the beauty salon was full for a change. All the parking spots, which were usually plentiful, were taken. But I figured J.J. could sit in the car for me, while I ran inside.

I turned the ignition off.

"Thanks for the lift." He put his hand on the door.

I hit the lock button. "You're not going anywhere until you tell me what you were doing in my yard."

He sighed. "It's really stupid, Dudette."

"Stupid is fine. I can use the diversion."

"Okay, well, just remember you asked for it."

"You are absolved. Lay it on me."

He sighed. "You know how me and my buds have our stash growing out in the woods by Highway Two?"

I nodded.

"Since we've been having so many warm days in a row, we wanted to throw a 'summer is back' party. So we went out there to weed our garden, if you know what I'm sayin'. But it was all freaking gone."

"What do you mean, gone?"

"Pulled up. By the roots. All that was left was some scattered buds and cuttings."

"So what did you do?"

He looked around, nervously, and scratched his head again. "We took what we could find and went home. Buddy and Moe wanted to cure it and smoke a spliff, but it was a righteous plant, so me and Rafe wanted to clone it."

"Clone it?"

"Yeah, it's when you plant the cuttings. So we leg-wrestled for it and me and Rafe won. Buddy and Moe have like, no appreciation of delayed gratification."

"And what does that have to do with me?"

"We decided we were gonna plant the cuttings where no one was ever gonna mess with them. And we knew you had a really cool—and private—piece of land."

I laughed. "You planted your pot at my house?" Gus was going to love that.

He nodded. "Not exactly *at*, because your house is a bitch, but in the *vicinity*. But we were stoned on some primo hash that Moe brought home from his trip to Mexico, and now no one remembers *where* exactly. We've been looking. I mean, since the weather keeps being so like, freakishly warm, it's gotta be growing, right? But we can't find it."

He looked out of the window. "Oh, shit!"

"What?" I looked around.

The local sheriff was coming out of the diner four doors down from the pharmacy, and Forrest, of all people, was going in. They stopped and chatted for minute.

"Don't let him see me," J.J. squeaked.

"I thought the sheriff was down with your weed proclivities." I squinted, trying to read Forrest's lips as he talked to the sheriff.

Not like I knew how to read lips, but I was willing to give it a try. The more I stared, the less sense it made, though. I tried to move my mouth to mimic Forrest's. All I got was something that looked like *hello, nice weather* and *yellow balls fart pecans.*

How did deaf people do it? I sucked at reading lips. So I switched to glaring at Forrest, hoping to push him out of this section of town by the force of my will alone. That seemed to work as well as lip-reading. He was completely oblivious. Either that, or he was very good at blocking.

The sheriff walked over to his patrol car and J.J. squeaked again.

"Use your words, like a big boy." I said, annoyed. "Don't make me read your mind."

Another squeak.

I looked over to where J.J. had been sitting. He was gone. In his place, was a large brown-and-white rat.

Chapter 30

I looked down at the rat, and it looked up at me.

"What happened to J.J.?" I asked.

The rat's whiskers quivered.

"Well, *hell.*"

Between the cargo pants and hoodie, J.J. had a lot of pockets. Was it possible he had stashed his pet rat in one of them? Had J.J. snuck out of the car and accidentally left the rat behind, while I was distracted with Forrest? Had I been that hyper-focused on trying to read Forrest's lips?

Oh, *crap.* Was it possible that J.J. told me he was leaving, fully expecting me to hear him? Could he have asked me to take care of his rat while my mind was otherwise engaged?

Or had J.J. somehow turned into a rat without my seeing it? But wouldn't I have sensed that kind of magic building up? Could it have been the cottage? Was it pissed off about J.J.'s visit? Or his missing pot plants? Did the cottage's reach extend into town? I looked around. I didn't see any abandoned clothes, just the rat.

I wrinkled my nose and stroked the rat's head. "Snap out of it Mara. That's just crazy talk. People can't really turn into animals." Of course, they couldn't turn into trees either, but tell that to J.J.'s great-great-grandfather.

It *had* to be J.J.'s pet rat. J.J. was just the kind of kid to keep a pet rat in his jacket pocket. With the smells emanating off the kid, the rat would feel right at home.

"What am I supposed to do with you?" I put my hand out for the rat to sniff and tried to look inside its mind.

It was a dark maze, lit up by images of food and grass.

Well, that was no help. Those images could belong to either J.J. or the rat. Gosh-dangit. Gus was going to laugh his ass off about this.

A tapping at the driver's side window made both of us jump. I clutched at my heart, while the rat jumped down and hid underneath the passenger seat.

"Miss? Are you okay?" The sheriff asked, tapping on the window again with his nightstick.

I rolled the window down and smiled at him. "I'm fine."

"You're parked in a loading zone."

"I was just dropping off..." Instinctively, I turned to the passenger seat, but remembered there was no one there. I turned back to the cop. "...a prescription. I'm sorry. I thought I could run in and be out in ten minutes."

"Last I looked, loading zone wasn't synonymous with shopping zone. You need to get moving."

"Yes, sir." I said, not about to argue. "I'll do that right now. Sorry about that."

I started the car and he moved aside. Thankfully, one of the cars ahead of me was just pulling out. I drove up a few feet, pulled into a parking spot, and turned off the ignition.

After the sheriff walked away, I cracked the windows so the rat could get some air. It was a gorgeous day out—which I was starting to get used to—but still a little overcast, so the car wouldn't heat up too quickly.

*   *   *

I ran into the pharmacy to get my prenatal vitamins. There was a line to check out though, and by the time I got back into the car, the rat was sitting on the passenger seat, looking at me accusingly.

"I wasn't gone that long." I said.

The rat chittered. It obviously disagreed.

"Okay, okay. I'll take you with me next time. Chill."

The rat settled down and I started the car.

"So, 'fess up, are you J.J. or J.J.'s pet?" I asked him.

The rat twitched its whiskers and chittered again.

"Seriously, that's the best you can do? Even Grundleshanks figured out how to talk."

The rat glared at me with its beady eyes and said nothing.

"Fine. Be that way."

*   *   *

I drove to the Trading Post but, Anna, the girl behind the counter, hadn't seen J.J. at all that day. When I told her I had his pet rat, she gave me his address, as long as I promised not to tell him where I got it from. As I was leaving, I noticed that the picture J.J. kept at the register of his great-great-grandfather Jarvis, was missing. I was going to ask Anna about it, but another customer came in, demanding her attention. I filed it away, to ask her about later.

J.J. lived in a beige brick apartment building, in the middle of town. It was just as drab on the outside as what my vision had shown of the inside.

I rang his doorbell, but there was no answer.

I rang his neighbors' doorbells, but no one had seen him. And no one knew if he had any pets.

By this time, the rat was perched on my shoulder like a furry bird. I turned my head and sniffed him. It did kind of smell like J.J. Wouldn't that be wild, if J.J. could shapeshift into a large rat when he panicked?

I mean, who knew what could happen in Devil's Point? Most of the town thought the cottage had turned J.J.'s great-great-great-grandfather into a rowan tree, and they seemed to be okay with that. And when I was looking up the history of the place, I learned that the Native American tribe who settled the area told tales of shapeshifting skinwalkers. But I always figured that was code for astrally shapeshifting, not physically shapeshifting.

Besides, J.J. wasn't a skinwalker or a shaman or a witch. He was just a barely-out-of-his-teens stoner. If a potted plant had suddenly appeared in my car, it stood a better chance of being J.J. than this

149

poor rat did.

I finally gave up, went back to the car and drove to the pet store.

* * *

The sun had come out and since it was too hot to leave the rat in the car, I opened my purse and looked at him. "Don't poop in there, got it?"

The rat twitched his whiskers at me, got in the purse and settled down. I zipped it almost closed, leaving a small gap. Big enough for the rat to get air, not big enough for him to escape.

With the rat nestled in my purse, I went shopping. I bought dishes, a water bottle, cedar chips and a rat habitat. If the rat was J.J., giving him pet food seemed kinda rude. So, I stopped by the grocers and stocked up on nuts, seeds, fruits and veggies along with chicken, beef and fish.

Gus was going to get a kick out of this—when he started talking to me again. I was feeding the rat a better balanced diet than I usually fed myself.

* * *

At home, I put the Dobes out in the run, then gave the rat a bath in a flat Tupperware container. It was definitely not happy about the entire thing. It started eyeballing my thumb with a carnivorous look in its eyes.

"Knock it off," I warned him. "You bite me, and I'll turn you over the humane society."

The rat twitched its whiskers and seemed to be thinking it over.

"I need a name for you." I said, as I rinsed him. "You seem pretty smart for a rat."

The rat poked his nose up and I stroked it.

"Let's go with Gronwy. Duke Gronwy of Rattenshire."

He squeaked and I turned the water off.

"Great. Duke Gronwy it is. Until you either turn back into a human, or J.J. shows up to claim you."

Once he was dry, I crafted a cloaking spell on the cage. It wouldn't work if someone was deliberately looking for him, but it should hold if someone (or some animal) was just passing by. But, just to be safe, I put Gronwy and his home up on top of the bookshelf in my room—out of the dogs' reach, and away from cat territory.

I debated knocking on Gus's still-closed door. I didn't want to bug him if he was still mad, but if he wasn't, we needed to talk. I tried the doorknob—although, I didn't know why, really. If Gus had been in there, he would be pissed about me walking in uninvited, and if he wasn't, I would risk letting his monster cats out for no reason. But Gus had locked the door.

I put my palm against it for a moment. Other than the cats, I couldn't feel anything on the other side. Either he was out, or he had tossed mega-shields up around the room.

*   *   *

When I brought the Dobes in for the night, they made a beeline for Gus's room. A cacophony of sound emerged—screeches, hisses and growls from the felines, earnest yips, barks and growls from the canines.

This had disaster written all over it. I ran to catch up to them. A closed door was the only thing between the dogs and death-by-cat and with the current assault from both sides, I didn't know how long it was going to hold.

Chapter 31

When I got there, the Dobes were hell-bent on digging their way through the door, scratching deep grooves into the wood with their nails. Above their heads, I could see the doorknob turning.

I grabbed the knob and held it, stopping its motion.

"Gus!" I yelled.

But the only reply was the yowling of the cats. Either Gus was still out, or they had killed and eaten him. Either way, I wasn't about to go through that door to find out.

I let go of the doorknob and it immediately started turning again—the only thing thwarting the cats' desires to emerge and engage was the lock. Although, for all I knew, the evil feline geniuses were on the verge of figuring that out.

I grabbed the Dobes by the collars and hurriedly dragged the fretting dogs into my bedroom, where I closed my own door and then read them the riot act. I wouldn't have expected most dogs to understand, but these Dobes were super-smart.

They had such guilty expressions on their faces, I was pretty sure they knew exactly what I was saying. And they tried their best to make their misbehavior up to me by becoming super affectionate.

But when they thought I wasn't paying attention, I would catch them glancing over at the door, torn between staying put and behaving or sneaking out and engaging the still-yowling monster cats.

I couldn't do anything about the cats, but I figured I could try calming the dogs. I sat on the floor with them and hummed, my thumbs rubbing between their eyes. I   pulled in their energy and hitched it to mine. I slowed down my breathing and vibrational rate. Then I used long, slow strokes over their heads and down their backs, until I could gently roll them on their sides. As I stroked their chests, they started to yawn and close their eyes.

Soon, they were both asleep. Even the cats had settled down and stopped screeching for the Dobes' heads on a platter.

I slid out of the puppy pile and checked on Gronwy of Rattenshire. He was curled up on his nest of shavings, sound asleep. The whole house was asleep except me.

*   *   *

I went downstairs to the library and looked through volume after dusty volume, trying to see if I had overlooked anything about the toad bone ritual.

I kept coming back to a sketch of a guy, kneeling on a riverbank, by the light of the full moon. And then it dawned on me. Gus was going to need a full moon.

I pulled out my iPhone and quickly looked up the moon schedule. We had a full moon earlier this month, so he wouldn't be able to do anything until the beginning of next month. That gave me some time to get the delivery from China. And from what I was reading, for the week before the ritual, he'd have to keep the toad bones physically on his person.

Well, there was a plan—wait until the week before the next full moon, slip Gus a Benadryl, or get him passed-out drunk, then roll him and see if any bones fell out.

It wasn't the best plan, but it was better than nothing. I filed it away as a last resort.

*   *   *

The next morning, Gus pulled up in Sally, my ex-little red Mustang convertible, while I was outside, picking up our delivery box of fruits and veggies.

As he got out, he glanced at me and looked away, his face still hard.

"Would you knock it off?!" I asked. "Aunt Tillie's the one who said you'll regret it. Not me. Stop hating on the messenger."

Gus faced me, his eyes narrowing. "That's calculated bullshit. You need to stop pulling your Aunt Tillie out as a trump card, every time I do something you don't like."

I set the box down and looked at him. "You don't like it, talk to her. If she's riding my ass about something you're doing, what do you want me to do? Keep it from you? She's perfectly capable of impaling you with garden shears if you ignore her. I have the scars to prove it."

Gus snorted. "Right."

"What does that mean?!"

"I think you're seeing what you want to see."

"Like hell. Look, I don't know why you can't sense her anymore, but Aunt Tillie is totally fixated on this." I said. "She's making my life miserable, trying to get through to you."

Gus rolled his eyes. "Fine. Let's assume you're right—for the moment. Let's assume you are actually talking to your dead, pain-in-the-ass, Aunt Tillie. Living with ghosts isn't like living with people. It's easier to misconstrue their messages—between their subtlety and your filters, she could be saying *do the ritual* for all you know. Not *don't do.* You can't be certain."

"Are you kidding? This is my Aunt Tillie we're talking about. She wouldn't know the meaning of subtlety if someone smacked her upside the head with a dictionary. And she has more words for 'no' than Eskimos have for snow. I'm telling you, she's talking to people on the other side and getting the low down."

Gus snorted again. "So, she's second-guessing me, because some dead Avon lady told her it was a bad idea?"

"I'm sure she's talking to people who've done the ritual," I said, annoyed. "Or who've studied it. She has access to everyone who's crossed over."

"You really believe that the most advanced witches and shamans are hanging around in the Otherworld, educating your Aunt Tillie about the perils of the toad bone ritual? The mere thought of that is ridiculous."

"Why? Because you think they're too good for her?"

"Because she's insane. Can I remind you, she tried to kill you? Just a few months ago."

"She was trying to protect me."

"Some protection. She's a lunatic from beyond the grave. And if you keep listening to her, she's going to make you as nutty as she is."

He started up the stairs to the front porch.

I put my hand on his shoulder, stopping him. "You saw how sick you got after the Supper for the Dead. Can you tell me that didn't have anything to do with what you're planning?"

"I ate a contaminated plum—one that *you* dropped into the garbage disposal and didn't throw out. Thank you very much. That wasn't the ritual's fault. I haven't done the ritual yet. That was yours."

"You took the garbage can away!" I said, exasperated. "You know damn well that one of the ways magic works is through serendipity."

He shook my hand off and slammed into the house.

I sighed and picked up the box. This was the first time Gus and I had been in a serious, ongoing fight and it felt horrible.

I wondered how long he'd continue living with me, if we didn't make up soon. Would he leave me and move into Forrest's home, full-time, once the cats had been delivered to Forrest's stepsister? The thought of not having Gus around made my stomach sink.

Chapter 32

The weather had been so warm, for so long, we beat a couple of national records—not only hottest days, but longest warm spell. It was impossible to turn on the TV and not hear someone discussing it. Weather people tried to figure out how long it would last, while religious zealots and conspiracy theorists claimed it was a sign the world was ending—albeit for very different reasons: *Hell has come to earth* versus *the poles are flipping* versus *secret government weather tests*.

No one mentioned anything about *spoiled rotten rogue witch wanting his own way and wanting it now.*

* * *

Once Gus saw the grooves in his door, and I filled him in on what had happened, he did something to it—either doused it in some kind of keep-away spray, or figured out how to put a hex on it. He didn't say which. But it was effective enough to encourage the Dobes to give Gus's door a wide berth, instead of trying to get in and meet those cats, face to face. Unfortunately, it didn't work on the cats. They were constantly trying to turn the knob, or poke their claws through the gap beneath the door.

While Gus and I were polite to each other on the surface, underneath, Gus was still pissed off at me for snooping and interfering and I was still pissed off at him for not believing me and honestly, for the cats.

If he wanted to make sure I was never going to go in his room again, he couldn't have picked a better weapon than those cats. The smell coming from his bedroom was insane. And it never ended. I got that it wasn't the cats' fault, they were sick. But, wow. It was totally stomach-turning. I had to hold my breath just to walk past his door.

It must have affected Gus as well, because he was rarely around anymore. He only came home to clean the litter box, feed the monsters and give them their meds.

I finally left Gus a nasty post-it on his bedroom door, telling him that he needed to clean the litter box more often—like maybe two or three times a day, or teach his monster cats how to use the toilet and flush.

The next day, I found a nasty post-it on my bedroom door, saying that if he could put up with my all-day morning sickness, *Princess Vomitron* could put up with his kittens.

*　　*　　*

Finally, I (intentionally) ran into Gus one day, after breakfast. He thought I had left—and I had. I slammed out the front door, then snuck in around the back. I was tired of him avoiding me. And sure enough, the minute he thought I was gone, he headed into the kitchen.

He froze when he saw me. He looked like hell. His feet and hands were covered in SpiderMan and Disney Princess Band-Aids, he had bags under his eyes and he wore old sweats that smelled like cat spray.

"What happened to you?" I asked, grimacing. "You almost look like a straight guy."

"Not in this lifetime," he snorted.

"Did you forget to tell the cats your extremities aren't on the menu?"

He looked at me, eerily calmly. "Those cats will be the ultimate test of the toad bone. Today, the cats. Tomorrow, the world."

It was my turn to snort. "Because if you can tame them, you can tame anything, is that what you're thinking?"

He nodded and carefully poured himself a cup of coffee,

yawning.

"Those cats are about as normal as a three-headed snake. Before you try world domination, maybe you should drop them off at a zoo."

Gus shrugged. "They don't like being held. They'll grow out of it."

I looked at his feet, where blood was seeping through one of the bandages. "I think they've developed a taste for human. You may want to start sleeping with your shoes on."

"They're just rambunctious."

"Are they even real cats?"

"Of course they're real."

"They seem like were-cats to me. Or demonic leopards. Are you sure Forrest got them from a breeder and he didn't conjure them up out of your Goetia?"

Gus sighed and hung his head. I didn't even have to try to hear him thinking that the full moon couldn't come soon enough.

Just then, the doorbell rang. "Police. Open up."

Gus looked at me, confused. "Did you call animal control on the cats?"

"Of course not!" I protested. It hadn't actually occurred to me that I could. But I tucked it away in my head as an idea to think about.

Chapter 33

I opened the door to Officer Brand and his female partner, Officer Chen.

Officer Brand was pretty cute. He reminded me of Gus's brother, all muscles and dimples. Officer Chen looked like she was being dragged around on a door-to-door against her will. She looked pissed and bored and ready to shoot someone.

I smiled at them. "Can I help you, Officers?"

Officer Brand held out a photo. "Have you seen this young man?"

Curious, Gus looked over my shoulder. It was a picture of J.J.

"Isn't that the clerk at the Trading Post?" Gus asked.

"Yes, it is." Officer Chen said, glaring at us. "We have reason to believe he was last seen here."

Gus looked at her, confused. "Here? Why would he be here? And what do you mean, 'last seen'—is he dead?"

"God, no," said Officer Brand. "At least, we hope not. His family reported him missing."

"I haven't seen him," Gus said. "Mara?"

Ugh. What was I going to say? I couldn't very well tell them I thought he had been turned into a rat. But when in doubt, go with the truth, right? Or at least, all the truth fit for human consumption.

"Yeah, I saw him. He stopped by, looking for something he lost and I gave him a ride into town. Is that when he went missing?"

"What was he looking for?" Officer Chen asked.

Crap. What was I going to tell them? J.J. misplaced his pot farm? If they found it, he'd go to jail. And they'd probably toss me in as well, since it's somewhere on my property.

"A…" I was going to say a necklace he bought for his sister, but what if he didn't have a sister? What could he possibly be looking for? I caught a glimpse of Gus's colorful Band-Aids, out of the corner of my eye. "Comic book. He borrowed a comic book from a friend of his and lost it."

"Why would he have lost it here?" Gus asked. "He doesn't hang out here."

I tried to think '*shut up*' at Gus as hard as I could. "He said he went to the little cemetery in the woods to pay his respects to Aunt Tillie and was wondering if he dropped it on the path."

Well, that was close enough to the truth, right?

"You said you drove him into town?" Officer Brand asked, writing on his notepad.

I nodded. "I dropped him off in front of the pharmacy."

"Which way did he go?" Officer Chen asked.

"I don't know."

"How can you not know? You dropped him off, right?" she said, giving me the cop equivalent of the evil eye.

"Yeah, but then I saw his boyfriend," I jerked my thumb at Gus, "coming out of the diner and I got so distracted, I didn't even notice J.J. getting out of the car. Much less which direction he went."

"How can you not notice someone getting out of your car?" Officer Chen asked, still giving me the stink eye.

Gus looked at me, annoyed. "She does that. It's this weird hyper-focused thing she does. It's a total pain in the ass. I can be in the middle of a conversation with her and then I realize she's focused on something else and hasn't heard a thing. It's like, *bam*, Mara's not only left the building, she's no longer on the planet."

Officer Chen rolled her eyes, clearly not impressed with my observational skills. "So, when *did* you notice the young man had gotten out of your car?"

"Another Officer came up and told me I was in a no-parking zone. I was about to tell him I was just dropping J.J. off, when I noticed he wasn't in the car. I figured he must have hopped out while I was glaring at Forrest."

"Seriously? Is that any way to behave?" Gus asked.

"I'm sorry. He may be your boyfriend, but I don't like him."

Officer Brand handed me a card. "If you remember anything else, or if the young man contacts you, please let us know. His family is worried about him."

As I closed the door after the officers, a god-awful ruckus started upstairs—thumps, screams, growls, thuds and screeches.

"Oh, fuck!" Gus hollered over the din. "Why didn't you put the dogs outside?"

"Because I wasn't really leaving! Why'd you let the cats out?"

"I didn't!"

The Dobes came galloping down the stairs and into the kitchen, clearly freaked out, the cats riding them like demented jockeys.

The bronze cat was facing backwards, spraying on Apollo's head.

Meanwhile, the white cat was biting into Aramis's neck, doing his best imitation of a furry Dracula.

It was simultaneously funny, scary and bizarre. Gus and I both looked at each other like: *this can't really be happening!* And in that instance, I knew Gus had finally forgiven me and things were going to be all right.

I turned and followed them into the kitchen, yelling for the dogs to halt. They skidded to a stop, whimpering. Both dogs had bloody gashes, and they were looking at me to save them.

I turned the water on in the kitchen sink, and with the spray attachment, I hosed the cats down. But they weren't about to relinquish their hold, water or no water.

"Knock it off!" I yelled at the cats. "Before I send you to a wild animal rescue."

They glared at me, with a look that clearly said: "You've got to be kidding. You have *no* leverage over us. None at all. We will do as we please."

I turned on the water full blast, and hosed down the demonic baby leopards again, until they slowly jumped off the dogs—giving me a slit-eyed cat look that left no doubt they were complying because they were *choosing* to comply, not because I had anything to do with it.

I quickly shoved the dogs into the mudroom, blocking them in with my body and tossed a pair of gardening gloves to Gus. "Grab those cats and put them away!"

"Patience, woman. I'm getting them." He put the gloves on and bent to grab hold of the hissing, biting, scratching, Ginsu-clawed cat-nadoes. Bright swaths of blood appeared on his arms, above the gloves. I could tell he was trying not to scream in pain.

Just then, the front doorbell started ringing again.

"What the hell?! Are the cops back?" Gus snapped.

"How should I know?" I asked, frustrated.

"Maybe you can start by answering the door."

The bell rang again and the Dobies turned into barking, snarling fiends. They shoved their way past me, knocking me to the ground, and setting the cats into new paroxysms of torture-induction.

Gus screamed as the bronze kitten sank its fangs into his arm, while the white one raked him with its hind legs.

"For the love of the Gods, would you get the door before these two kill me?" Gus hollered as he picked up the cats—who were making sounds I'd never heard a cat make.

He hustled them upstairs to his room, hissing with pain at every new injury they inflicted, leaving a trail of blood in his wake, while I got up from the floor and limped after the dogs.

Chapter 34

I pushed through the Dobes and opened the door to find Paul standing there.

"Your timing sucks," I snapped. "What do you want?"

He looked completely taken aback. "I'm here to pick you up."

"What for?!"

"Are you kidding me? You forgot?!"

I looked at him, exasperated. With everything that had been going on today, I didn't have the patience for guessing games. And I really needed to check on Gus.

"The 3-D ultrasound? Remember?"

I closed my eyes. *Crap.* I had totally forgotten.

"Sorry," I said. "It's been a rough day. No caffeine. Cats gone wild. Too much stress. I'm a little cranky."

"I'm sure I've been part of the stress," Paul said. "I want to apologize for that. Wait. What do you mean, *Cats Gone Wild*? What do topless cats have to do with anything? Or is that code for something else?"

I laughed. "You've been watching too many cable commercials. Come in, sit down, I'll tell you all about it in a minute. I have to go check on Gus."

I stood back so he could enter. The Dobes immediately switched personas from ferocious guard puppies to laughing, smiling, leg-rubbing, *'pet me'* fools. And this time, instead of being paralyzed with anxiety, Paul walked right in and started playing with them.

* * *

I left Paul with the Dobes and ran upstairs to check on Gus. The cats were yowling in his bedroom. The knob was turning like a possessed thing, but the door stayed closed. Gus must have locked it. I walked down the hall and found him in the bathroom, staring at his bleeding arms. I glanced at the trashcan, where two empty Neosporin tubes and empty Band-Aid boxes were getting cozy with each other.

"Need help?" I asked.

"I need a third hand. The Band-Aids keep sliding on the Neosporin and smearing it off my skin."

"You're lucky you don't need stitches," I said. The gashes and bites on his arms were angry, the skin around them pink and inflamed. "Are you allergic to cats?"

"I don't think so," Gus said. "Why?"

"Your arms look like my back did, when I got tested for allergies. A few stitches on that big gash may not be a bad idea."

He shook his head. "If the Band-Aids don't work, I have super-glue in my bedroom."

I rolled my eyes. I knew super-glue was a viable alternative to stitches, but I had a hard time wrapping my head around using it, after a lifetime of being told not to get it on my skin. "Move over."

Gus moved aside and I dug around in the medicine cabinet until I found giant gauze pads and tape, as well as hydrogen peroxide, the last tube of Neosporin, and a box of butterfly bandages.

"Hold your arms over the sink," I said, opening the bottle of hydrogen peroxide.

"Are you kidding me? That's going to hurt!"

"It is not. If you want pain, I can pull out the rubbing alcohol."

Gus narrowed his eyes, but complied. "You are a cruel and unusual woman."

"And that's why you love me," I said, pouring the hydrogen peroxide over his arms. It fizzled and bubbled, cleaning out whatever infection had set into his wounds. A lot of people don't like hydrogen peroxide, but it was the most effective thing I had found to clear up cuts that were bordering on infections. I dried his arms off, then squeezed the Neosporin on a cotton swab and started applying it to Gus's wounds.

"Who was at the door? Was it the cops again?"

"Nope. Just Paul."

"Figures. His timing sucks."

"That's what I told him."

"That was so weird about J.J., wasn't it?"

I nodded.

"You know, it's just you and me, now," he said. "You can tell me what's going on."

"What does that mean?" I asked, applying fresh Band-Aids.

"I know you know something about that kid. Cough it up."

I sighed. "I think he may have gotten turned into a rat." Okay, that sounded crazy even to me.

"I'm sorry," Gus said. "What did you say? I think I may have gone deaf in that ear."

I made a face. "You heard me. I don't think he got out of the SUV, I think he got turned into a rat."

"Seriously? That's... crazy talk. People can't physically turn into animals."

I shrugged. "I don't know what to tell you. I have a rat in my room and it's either J.J. or J.J.'s pet. I can't decide."

Gus howled with laughter. "This I have to see."

"Hold on. Let me finish." I fastened the gauze pads around his arms with tape. "There."

By the time I was done, Gus looked like he had morphed into a very colorful, Son of the Mummy.

*   *   *

In my bedroom, Gus and I both stared at the rat. It twitched its whiskers at us, then grabbed a piece of lettuce and started gnawing on it.

"I named him Gronwy of Rattenshire, just in case it's not J.J. Maybe he slipped out of the car and left the rat behind."

"That gets my vote. Although turning into a rat would be way cooler."

"The problem is, ever since then, no one's seen J.J. Not his co-workers, not his neighbors, he hasn't returned home. So... I don't know."

Gus leaned closer and held out a finger for Gronwy to sniff through the bars.

"Careful. He got a little bite-y when I gave him a bath."

"Are you even supposed to give rats baths?"

I stopped to think. "I don't know. But he was pretty smelly—kinda like J.J.—so I did."

"Hmmm. I don't think it's J.J."

"Why not?"

"Well, he's straight, right? When a pretty girl gives a straight guy a bath, he's not thinking about defensive biting. His brain is somewhere else, entirely."

"You may have a point. But it may not work the same way when that brain is shrunk down to rat-sized." I opened the cage and Gronwy ran up my arm and hid in my hair, chattering at Gus.

Gus tried to grab him by the tail, and Gronwy turned and promptly bit his thumb.

"Ow! What the hell?! I get enough of that from the cats."

"At least the dogs don't bite you," I said. "So it's not like you're pissing off the *entire* animal kingdom."

The clock radio went off, playing—of all things—Michael Jackson singing *Ben*. A song about a rat.

"What kind of radio station are you listening to?" Gus asked. "Show tunes from the last century? Oldies-R-Us? Top 100 Hits From The Crypt Keeper?"

"Don't look at me. I have no control over the radio." I pointed at the unplugged cord that was sitting, curled up, on the dresser. "It plays whatever and whenever it wants. I can't do a thing about it."

As *Ben* finished, *Bad Moon Rising* by Creedence Clearwater Revival started.

Gus picked up the clock radio and examined it. "That's just weird. Not as weird as J.J. being a rat, but still..."

"I know. I unplugged it before Misrule, but it still keeps playing." I picked Gronwy up off my shoulder and returned him to his cage.

While Gus started taking apart my possessed clock radio, I grabbed my purse, a light jacket, and mentally prepared myself to get snapped at for making Paul wait.

Chapter 35

I forced a smile as I headed down the stairs to join Paul. "Okay, let's do this. We have a baby to look at."

I fully expected him to be livid. Instead, he was playing with Apollo and Aramis.

"Are you sure? Nothing else you need to do? Shed you need to paint? Stocks you need to buy or sell?" he asked—in a joking, not pissed-off, way—as he tumbled around on the ground with the Dobes. When I didn't answer, Paul looked up at me, his blue eyes full of concern. "Everything okay?"

I nodded. "Sorry about the wait. Gus went a few rounds with his attack cats and lost, so he needed my help getting bandaged up. But he's fine, so we're good to go."

"As long as he doesn't need a ride to the E.R., it's all good, right!" Paul asked, giving Apollo one last chest rub.

I stood there, not quite sure what to say next. I mean, it's easy when someone's consistently a jerk, because you know what to expect. But when they're unexpectedly nice, it throws you for a loop. I had gotten so used to our interactions being barbed, I didn't know how to respond to his attempt at levity and sincerity. But boy, was I relieved this car ride wasn't going to wind up being me, trapped in a small space and lectured non-stop on what an insensitive ass I was.

Then, Paul stood up and actually helped me into my jacket.

I couldn't take it anymore. "What's going on with you? Why are you being so nice?" I asked.

"Hey! I'm a nice guy. Nice is my default setting."

I snorted—not intentionally, it just kind of escaped me before I could stop it.

Paul sighed. "Okay, I deserved that. I've been... a little stressed lately." He stood up and brushed his hands against his jeans. "I'm sorry for being a jerk to you. I've been blaming you for everything, and that's just... really unfair. You were as much a victim as I was—more actually."

I looked at him, warily. Of course, he should blame me. *I* blamed me. I had made so many stupid mistakes over the last year. At least we both survived my stupidity—unlike my Aunt Tillie.

"What's going on?" I asked. "Men never admit when they're wrong. Apologies are usually a tactic to get sex."

He shrugged. "I'm not a typical man."

That was for sure. Not many men would have been able to go through the hell I had accidentally put Paul through, and still be sane.

"Besides, I have good news." He glanced at his watch and frowned. "Which I'll have to tell you about in the car. We're running later than I thought."

*   *   *

The car ride was a little odd. We were both on our best behavior, talking about mundane things, as Paul sped down the country roads. I made sure my seat belt was on and tried to relax, in case he hit anything.

Finally, I asked him about his news, hoping the question would distract his foot from the gas pedal.

"I didn't want to say anything until it was official, but I landed a teaching position at OMU. Old Main University in Oldfield. I'm the new Creative Writing Professor in their MFA program."

"That's great!" I said, truly thrilled for him. "But what about the high school? I thought you loved teaching there?"

"I do. But this is more money, better insurance, a more flexible schedule. And even better... are you ready for it? I was able to get you and the baby on my insurance plan."

"What?!" This conversation was happening entirely too fast for me. "What do you mean?"

"I wrote you in as my significant other." He slammed on the brakes as the car in front of us slowed to a stop.

Paul leaned on the horn and the driver flipped him off.

"What the hell is going on up there?"

I rolled down the window and craned my neck. I could see flashing lights up ahead. "Accident," I said. "They're blocking the lanes to let the ambulance through."

Then I turned my thoughts away from it—before my 'sight' decided to wade deeper into what was going on. I didn't want to know if anyone died or what their injuries were.

I focused on what Paul had just said. Insurance would be a good thing—a very good thing. Insurance would mean regular exams and I could deliver the baby in a hospital instead of in a blow-up pool in my backyard. Insurance was like the Holy Grail.

"Why would you do that for me?" I asked. I could feel tears welling up. Damn pregnancy hormones. I cried at everything—even TV commercials.

"If it's my baby, it wouldn't be very responsible of me to leave you both out in the cold, fending for yourselves, would it?"

"Even if it has hooves and horns?"

"You're still planning to raise it, right? I can't talk you out of it?"

"I am. But it's okay. You don't have to be part of the baby's life, if the thought of its existence upsets you." Oh, man. Even saying that hurt.

I felt my chest tighten and those tears that had been threatening, finally spilled out. I pulled a tissue out of my purse and tried to staunch the flow before Paul noticed.

Paul put his hand on my leg and gently squeezed. "I'm trying to do the best I can. Why else would I be going out of my way—and courting a fraud lawsuit—to get you health insurance? You've had awhile to get used to this. I just found out. Jeez Louise, woman. You don't give a guy much time to process."

"You're right. I'm sorry. I'm just stuck in defensive mode." I said, sniffling and wiping away tears. "I'll stop."

I took a deep breath, closed my eyes and tried to relax, letting the emotions flow out of my body and ground into the earth.

Paul squeezed my leg again.

I looked at him and smiled.

Cars slowly started moving and Paul returned his hand to the steering wheel. The sudden absence of physical contact made me feel chilly. I wished I was still wearing my jacket instead of tossing it in the back seat.

"It's a long ride, so I figured we could spend the night there. Maybe we could go to dinner and a movie after the doctor visit."

I opened my mouth to say that was great, but Paul interrupted. "I'll spring for separate rooms. You don't have to worry about me making advances on you."

Who was worried? I thought to myself. I would have welcomed an advance or two. Oh, who was I kidding? A night of hot sex sounded heavenly. Being pregnant had put me in a state of horny frustration for months—either that, or maybe it was the sudden and prolonged lack of sex, after all those wild escapades with Lisette and Lucien.

*   *   *

As Paul drove faster to make up for lost time, I tried to slow him down by commenting on the speed limit, nearby cop cars and the probability of speed traps. But soon, he'd be pressing down on the gas again.

"Why are we in such a hurry?" I finally asked.

Paul looked at the time display on the dashboard. "It took twenty minutes to get out of your house, then we were stuck in traffic for another ten minutes. I don't want to drive all the way out there, just to miss your appointment. We have the last appointment before the office closes for the holidays."

Oh. Well, that sounded reasonable, but I was a firm believer in better late than dead.

"Besides, I'm not *that* kind of guy. I'm known for being early. And I don't want to start being the type of guy who barely makes it anywhere on time."

He sped up some more.

I closed my eyes and reached out to the Lady with my thoughts. *"Show me what to do to keep us safe."*

Images started spinning in my head. A *fetch*. Of course. In my mind's eye, I reached into the void, taking a piece of it, and crafted a fetch with it. A giant serpent that I coiled around and around the car, like an astral bumper. I tasked it with keeping our SUV safe and keeping the cars around us at a reasonable distance.

I was so focused on what I was doing, I didn't notice when we arrived.

Paul, on the other hand, thought I had spent the drive sleeping. "Wake up, Sleeping Beauty. We're here," he said, as he parked the car.

I smiled to myself. *Sleeping, my patootie.*

Chapter 36

In the doctor's office, we had to fill out a bunch of forms and then wait to speak to a genetic counselor. It wasn't until I asked Paul for the date, that I realized it was Yule.

Since Yule happens on the solstice, it arrives a few days before Christmas. No wonder they were shutting down for the holidays after my appointment. I was surprised Gus hadn't reminded me, but we had been a little distracted with the cats.

I told Paul that I was going to have to turn down his offer of an overnight stay. Gus and I had standing plans for the Sabbat. I just hoped Forrest wouldn't be joining us.

Since Yule was the longest night of the year, in addition to whatever ritual Gus cooked up to honor the event, we stayed up all night, tending to the Yule fire until the sun came up. It was an old pagan superstition. A bit of sympathetic magic, giving fire to the night to make sure the sun returned in the morning without any problems, and kicked off the next Wheel of the Year.

Then, after Christmas, we'd chop the branches off the Christmas tree and keep the trunk. That would become next year's Yule log.

* * *

When we finally met with the genetic counselor, we had to go over our complete medical histories, as well as answer a bunch of questions about our parents and grandparents. Not that I knew much about my family, but I filled her in on what I could.

Paul, on the other hand, was a walking encyclopedia of his family's medical history. He had the counselor practically trilling with delight at the way his mind categorized and stored every pertinent piece of information—until he started asking her if a baby could have three genetic parents and if there was such a thing as spiritual DNA, as opposed to physical DNA, and how would it affect DNA mutations if the third string of DNA was non-human.

I discretely stomped on Paul's foot and told the counselor (who looked like she was on the verge of calling Security) that Paul was fascinated by theoretical science and he couldn't keep his mind from spinning off into fun tangents that had absolutely no grounding in reality. But if she indulged his wild flights of 'what-if' fancy, we'd be here all night.

As we returned to the waiting room, I punched Paul in the arm and told him to knock it off before they kicked us out.

There was a pitcher of citrus-infused water on a nearby table, so I poured Paul a cup and handed it to him. "You really need to start cutting back on caffeine. You're about to jump out of your skin."

"I'm just nervous. Aren't you nervous? This is where we find out if we're having a normal baby or a mutant."

"Paul! This isn't the X-Men. Of course, we're having a normal baby."

"No, you're right. Of course. I'm just... being silly." But he didn't sound like he believed his disclaimer. Instead, he seemed to be getting tenser.

I poured myself a cup of water and sipped it. I was pretty sure the baby would be normal. At least, mostly normal. Maybe on the witchy-side of normal. Just a little extra-special.

But Paul really didn't need to hear that.

* * *

Soon, it was time for the ultrasound.

I sat back on the table. Paul pulled a disc out of his pocket and gave it to the technician. I looked at him, quizzically.

"So they can make us a copy," he explained.

I felt my face light up. Normally, I only got fuzzy print-outs from ultrasounds. "How cool is that? A 3-D digital image. I can't wait to show Gus."

Paul's face darkened. "Don't tell me Gus's DNA is in the mix too."

"Of course, it's not." I said. "We're just friends."

This was not the time to tell him that Gus had always been there for me and he was acting more like a father-to-be than Paul. Now that Paul was starting to get invested in the pregnancy, I didn't want to say anything to jeopardize that.

I was hoping, by the time the baby was born, Paul would realize that he had been all worried for nothing. It would be great for the baby to have two dads in her life as well, instead of just me. Because, really, when it came to babies, I had no idea what I was doing.

"Fine. I'll email you a photo so Gus can see it."

Of course. His disc, his copy. I should have realized.

The technician must have seen the look on my face. "I think we have an extra disc here. I can make you both copies of today's visit," she said.

She started up the machine and smeared my exposed belly with goo. The doctor walked in, and the procedure started.

"First, we have to take some measurements," the doctor explained, in his lilting Indian accent, as he moved the ultrasound wand in various patterns, sliding it through the goop on my skin. "We're checking to see if there are any abnormalities in the baby's development. We're looking for anything out of the ordinary that may signify genetic defects or Down's syndrome. Once we're done, we'll show you the baby on the monitor."

"I'd like to see the entire process. I don't need to wait until the baby is ready for its close-up." I could have said, 'the garbage can is on fire,' for all the mind the doctor paid me. He was riveted on whatever he was seeing, directing the technician. She clicked computer keys, recording data and freezing images.

"I'd like to see the entire process too. I want to know if there's anything at all odd about the baby. Even the tiniest little thing." Paul said, tersely.

I frowned. No matter how nice he was trying to be, deep down, he was still afraid that this baby was going to be some kind of mutant. That we would somehow trap him forever, tied to us by an accident of genetics.

If I could have kicked him in the nuts without disturbing the doctor, I would have.

The doctor nodded and the technician turned the monitor to face us. The baby was curled up, floating in profile.

"Do you want to know the gender?" The doctor asked.

"Sure," I said.

"Me too," the doc said, laughing.

Just my luck. The doc was a comedian. He turned a dial and a swishing sound filled the room, punctuated by rapid thumps.

"Hear that? That's the heart beat."

"Is it supposed to be that fast?" Paul asked. He looked like he was about to jump out of his skin, he was radiating so much tension. "It sounds like a galloping horse. The baby doesn't have hooves, does it?"

"It's a strong, healthy heart. Nothing to worry about."

"What's the swishing sound?" I asked. "It sounds like an ocean."

"It's the sound of your blood flow."

"How cool is that?" I said, thinking about a song Gus often sung. *The ocean is the beginning of the earth, all life comes from the sea...*

"So is it a boy or a girl?" Paul asked.

The doctor shook his head. "This baby is crafty. It keeps hiding the important bits."

Come on, baby, I thought. *We're all waiting for you.*

The baby turned its little butt and mooned us.

"You may have to come back next month."

Paul looked irritated. "Are you kidding? That's all we're going to see? A profile and a butt?"

I frowned at him.

"Normally, babies respond to the wand's sound waves." The doctor shifted the wand around. "I'll see if I can encourage your little one to move."

I turned my thoughts inward. *Turn around, baby. Show me your face.*

There was no movement for ten, very long, seconds.

The doctor was just saying we should schedule another appointment, when the baby started to move... We had a three-quarters profile... And then a full on face shot, as the baby floated away from the ultrasound wand.

The doctor smiled, pleased. He pressed a button and the ultrasound machine spit out a picture.

"Wow. Look at her. She's so beautiful," I said and felt tears of joy starting. I was so happy, it was literally leaking out of my eyes.

"Is it a she?" Paul asked.

The doctor shrugged. "We never got a clear view of the genitals. The face on the other hand... This is what your baby's going to look like when it's born."

Paul looked at the photo, still nervous. "It's normal, right? No extra parts?"

"As I said, we'll have to try for gender on a different date."

"No hooves, horns, wings or claws, right?"

"Paul!" I snapped.

"I can't help it! It sounds like a centaur."

"That was a heartbeat, not hoofbeats, you moron."

The doctor gave him an odd look. "Sir, you're reading too many tabloids. Your wife is having a baby, not a mythological creature."

"She's not my wife," Paul muttered.

I turned to the doctor. "I'm sorry. You'll have to excuse him. He's an idiot."

The doctor laughed. "I understand. Fathers often get nervous. No, sir. No extra, non-human parts." He moved the wand, as the baby turned. "Hmmm."

"What?" Paul asked, sounding worried. "Hmmm is never good."

"It's nothing. It's just..." He looked at the monitor again. "For a second, I thought I saw something on the baby's forehead."

"It's not horns, is it? Was it nubby horn roots?" Paul shouted.

"Paul, stop it!" I shouted back at him. "You're being ridiculous."

"Calm down, sir. It was only a shadow. Nothing to worry about. It's gone now. If the baby had horns they wouldn't have vanished."

"Did it look like the mark of the devil? Was it in the shape of a 666?"

The doctor looked at him, annoyed. "Your young woman here is going to give birth to a child, not a goat or a demon. You'd do well to stop your subscription to the National Enquirer, turn off whatever fanciful TV shows are filling your head with impossibilities, and start reading parenting manuals," he said, glaring at Paul.

Paul cleared his throat and gave him a nervous smile. I rolled my eyes and went back to looking at the monitor and my beautiful baby.

Chapter 37

"That whole forehead thing was weird. What do you think the doctor saw?" Paul asked, still nervous as we left the office.

"No idea," I said, shrugging.

Actually, I had a pretty good idea of what the doctor had seen, but I knew better than to tell Paul. What had popped into my head, was that it was a Witch Mark.

It made me happy, because it meant I was going to have a baby witch on my hands, but it would freak Paul out.

As it was, Paul had freaked out the technician. When she pulled me aside to give me a folder with my disc and print-outs of the pictures, she also slipped me a business card for a family therapist.

She told me he specialized in Peter Pan syndrome, and suggested I set Paul up with an appointment, stressing how important it was for him to get his feet grounded in reality before the baby arrived. I assured her he had recently started therapy. Obviously, it wasn't enough, but maybe he could up it to twice a week instead of once.

*   *   *

As Paul drove us back home, I looked at the pictures of my baby. There was no gender reveal, but the face was beautiful and the tiny little body was amazing. I stroked my belly. *You did good, little one.*

I felt the baby turn and stretch in response.

When I looked up, Paul was—as usual—driving like a maniac.

But when he swerved too close to the edge of the lane, the car next to us also swerved, so it kept a consistent distance. When he got too close to cars in front, they moved to a neighboring lane. No one behind us was tailgating. It was like our SUV was protected by an invisible bubble.

I grinned. We were going to be okay. The fetch I had made was working. Since Paul was focused on driving, I took out my cell phone, texted Gus and we filled each other in on our days.

Me: I have gorgeous baby pics. And guess what baby has?

Gus: A penis?

Me: Ha. Funny. A witch mark.

Gus: Cool. We have a baby witch. I never doubted it.

Me: What R U up 2?

Gus: Forrest showed up. Took cats.

Me: Thank the Gods. U were running out of blood.

Gus: Very funny. Now I have no toad test. How was Paul?

Me: Kept asking doc if baby had horns, hooves or a tail.

Gus: Are u sure no horns? Becuz that would be wicked cool. We could hang ornaments on them. Or paint them in neon stripes.

Me: I'm good w/the witch mark.

Gus: We'll have to burn Yule log in fireplace. Raining heavy out here.

Me: Not here. :-p

Gus: Yuck it up, mama lama. Keep up that attitude and you'll call it to you. Just u wait.

"It's such a pleasure driving with someone who completely ignores you to text her non-boyfriend." Paul said, giving me an irritated look as he muted the radio.

"Sorry," I put the phone away. "I didn't want to distract you."

"Right," Paul snorted, clearly not believing me.

"Besides, you've been in a weird space. What was that about, back at the doctor's office? The technician was ready to turn you in to Family Services as a potential danger to the baby."

"I'm sorry. I just... flipped out. When I heard that heartbeat, I started thinking about Ichabod Crane—"

"—The Headless Horseman?—"

"And it all went downhill from there. I know what I was saying was rude and possibly idiotic, but it was like I had no control over what was coming out of my mouth."

"Was it the PPSD?"

He looked at me, quizzically.

"Post-Possession Stress Disorder. It's what I think you've been struggling with."

"I don't know. Can we please stop talking about it? I apologize, from the bottom of my heart. Can we move on now?"

I nodded. But, crap. If he was going to flip out like that at an ultrasound, there was no way I could risk having him in the delivery room. Thank the Goddess that Gus wanted to be there, or I'd be delivering this baby completely on my own.

So, we made small talk. Not about anything important. Not about the baby. Just about books, TV shows, the freaky weather.

As night fell, an overwhelming sense of exhaustion washed over me, and I had to close my eyes. I tilted my seat back, thankful that Paul was driving—even if he could use a few stints at a driving school. At least he was able to stay awake, which was more than I could do.

A few minutes later—at least, it felt like a few, but it was probably more like twenty—Paul nudged me awake.

"I was thinking we could go to the Fortenberry Mansion off Route Ten for dinner."

The Fortenberry Mansion had been converted into a restaurant and it was supposed to be spectacular. It had been built in the 1800's, and had been remodeled in the early 1900's, with a bowling alley and a private distillery in the basement a key club for the upper class, to get around prohibition restrictions.

"Isn't that expensive?" I asked.

"It's my way of apologizing for being a jerk. Hey, look at that."

The moon was just rising, huge and glorious. It was close to Earth and it looked amazing. A warmly glowing fruit that you could almost pluck out of the sky. It took my breath away.

"That's the most gorgeous moon I've ever seen," I said.

Paul agreed.

Suddenly, my blood ran cold. "Wait... is that a full moon? Totally full? Not even one little sliver off?"

"Look at it. That's as full as it gets."

Oh, no! I closed my eyes and tried to feel for Gus, but we were still too far away. Either that or he was deliberately blocking me. Was that what the radio had been trying to tell me with its song selection? *Bad Moon Rising.*

"How could it be a full moon?! We had a full moon, at the beginning of the month. And it can't be a blue moon. It's too early."

"You're losing your days, Mara. The last full moon was after Thanksgiving, not at the beginning of December."

I sat there, stunned. What kind of an idiot witch was I, letting the moon phases slip by, unnoticed? What the hell was wrong with me?! I mean, granted, I kept falling asleep at ridiculously early hours these days, but if I wasn't going to look up at the night sky, why didn't I check a damn almanac? Or a calendar?

Wait. I *had* checked the dates on my phone.

I pulled out my iPhone. *Yes.* I had bookmarked the site. I clicked on the bookmark.

"It can't be. The next full moon isn't supposed to be until the beginning of January."

"Tell it to the moon," Paul shrugged.

I made the site larger. "Damn!"

"Did you figure it out?"

"It defaulted to the wrong year. I was looking at the wrong damn year." Why hadn't I just charted it, looking out of the freaking window? Why did I believe a stupid app? Why had I stopped paying attention to nature, when I knew how much was riding on this moon? How could I have been so stupid?

So what I thought had been a waning moon during the Supper for the Dead, was actually a waxing moon.

Great. The full moon hit on the longest night of the year. Knowing Gus, he was going to be all over it. Unless it was still raining, he'd be getting ready to do the toad bone ritual. At the stroke of midnight, he was going to drop those bones in the stream, under the light of the full moon, and the horrible predictions, nightmares and visions Aunt Tillie had been flinging at me would come true. We'd get winter back and I would lose Gus forever. He'd either go mad and I'd lose him in this world, or he'd follow the bones into the wasteland and I'd lose him to the Otherworld.

"What is your problem with the moon?"

I shook my head. "I have to get home. Can we go any faster?"

"Okay…" Paul said, but he was thoroughly confused. "So you've turned down a fancy dinner, a movie and an overnight hotel stay for… what, exactly? Your gay roommate? The moon? Is this your way of telling me to get lost?"

"It's not you. It's Gus. He's in trouble. I mean, he's not yet, but he will be unless I get home."

"Did he text you or something?"

"No, but that's a great idea." I pulled out my phone and started texting.

Me: Is it still raining there?

Gus: Nope, clear and booty-ful.

Me: We're doing Yule tonight, right? I'm on my way home.

Gus: You'll have to start Yule without me. - I see a bad moon rising

Me: Ack! No! I know what U R up 2. Don't do it. Please.

Gus: Sorry, can't hear you. Too much static on this line. Call back later.

Me: Gus! I'm serious.

Gus: The party you have dialed is not home. Try again 2morrow.

I tossed the cell phone in my purse, annoyed.

"Can we please go faster?" I snapped at Paul.

He looked at me, surprised, but hit the gas, while I prayed for winged Hermes to grant us additional speed.

Chapter 38

As we drove, clouds moved in, obscuring the moon, and the wind picked up. It was as if the night was screaming, *"Danger."* The storm that had passed through Devil's Point was about to hit us.

Soon, the winds were at gale force and the moon had completely vanished behind storm clouds. Lightning raced along the horizon. Thunder shook the car. Rain pelted down in sheets and a gust of wind blasted the SUV.

Paul slowed down to a crawl as he struggled to keep us on the road. He turned on the wipers, but even at the fastest speed they couldn't keep the windshield clear.

"Weird fucking weather," Paul muttered. "Freaking summer storms in the middle of winter."

The slower we went, the more I struggled to keep little screams of frustration from erupting out of my throat.

Paul glanced sideways at me. "Mara, what is your damage?"

"Sorry," I said. "I'm worried about Gus. I just have this feeling that something is wrong. Can you go any faster?"

"I could, if I wanted to kill us. But I don't."

"Not even a teeny tiny bit faster?"

The rain, if anything, got heavier. I pounded my leg in frustration. I turned the radio to an AM station to get traffic and weather info. Maybe there was some kind of ETA on when it would blow over. But all I could find were commercials and religious pontificating.

"It's not raining in Devil's Point. So, the faster we head in that direction, the faster we'll be out of this storm."

"Nice try. Not happening." Paul said, pulling into a diner parking lot. "It's not the Mansion, but we may as well stop and get something to eat. We're going nowhere fast tonight."

"Oh, come on! This is ridiculous. Don't tell me a little bad weather is going to scare off your big strong he-man self."

"You're going to have to tough it out," Paul shouted over the pounding rain as he opened the car door. "Gus is a big boy. I'm sure he'll be fine."

He took off his jacket and held it over his head. Then he ran over to my side and opened the door. "Let's go. I'm starving."

Together, huddling under his coat, we sloshed through the rain and into the diner.

*   *   *

The small restaurant shook in the storm. Paul wanted to stay away from the windows, but I forced the issue. There might not have been anything Paul could do about the weather, but there was something I wanted to try. Finally, he agreed and the hostess led us to a window seat in the mostly empty diner.

While Paul was studying the menu, I closed my eyes and slowed my breathing. I started running my finger around the top of my water glass, in clockwise circles.

Hekate, Lady, I call on you.

I waited until I could feel the tingling on my skin that meant she was paying attention. Then I continued.

Tame these winds around me.
Soothe the savage beast.
Tonight, grant me peace,
And tomorrow we'll feast.

It might have been my imagination, but it seemed like the wind died down a bit. The window glass wasn't rattling as hard as it had been when we sat down. But the rain was still coming down in sheets.

I was about to continue the spell, when the waitress came over to get our order.

"We're in a hurry. What's the fastest thing your chef can whip up?"

"Probably a salad," she drawled.

"We're not in any hurry," Paul said. "I'm not driving in that storm. We're going to stay here until it dies down."

"We close at ten. But there's a hotel on the other side of the parking lot," the waitress oh-so-helpfully chimed in.

"Fantastic. That's the only place I'm going." Paul said.

"No freaking way! I didn't sign up for an overnight stay," I protested.

"So, you know what you want?" she asked, popping a piece of chewing gum.

"Just a tossed salad, no dressing."

"Steak, baked potato and green beans," Paul said. "And she'll have grilled salmon, a baked potato, and a cup of cream of spinach soup with that salad. I want coffee and she'll have a large milk."

I looked at him, furious. I didn't know whether to kick him in the kneecaps or be impressed that he managed to order food I wanted to eat.

The waitress finished writing the order, then took our menus and left.

Paul looked at me, daring me to bitch at him.

I glared at his reflection in the window.

When he got up to use the restroom—taking the car keys with him—I continued my spell.

I closed my eyes and circled the top of the water glass, until a childhood rhyme popped into my head. It was silly, but I figured there had to be a reason it showed up, so I used it:

Rain, rain, go away,
Come again some other day.
By the crossroads three,
As I will it, so mote it be.

"Ow!" I yelped as I felt a sharp pain in my fingertip. Blood dripped and blossomed into the water glass.

"Fuck!" Paul swore, returning in time to see the bloody water. "Are you all right?"

"Right as rain. Could you get me a Band-Aid?"

I wrapped a napkin around my finger and applied pressure, while Paul went to find the manager.

I closed my eyes and desperately bargained with the Lady, asking her what she wanted to quell the storm. The image of a fire opal popped into my head. I grimaced, hoping I could find a less expensive version online, and agreed to the exchange.

By the time Paul got back with the apologetic manager, concerned waitress and a Band-Aid, the rain was starting to lessen in intensity. It had turned the corner from biblical deluge to standard downpour. The waitress whisked away the offending glass, the manager offered to comp our meals, and I smiled at the success of the rhyme.

After we finished eating, the rain downgraded from downpour to normal rain storm. I talked Paul into skipping dessert and dragged him out into the parking lot, so we could get back on the road. I offered to drive, but he said he'd rather race a freight train than trust me with his car, in the frame of mind I was in.

As we traveled, I kept up a running dialogue to Hekate in my head, to continue dissipating the storm. The rain slowed to a light drizzle and the winds quieted down. We were still feeling small gusts, but they no longer threatened to topple the SUV.

I looked at my watch. "Can we go faster, please?"

"Mara, I'm not going to hydroplane the car."

"There's got to be a speed between meandering and hydroplaning," I snapped.

Paul grumbled, but he pressed down on the gas pedal.

Now all I had to do, was come up with a plan to keep Gus from leaving the house and heading to the stream. I had found a pair of fuzzy-covered handcuffs in the trunk in Gus's room, when I was looking for the bones. Maybe I could sneak up on him and handcuff him to a chair until morning. Although, knowing Gus, that wouldn't stop him for long. Maybe I could shove him into the basement altar room and lock him in until the full moon passed. It only lasted a few days, right?

Chapter 39

It took longer to get home than I anticipated. By the time Paul dropped me off, it was twenty minutes to midnight. I raced through the cottage, calling Gus's name. All that accomplished though, was waking the puppies.

Since the cats were gone, I risked going into Gus's room, and boy, did I regret that. As soon as the smell of cat hit my nostrils, I wasted precious minutes running for the bathroom. Stupid morning sickness.

The dogs, however, were having a field day rooting around in the cat toys. I had to drag them out by their collars. I locked them in my bedroom and I quickly checked on Gronwy of Rattenshire. He was sleeping in his cage, showing off a full round belly, his whiskers and paws twitching as he dreamt. His food dish was completely empty. If Gronwy was J.J., he certainly seemed to be enjoying his stint as a rat.

I tried to sense Gus, but the wards he put up when he was pissed at me effectively blocked my sight. So, I had to rely on logic and reason—two of my least favorite tools.

Gus would be at the stream, but where? It was an awfully large stream, and it meandered quite a distance.

Think, Mara, Think.

The stream was fed by a waterfall. At the bottom of the cascade, once you got beyond the rocks and roots and fallen tree trunks, about ninety yards out, the stream grew wider and not as rocky. An enormous weeping willow grew there, its roots dipping deep into the water, and there was a dusting of toadstool mushrooms that grew in its shade.

Gus called it his fairy garden, because of the importance of both the toadstool mushroom and the weeping willow to the Queen of the Fae. And since that was the widest section of the stream, that's where he was most likely to incorporate the full moon into his ritual.

That's where he *had* to be.

*   *   *

I raced out of the house and through the woods, sliding in the mud and catching myself on trees, trying not to trip on rocks and exposed tree roots. By the time I reached Gus and his faery garden, my palms were bloody and stinging.

"Gus, don't!" I yelled from the top of the hill. The waterfall was beating down, churning the swollen stream into a frothy dance. I wasn't sure if Gus could hear me over the sound of the rushing water. But somehow, he managed to sense me.

He turned and looked up, as I slid down the hill towards him.

He was wearing a shorty wetsuit and his face was handsome and determined in the moonlight. "It's not your decision to make," he hollered. "You can help me or leave me, but don't get in my way."

I kept moving forward, trying to get closer to him, but I was terrified I was going to lose my footing over the slippery tree roots, mud and large stones, and fall into the thundering stream below.

"Gus, be sensible. Look at the water. At least wait until next month, when it goes back to normal." That would give me a chance to get the other toad bones delivered from China.

"Are you kidding? This is the perfect time. You heard the radio. It's a Bad Moon Rising. I'm not wasting it."

Gus's watch alarm went off. He must have had it set for the stroke of midnight. He raised his arm...

"Fine! I'll help. I can't let you do this alone. You'll kill yourself."

...and he threw the bones into the river.

I heard a high-pitched scream come from the rushing water. "What the hell was that?!"

"It's the toad bone!" Gus said, and promptly jumped into the stream, slipping on a submerged tree root.

He fell on all fours, completely going under the water, but he quickly emerged and regained his footing, holding on to a large rock to help him stand against the current.

"Do you see it?! Where is it?"

I looked around. I was on higher ground than Gus, so I had a slightly better view. Gus was looking for the one bone that would go against the tide and float upstream. Although, with the strength of the current, I doubted anything as lightweight as a toad bone could fight its pull.

But in the moonlight, I thought I saw a small shadow coming toward me, spinning off one of the rocks.

"I see it! At least, I think I see it!"

"Where?!" Gus asked, splashing around.

"There! By the roots of that river birch."

I slid closer to the stream. I could barely see a small, shovel-shaped piece of bone in the moonlight. It was standing still. I wasn't sure if it was caught on something, or if it was resisting the pull of the stream.

"I think it's stuck."

But then the bone began to move. It was definitely going upstream!

"It's moving! Hurry!" I yelled, completely focused on the bone.

Gus pushed through the current towards me, fighting hard to keep moving forward, swimming through the deeper sections, wading and running through the shallower sections. Finally, he made it to a nearby grouping of rocks.

"It's just ahead of you, slightly to your right."

Gus lunged for the bone, but his foot got stuck in one of the rock piles. He fell forward, cursing. "Son of a bitch!" he howled in pain and anger.

"Hurry!" I said, all thoughts of Aunt Tillie and her warnings completely out of my head. All I could think about was getting that toad bone.

I slipped and slid up the bank, trying to keep the bone in sight. "It's moving faster!"

"Ow! Fuck!" I could hear Gus splashing, as he waded through the water towards me.

I glanced over at him. The water was up to his chest and rising.

"This stream is freezing cold."

So was the night air, for a change. My teeth were chattering and I was shivering, for the first time in weeks.

"Gus! The weather's turning. We have to get out of here."

"I'm not leaving without that bone!" He grunted.

"Look to your left! It's in that shaft of moonlight."

He lunged, grabbing it up with a war whoop. "I've got it! Mara! I've got the toad bone!"

I heard a shriek—I don't know if it was from Gus or the bone or the churning water—as the stream seemed to rise up and shove him. He fell backwards, his feet losing their purchase on the bottom.

The current was angry and moving faster than I'd ever seen it. It slammed his body downstream, bashing him against rocks and roots.

"Gus!" I slid down the hill, trying to follow him as quickly as I could.

Gus's screams made my blood run cold. I don't think I've ever heard him make sounds like that in his entire life. Not even when the cats were carving him up. I didn't want to think of the damage the rocks were doing to him.

The stream had turned into a writhing, living thing, punishing Gus and dragging him under the water at every opportunity. If I didn't think of a way to save him soon, Aunt Tillie's prediction was going to come true. I would lose him forever.

Lightning strikes lit up the sky, rain pounded down and a big, thundering book shook the ground under my feet. The hill seemed to shrug, and the next thing I knew, I was tumbling into the water.

Gus was rapidly heading towards the river birch and I was following close behind, spinning off of partially-submerged rock formations. I had to do something, before the stream killed both of us.

Without thinking, I opened my sight, turning my entire body into a conduit. The world looked different, like a weird, surrealistic representation of itself. In the sky, I could see electrical energy crackling through the clouds,

I reached up and called on Hekate to help me.

Hekate's fire, Guide my hands,
as I this bolt of lightning send...

I gathered the spirit of the electrical sparks, and threw it as hard as I could, into the river birch. The tree moaned and shrieked, swaying in the wind.

Lightning struck the tree, in the same spot, and the trunk splintered. The tree fell across the stream, stemming the tide.

Gus caught himself on the trunk, seconds before I slammed into him.

"I've got it," he said, weakly, holding up the toad bone. "I've got it."

I nodded, trying to catch my breath, and felt a cold chill run through my body.

Gus may have the bone, but nothing ever came without a price tag—whether it was for a pound of currency or a pound of flesh. If Gus had the toad bone, who now had us?

Chapter 40

The rain petered out as the storm cell moved on. Gus and I hugged the tree, using it as a lifeline to get up to the shore. I climbed out of the stream, my feet squelching in the mud. Gus tried to climb out but fell back into the water. I grabbed onto his arms and dragged him onshore.

"We can't climb back up the hill. It's too slippery. We need to keep going forward, down to the old willow tree and over to the east side of the forest. Even if it's muddy, the land's flatter there and there's a back way to the cottage that's not as steep."

Gus nodded. He tried to stand up and yelped.

"What's going on?" I asked.

"It's my knee. I must have bashed it into the rocks or twisted it."

"Can you walk? Here, lean on me."

"Forget it. I'm a man. I'm hardwired to eat pain for lunch and keep going. I'm not going to lean on a pregnant chick." He said, wincing.

I picked up a downed tree limb that looked like it could double as a walking stick. "Can you use this without losing your he-man status?"

Gus nodded. "Thanks."

He took it from me and, with some cussing, used its help to step out of the muck and go further up the bank.

*   *   *

As we got closer to the tree, I noticed the weirdest thing I've ever seen. The toadstool mushrooms under it were huge. And by huge, I mean enormous. Like, house-sized.

"Holy crap! Are you seeing what I'm seeing? That's fucking amazing." Gus said.

"Oh, my gosh. They are so pretty." I know it was an inane comment, but I was struck with it all of a sudden. Toadstool mushrooms are generally pretty, but wow, when they're twelve feet tall, they're really gorgeous.

"Did they grow or did we shrink?" I asked Gus.

"I don't know," he said, examining the ten-foot wide stem. "Is this a door?"

I looked to where he was pointing. At first, I didn't see anything. But when I shifted my vision—like with those weird three-dimensional pictures—I could see lines in the stem intersecting to form a door.

"It definitely could be."

"I'm going in."

"Wait!" I said, putting my hand on his arm. "This seems like a really bad idea."

He shrugged. "When else are we ever going to have the opportunity? Can you imagine telling the baby about the time we went inside a toadstool?"

I couldn't. Not unless the sentence following that declaration was: *we were so stoned, completely out of our heads on some kind of bizarre acid trip.* This was way beyond the scope of normal, even for *my* life.

"This kid's going to grow up and have us committed," I muttered. "What color do you want your rubber room to be?"

Gus frowned. "There's a reason that pessimists don't rule the world. Life is all about optimism, baby. So get on board the Sunshine Express."

I snorted. "I'm not a pessimist. I'm a realist."

"We're about to go where no man has ever gone before. We're

like the Star Trek captains of witchery. Kirk and Picard. Janeway and Archer. Mara and Gus."

"Did you just call me Janeway?"

"Seven of Nine and the Borg Queen." Gus pressed his hand against the door, but nothing happened.

He tried knocking against it with his walking stick. It just dented the door for a few seconds, before the fleshy skin of the mushroom sprang back.

"Try the toad bone," I suggested. After all, if anything should unlock a toadstool door, it should be a toad bone, right?

Gus took the bone out of his pocket and pressed it against the door. It solidified into wood and swung open.

*   *   *

Inside, was the cutest little cottage I'd ever seen. The floor was dirt and the furniture was made of twisted and gnarled branches of living wood, as if it had grown in those shapes and was still humming with vitality. Even the cushions were thick plant growth—soft moss, leaves and flowers. There was even a table-shaped tree, with a giant flat rock balanced on top of it and sturdy-looking mushrooms providing seating around it. Beeswax candles were nestled into candle holders made of crystal formations. Everything seemed alive. Even the hanging lanterns were made of spun sugar.

Gus pushed me, "Ladies first."

"Stupidity before gender," I said, backing into him. "You opened the door, you go first."

"I need to bring up the rear, in case anything attacks you."

"Like the Travelocity gnome, maybe?" I asked. "Or a fairy on steroids?"

"Don't mock the Fae. They can be terrifying." Gus said.

Knowing Gus, I was sure he had first-hand knowledge of that.

"Coward." I stood at the threshold, looking around in wonder.

In my wildest dreams, I had never seen anything like this cottage. In the kitchen, the sink area was a small waterfall that fed into a round, flat basin, large enough to bathe in, and then down a smaller waterway that went under a small arch, out of the house and probably re-emerged in the back garden.

203

Suddenly, something shoved me, hard, and I was all the way in the cottage. I turned my head, furious, as the door slammed shut behind us.

"Why did you do that?!" I hissed at Gus.

"I didn't do anything!" Gus protested. "Something shoved me."

He looked around. "Talk about landing in the Enchanted Forest. Could this place get any creepier?"

"It's adorable," I said.

"You need to get your head examined. It's like the forest is absorbing the cottage. The wild things are taking over."

"Don't you think you're exaggerating? I'd love a little hideaway like this on our property."

Gus shuddered. "Count me out."

"Whatever happened to boldly going were no man has gone before?"

"We went, we saw, let's go back. This place gives me the creeps." He turned around to open the door, but it was gone. In its place was a smooth expanse of wall.

Gus tried putting the toad bone against it, but nothing happened. Then he got irritated and whacked it with his walking stick. The wall boomed and the sonic wave threw Gus backwards, bouncing him off the table and onto the ground.

Chapter 41

"Ow!" Gus howled in pain. "Son of a bitch!"

"Are you okay?" I asked.

"No, I'm not freaking okay."

"Can you stand up?"

"Give me a minute," he grunted. But as soon as he tried, his right leg started buckling, and he collapsed on one of the mushroom seats. "It's my fucking knee. I can't put any weight on it."

His knee was exposed under the shorty wetsuit and it looked even more swollen than it had been before. There had to be something I could do to help him.

I had been reading up on energy healing and quantum touch while Gus was in Chicago, figuring it would be useful when the baby arrived. Maybe it was time to put theory into practice.

I looked around. There was a wooden pail next to the fireplace. I filled it with water from the miniature waterfall in the kitchen, and brought it over to Gus. I centered myself and focused on pulling energy up from the ground, through my body and into my hands. Then I rubbed my palms together, increasing the vibration of the energy.

"What are you doing?! Don't touch my knee!"

"I have to touch it, you big baby. I'll be careful."

"Forget it!" He shook his head. "Not while you're pregnant. Healing spells are dangerous. I don't want you accidentally harming the baby."

"Either this is one kick-ass hallucination or we're inside a freaking toadstool, in the Faery Realm of the Otherworld. *Anything* could happen. I need you ambulatory. The baby and I can't get out of this place on our own."

Despite his misgivings, he finally agreed to let me try. When my palms were tingling, I laid them on Gus's knee. As my fingertips explored his skin, I used my 'sight' to see what was going on. The spongy layer under the knee was torn and bulging, and a secondary ligament on the outside of the knee was partially torn. That explained why the front and side were swollen and hot to the touch.

I visualized the pain Gus was having as a living object, a black ball of agony. I gently coaxed the ball of pain up and out of his knee. Then, holding it carefully, I plunged it down into the pail of water and held it there, drowning it. Gus shuddered, a small cry ripping out of him and dying off with the pain ball's submersion into the pail.

Gus opened his eyes. "Wow. You did it. My knee feels better." When he tried to stand up though, it buckled underneath him. "Better than it works, apparently."

"We're not done yet. I need to rock your leg back and forth just a little. Don't worry, it'll be a gentle movement."

Gus made a face, but closed his eyes and let me manipulate his leg. I visualized the interior of the knee as a liquid environment and used it, along with the motion, to ease the white, spongy meniscal disc back into place. Then, I flooded the knee with warm, healing energy, increasing the blood flow and pushing the tendon into repair mode.

As the ligament knitted itself together, I could feel my own energy levels depleting. *Damn.* I hadn't been able to draw up enough outside energy. Soon the working would be pulling it from my personal stores and then the baby's. I couldn't let that happen. But when I tried to disconnect, I felt something sinewy wind around my hands, holding them in place.

I opened my eyes and saw that vines had come up from the floor of the cottage and wrapped themselves around my hands and Gus's knee, anchoring us together.

"Gus, help!" I yelled. I wrenched backward with all my strength, but the vines held fast.

He opened his eyes and saw my predicament. He tried to pull the vines off, but they got tighter. "I told you this place was creepy!" he snapped. "I need a knife."

I could feel the cottage cringe when he said that, and I knew there wasn't a knife to be found on the premises—even if we had the ability to go searching for one. "If you can magic a knife up out of thin air, I'll be really impressed."

"Be ready to be amazed." Gus said. He unzipped a small pocket on the thigh of his suit and pulled out a Leatherman all-purpose multi-tool and a waterproof lighter.

"Don't damage the vine, if you can help it," I said. "I think it's tied into the rest of the cottage somehow."

"Fine. Fire before steel." He lit the beeswax candle and held the flame to the vines—close enough to singe the plant without actually lighting it on fire.

The vine shrieked and let go of us, descending back down into the dirt floor.

"I knew this pocket would come in handy," Gus said, sounding pleased as he zipped the lighter and Leatherman back into it.

"Good planning," I agreed.

I felt kind of fuzzy. I leaned against the table, feeling woozy and a little nauseous. The room seemed darker than before, and slightly out of phase, like there was actually multiple rooms, all on top of each other, but they weren't quite lining up anymore. It was starting to make me dizzy. Sleep sounded really good. I just needed to take a nap. Like, maybe for a year or two, and I'd be fine.

"Don't you dare, Mara!" Gus said, forcing me to wake up. "Don't you dare fall asleep in a faery realm! You could trap us here."

"Just for a minute. I'm so tired." I yawned.

"Mara! Don't make me throw that bucket of pain water at you."

I shuddered. That was the last thing I needed. Gus enveloped me in his arms, pushing energy into me, rubbing my arms and back, trying to get my vibration rate up.

"Don't," I croaked. "You need that energy to heal."

"So I'll limp a little. My knee feels great. I can't go dancing on it yet, but look at me—I'm standing! I can walk!"

I smiled. "Yay, me."

"Come on, Mara! Knock it off. You need me to be walking, and I need you to be awake, to help me find a way out of here."

I nodded, trying to open my eyes. It was just so difficult.

"Mara! Listen to me. That little witchlette inside of you doesn't want to be stuck in your womb for the next six decades. You need to stop fighting me and wake up! Now!"

He slapped me and the sudden pain jolted me awake.

I pushed away from the table, still a little shaky, but better than I had been.

"Now what?" I asked, shaking my head to clear it.

"Since we can't go back, we'll have to keep going forward."

I nodded and rubbed my eyes to get the last of the sleep out. A sudden movement caught my attention. "Did you see that?"

"What?" Gus looked around.

"I think… Grundleshanks just hopped into the back room!"

"Seriously? Grundleshanks is *here*?" Gus asked, his voice strained. "Why do you think it was Grundleshanks?"

"It was a giant toad wearing a witch hat. And whenever I think of Grundleshanks, I see him wearing a witch hat. Whoa! Do you think we accidentally ingested some of the mushrooms? Or got hit on the head with a falling branch? Maybe this *is* just one giant hallucination. I mean, toads don't generally hop around with witch hats on their heads, in any realm. Do they?"

Gus smacked me on the arm with his walking stick.

"Ow! What the hell is wrong with you?! That's going to leave a bruise."

"If this was a hallucination, that wouldn't have hurt."

I slapped Gus, as hard as I could.

"Ow!" he said, his hand rising to his cheek.

"Sorry, had to check." My hand could use an ice pack, so that had probably hurt Gus more than I intended. "Now, we're even."

"You're just vindictive."

I shrugged. "Guess it's not a hallucination."

Then I saw Grundleshanks again.

I nudged Gus's arm and pointed. "There he goes! Follow that toad!"

Chapter 42

We hurried after Grundleshanks, through the kitchen and out the open back door. The full moon hung low and bright, and the night was full of music. Crickets, tree frogs, owls, foxes and wolves serenaded us from every direction.

We were worried we'd lose Grundleshanks, but he was waiting for us in the yard, his tiny witch hat at a jaunty angle.

"I told you it was Grundleshanks! Even if he is bigger than he used to be. Talk about freaky!"

"More like awesome!" Gus said. "And we're finally out of that horrible cottage."

"What do you mean, horrible? Except for the end bit there, I thought it was charming."

Gus gave me a look like I was crazy. "You are one weird chick."

As soon as we caught up to Grundleshanks, he was on the move again, leading us down a very familiar path.

I looked around and goosebumps rose on my arms. "Gus, do you notice anything odd?"

"Other than we've gone into a toadstool, wound up in some kind of weird faery land and are now following an oversized, not-so-dead, magickal toad?"

"Yeah. Other than that," I said.

"Nope. My brain's been pretty preoccupied with just that. This place is like some kind of fever dream."

"This is our backyard."

"What? How can you tell? It doesn't feel like home."

"Look! There's our cemetery." I pointed to the ornate gate, which in this realm, was an elaborate wooden structure wrapped in ivy. In the center of the cemetery, instead of an angel statue, an old tree grew in the shape of an angel, with the branches forming the hair and wings.

"Fantastic. I need to be in a cemetery for the next part of the ritual anyway. Maybe this is all part of what's supposed to happen."

I snorted. "I seriously doubt that."

"How do you know? Neither of us have ever done this ritual before."

"If anyone else had wound up in a parallel Toadstool World, they'd have totally written a book about it. Or a script. Or at the very least, put an article on the Internet. Nobody does anything nowadays without telling the world about it."

As Gus opened the gate, a huge, beautiful Doberman ran up from inside the cemetery, barking and snarling.

Gus slammed the gate shut, and backed up a few steps.

"Awwww, look at the cute little doggie," I said. "He looks like Aramis, but all grown up."

"Are you kidding me? He could eat Aramis and still have room for Apollo—and possibly us."

I squatted down in front of the gate and held my hand out for the dog to sniff. "You're so beautiful. What a pretty boy."

The Dobe got down on his front end, his hips in the air, his lips bared in a grin, making *play-with-me* noises.

"What a good doggie," I said, standing and unlatching the gate.

"Mara! Stop! Are you crazy?" Gus hollered. "Don't go in there!"

"He's not going to hurt me."

"Mara! Don't! I mean it!"

I ignored him and went into the cemetery.

From behind the safety of a tree, Gus's voice called out to me again. "Mara, please, I'm begging you. Step away from the snarling beast! For your own safety."

"Don't be silly, Gus. He's a sweetie." I sat down on the ground and started playing with the dog.

"He's going to eat you alive."

"No, he's not. Are you, boy?" I asked the puppy. I turned to Gus. "Having those cats at home has changed you. You've never been this weird around dogs before."

The Dobie wagged its stumpy tail.

"That's because he's not a dog. He's a giant, slavering Hell Hound who looks like he snacks on linebackers."

"Oh, please. He's just a sweet, oversized Dobie, who likes getting his chest scratched," I said, as the dog rolled over on its back.

As I petted him, the oddest thing happened. It was like my perception shifted and I was suddenly able to understand the different sounds around me, in a way that I've never understood them before. The animal calls, even the whispering of the wind, they were all part of a song that made exquisite sense. They were all different vibrations, different strings on the same instrument, and their song was heartachingly beautiful. It resonated in my soul at a profound level. I tried to grab hold of a phrase here and there, to take what the wind was singing and translate it into English, to fix it concretely in my head, but it was like trying to hold onto quicksilver.

It's all in your perspective, I heard a whisper in my head say.

Was that Aunt Tillie's voice?

As Gus tried to sneak past us and into the cemetery, the dog sprang to its feet, snarling. Gus screamed and ducked behind a tombstone.

"Hey, stop that!" I said, tapping the dog on the nose with a finger. "He's a friend."

The dog sat down next to me, but he continued to softly growl in Gus's direction.

Gus peeked out from behind the tombstone. "Tell me you did not just tap a *hell hound* on the nose?"

"What is wrong with you? Ever since we got here, you've been weirdly overreacting."

"And you've been weirdly under-reacting," he snapped.

"Whatever happened to Captain Kirk and the Starship Pie-Eyed Optimist?"

"Hasn't anyone told you it's not nice to mock someone when they're down?"

"No," but that made me think about what the voice had whispered to me. It's all about perspective. "Gus, when we went into the cottage, what did you see?"

"The place was in ruins. Everything was broken. I have no idea why you liked it so much."

"And when you look at this dog, what do you see?"

"A black hell hound with red eyes and teeth like daggers."

Well, that explained it. "I'm not seeing what you're seeing," I said. "Somehow, we're out of phase with each other."

"Fine. You hold onto your pet while I go over to that broken-down angel statue in the middle of the cemetery."

"You mean the angel tree?"

"No, I mean the broken statue. I'm going to climb up on the base, so I can get an overview of the cemetery and figure out where I need to be in this blasted place. But I don't want Fluffy there to use me like a chew toy."

"Wait here," I said to the dog. Then I walked over to Gus's hiding spot. "We need to get back in sync with each other. You would not believe the awesome world you're missing out on."

He looked up at me. "Just how do you propose we do that?"

"I think we need to get on the same vibrational rate." I carefully sat down and entwined myself around him. "Match your energy to mine."

He held onto me, and we synchronized our breathing, until it felt like we were one organism, breathing together, our vibrations merging and smoothing out. It was all very up-close and sensual, and I don't know at what point I realized Gus was kissing me. The kiss went on for a little while, sensual but not sexual. Luxurious but not heated. A feast for the senses. It felt like a merging of spirits, like I had returned home after a long absence and I was being welcomed back into the fold, made one again with the whole.

I opened my eyes and pushed him away. "Okay, I think we're

done."

He nodded. "I think you're right."

"What was that kiss for?" I asked. Gus had never kissed me like that before.

"I thought it was important to merging our energies together. Kisses play an integral part in fairy tales."

"Oh." Well, that made sense. It had felt so right, I had almost hoped there was more to it than that. "You're an excellent kisser."

"So, I've been told." He peeked over the tombstone and turned back to me. "I don't think it worked."

I stood up. The beautiful world of nature that I had seen before was gone. In its place was a giant, broken, overgrown ruin. Even the gorgeous angel tree in the middle of the cemetery was gone, replaced by a broken, water- and time-damaged angel statue. The once-lush grass was now an overgrown menace, resembling a jungle, with knee-high, sharp-edged blades of grass.

"Oh, no freaking fair!" I said, tears pricking my eyes. "You dragged me into your world! It was supposed to work the other way around!"

The sweet dog I had been playing with just moments before, stood and growled. It was huge and terrifying. Its eyes and the inside of its ears were blood-red, and as it got closer, I could see drops of blood dripping off of fangs as long as daggers.

Chapter 43

I promptly ducked behind the tombstone. A sudden, very unwelcome thought occurring to me. "Gus, is it possible that we're dead? Did we drown in the stream? If that's a Hell Hound, is this the Underworld?"

Gus hesitated, then shook his head. "No... I really think we're in some kind of weird, dark, Faery realm. The Otherworld not the Underworld. Although we may be at some kind of odd juncture where the two meet."

"Are you *sure* we're not dead?"

"We'd know if we were dead. Tunnels of light, dead relatives, the whole shebang. Do you see a crowd of dead people? Because I don't."

I shook my head. "You're right. If anyone would be here, waving a pitchfork and trying to skewer us, it would be Aunt Tillie. She's decided she does not want us on her side of the veil, under any circumstance. But that is one scary-ass dog out there."

"I know," Gus said. "Which is why I very sensibly chose to hide. You're the one who was babying it."

I peeked around the tombstone. I couldn't imagine doing that now.

"What if we split up and go in different directions?" Gus asked.

"It can't take us both out at the same time."

"I wouldn't count on that. It looks pretty damn fast to me."

"We can't sit here all night. I should have gone while you were on its good side."

"I tamed it once, maybe I can do it again," I said, steeling myself.

"Are you nuts?"

"I'm being totally serious. Instead of both of us running, I'll distract him while you get over to the statue and figure out where you need to be."

Gus thought about it and nodded. "You're sure about this?"

"Sure," I said, but my voice was kind of shaky. "I treated him like one of the Dobies and he seemed to respond to that before. I just need to do it again."

"Can you pull it off with the same degree of conviction, now that you can see what he really is?"

"I don't know. But you're the one with the toad bone. You're the one who has to be in the cemetery. I'm just along for the ride. So, I'll... stay here and play with Fluffy."

Before Gus could stop me, I stood up and walked toward the growling beast. "Who's a good boy?" I asked, my tone bright and chipper.

The growling got stronger as the beast fixed its eyes on me.

I continued to talk to it, skirting the edge of the cemetery, heading towards the gate. As I moved, it turned its head, its eyes staying on me. Behind the beast, I could see Gus slinking off towards the middle of the cemetery.

It must have seen a shift in my eyes, because it started to turn its head to where I was looking.

"Here, Fluffy!" I hollered, "Wanna play catch?" Then I turned and ran away from it as fast as I could.

With a *whumph*, it turned and started chasing me.

I was really tempted to look over my shoulder, to see if the beast was closing in, but I kept thinking about the myth of Orpheus where, because he looked over his shoulder, Eurydice was lost to him forever, pulled back into Hades. What if I looked over my shoulder and that was the hesitation it needed to bring me down? If anything happened to me here, would I be trapped here forever? Would Gus?

I must have slowed down while I was thinking, because in my head, I heard Gus's voice saying *"Don't look, Mara. For fuck's sake, just keep moving!"*

So, I did. I ran and ducked between tombstones, until I ran out of them.

I ran in circles around the last large, crumbling tombstone in the row I was in, trying to keep it between me and the Hell Hound. But the beast didn't respect the boundary. He leapt over the grave and landed on me, knocking me off my feet.

As he stood over me, his front paws pinning my shoulders, his fangs getting closer to my face, the smell of blood and decay was almost overwhelming.

I closed my eyes and tried to hang onto that moment of perfection when we first entered the cemetery and I had been petting that sweet-faced dog. When it felt as if I could suddenly understand the whispers of the wind and the calls of the animals, as they wove around me in a grand symphony. That brief moment in time, where the language of nature merged with the language of humanity and they vibrated in complete harmony. And then I thought of the child within me and the unspoken language we shared, and tears started streaking down my face.

I opened my mouth to—cry? yell? scream?—and instead, what came out was music. Not a song. Notes. Tones. One after another. A deep vibrato, a soaring soprano lilt. The pressure on my shoulders eased, and I sat up, still singing. The beast lay down next to me, its head on its crossed front paws, listening. Its eyes seemed to tear up and it closed its eyelids, with a heavy sigh. As its breathing became deeper, and it lost itself into whatever dreamscape the music was evoking, I slowly stood up and crept away, still singing notes, but making them slower and longer, more of a lullaby. I didn't stop singing until I reached Gus at the angel statue.

As Gus gave me a hand up onto the base of the statue, I looked around and noticed the tombstone arrangement wasn't the same as home. Instead of looking like a haphazard smattering, the tombstones formed corridors, in every direction, with the giant Angel in the middle of the graveyard compass.

"We should totally do this with our cemetery." Gus said.

"I am not digging up graves and moving tombstones, just to give you an *isn't-it-cool* thrill."

"*Eh*, win some, lose some. Nice job with Fluffy. Guess it's true that music soothes the savage beast. How'd you come up with that?"

I snorted. "I have no idea. The notes just bubbled up from somewhere inside me."

Gus shrugged. "Maybe it was the baby."

"If it was, then she's already a heck of a lot smarter than I am, and she's not even born yet."

"You mean, 'he'."

"Knock it off."

"Not until the baby is born without a penis."

I rolled my eyes.

"I have some good news for you," Gus said, looking around. "I know why Grundleshanks was leading us here and why the Hound of Hell tried to stop us. I think we're right where we need to be."

"How do you know?"

"The layout of the tombstones. All paths lead to the center. This is the crossroads. Not just a three-way or four-way. This is an eight-way crossroads. It's the Cosmic Crossroads, where you can turn the Hand of Fate. This is where the ritual will be completed."

"Great. So there's no more running around, trying to avoid being chomped on by Fluffy. What do we do now?" I asked.

"You sit at the Crossroads and wait for the Devil," a deep voice answered.

Chapter 44

I made Gus hide behind the base with me while the Devil stepped out from the other side of the broken angel statue. He was enormous, his cloven hooves shaking the ground, like an earthquake.

He was the most alien-looking thing I had ever seen. His body was so well-defined, he could have been a statue, his muscles hewn from meteoric rock. He had horns on top of his head and enormous bat-like wings. No wonder Mrs. Lasio had freaked when she saw the statue of Baphomet in my apartment last summer. There was definitely a resemblance there.

"You worked so hard to get my attention. Aren't you going to come out and play?" He asked, his voice loud and deep and echo-y.

I was flattened by how incredibly sexy that voice was. It sounded like hot fudge, generously poured over naked bodies, which were then covered with whipped cream and topped by rum-soaked cherries. Even though I was terrified, all I wanted to do was hear him speak again. The vibration of his voice went through my body to my very soul, like listening to the best radio in the world with the bass cranked all the way up. I was pretty sure if I listened to him long enough, I would have a spontaneous orgasm. I looked over at Gus and could see he felt the same way. That shorty wetsuit didn't hide much.

"I can't believe we're talking to the Devil," Gus whispered. "This is so cool."

"I can't believe you dragged me with you to talk to the Devil." I replied.

"Come on, children. What will it be? Don't you have some kind of offer to make me? Some kind of interesting trade?"

Holy moly, it was starting to get hot in that cemetery. I was thinking of all sorts of trades that were entirely inappropriate. It was like my thoughts were running away from me and I had absolutely no control. There was a deep chuckle, as if the Devil was reading my mind. Well, he *was* the Devil after all. He probably was.

"This has got to be negative karma points, for sure." I muttered.

"No one asked you to come. I was fine, doing this on my own."

"You would have been knocked unconscious and drowned on your own," I pointed out.

"Maybe. But look on the bright side. We're in a funky toadstool world and we get to meet the Devil. Who else can say that?"

"Who else would want to?" I muttered.

"Children, it's rude to make the Devil wait. Are you intentionally trying to anger me?"

I could tell he was getting pissed, because his voice had changed from the sound of guilty pleasures to the sound of painful torture, promising worlds of hurt if we didn't conclude our business.

It made me cringe but at least it brought me back to my senses.

"Before we come out, we want some assurances," I yelled.

"And what would that be?" The dark voice replied, back to its silky, cloying self.

"No soul-stealing, soul-contracts, soul anything," I said. "No blood pacts, blood oaths, blood vows."

There was a long pause.

"Fine," the Devil said.

"Swear by the light of Lucifer," Gus yelled.

"You do know how to ruin a fun time," the Devil sighed. "All right, I swear by the light of the Morning Star, I won't steal your souls—at least, not tonight. However, I reserve all future rights."

I peeked around the base of the statue. "We're not negotiating with you while you're Jolly Green Giant-sized and we're Munchkins," I said. "You should at least give us an illusion of a level playing field. It's only polite."

The Devil roared with laughter. But a few minutes later, he was down to our size—almost. We came out from behind the base and we were at eye-to-nipple height with him, which was better than the eye-to-giant-disturbing-penis height we had been at before. Although it didn't seem to make much of a difference, as far as Gus was concerned.

"Va-va-voom," said Gus, staring at the Devil's dark, muscular chest.

"Are you kidding me?" I smacked Gus's arm. "That's the Devil."

"And yet, somehow, my libido doesn't care. Penis and boobs? Total wet dream combo."

"Excuse us for a sec," I said, and dragged Gus back behind the statue, while the Devil chuckled, amused and flattered by Gus's predicament.

"Don't tell me you're not thinking about having sex for days," Gus said, dreamy-eyed.

"Of course I am," I said, frustrated. "The Devil is every vice rolled into one convenient package. But you can't get sucked into that, or you'll be subjugated by him. Try focusing above his neck."

Gus peered out from behind the statue. The Devil's face wasn't remotely human. More like a cross between a human and a bull, with fierce looking horns

"Holy fuck. Look at those awesome horns. And the wings. Is it wrong that I want him even more?"

"Seriously? He's got the calves of an oversized goat!" I threw my hands up, frustrated. "Why do women even bother shaving? We should swap razors for strap-ons."

The Devil laughed again, the sound reverberating in his chest. "You two are a hoot. It'll be a shame if I have to kill you for your unbearable rudeness. No one's amused me this much in aeons."

"Let's not be hasty." I said, as we hurriedly emerged from behind the statue. "We have a lot of funny left."

"And I'm looking forward to every minute." The Devil turned to

Gus. "I have a special place in my heart for you. You are my poster child for the seven deadly sins. Lust, gluttony, greed, sloth, wrath, envy and pride. I can't wait to see what new and exciting thing you come up with next," he said, his fiery red eyes glowing. "All you have to do is hand over the toad bone. I will return you to your world, and we can continue making memories together."

Gus's eyes narrowed and his grip on my shoulder tightened. "Wait just one toad-pickin' minute, Mister. I don't care how disturbingly hot you are, that bone is mine. My toad. My bone. I didn't go through hell just to hand it over to the Devil."

"Personally, I think the bone belongs to Grundleshanks," I muttered.

Grundleshanks, who was chilling out by a tombstone, croaked his agreement.

The Devil narrowed his eyes. "My demon, my bone. Get yourself another toad."

"Grundleshanks isn't a demon," I protested.

Both of them turned and looked at me, like I was an idiot. "What?" I asked, looking from one human face to one inhuman one.

"Lucien?" Gus reminded me.

"Oh. Of course." Back when Paul and I had been possessed, we had to get Lucien out of Paul's body, and we used Grundleshanks to do it. Obviously, the fact that Lucien and Grundleshanks had shared the same bones for a fraction of a moment must mean something.

While Gus and the Devil faced off, I heard a voice in my head.

Of course, it means something, you stupid girl. I told you to stop him.

Aunt Tillie! I thought, overjoyed.

Hush! Have you learned nothing?

I quickly stilled my thoughts, before they caught the Devil's attention. But just that little interaction with her made me feel a lot better.

"You and I have been flirting for quite awhile," the Devil said to Gus. "I particularly enjoyed how you went all out, and courted the wrath of the Winter Queen, to flip the seasons. I haven't laughed so hard in centuries. I could use a talent like yours on my side. And I can make it worth your while."

The Devil snapped his fingers and turned from a massive archetypal being into a hot rock-and-roll guy with flowing blond hair, dimples and muscles for days. I could practically feel Gus's eyes pop out.

"So, what'll it be?" asked the Devil. "Do you keep the bone and come work for me, in the Underworld? Or do you stay in your realm and make a trade for the bone? You can have whatever your heart desires. This is your chance to drastically change your life. Do you want to be a movie star? I can make that happen. All you have to do, is give me the bone."

What's going on? I asked Aunt Tillie. *Why doesn't he just take the bone?*

Even the Devil has to play by the rules, Aunt Tillie responded. *His game is persuasion, seduction, exploiting existing weaknesses to create new ones.*

"Tillie!" The Devil roared. "Shut the hell up, before I roast you on a spit."

Aunt Tillie immediately vanished. *Crap.* I hoped her spirit was safely in the Summerlands and out of reach of the Devil.

"So, handsome, what do you want, in your heart of hearts?" the Devil purred. "Fame? Fortune? Immortality? Unending pleasures of the flesh?"

"With you? The Devil's gay?" I asked. "That's not very P.C."

He roared with laughter. "I'm the Devil. I am the original pansexual being. Men, women, transgenders, intergenders. Don't try to pigeon-hole me, or limit my enjoyment of your species with your puny restrictions," the Devil said. "Now, about this bone..."

"No..." Gus shook his head, his face wearing that stubborn look I knew all too well. "I appreciate your offer, but the bone's mine."

"Isn't that adorable? You think you actually have a choice."

"We do," I said. "It's called Free Will."

"No, darlin'," the Devil chuckled, returning to his original form. "Free will is an illusion."

I frowned. "No, it isn't."

"Not only do we have free will, we are witches. We can change the hands of Fate and bend the future to our Will." Gus said.

The Devil laughed. "Your will isn't as free as you think. If it was, it wouldn't be so easy to bend it in my direction."

"I control my own destiny," Gus said. "You may be able to toy with mere mortals, but I am Witch—hear me roar."

The Devil chuckled and expanded out to his original size, which was scary as hell. "By the time I'm done with you, you'll be begging me to take the bone, and you'll get nothing in return but the mercy of death," the Devil said. "The opportunity for you to make a trade is over."

He snapped his fingers and zapped us with some kind of explosion that flung us, screaming, out into space and through a swirling portal.

Chapter 45

When I came to, I was in a field of toadstool mushrooms. I turned to Gus and shook him, until he sat up.

He looked around. "I love this place. Just being in proximity to the mushrooms, sent me flying. I had the best hallucination of all time."

"Did it involve a weirdly sexy Devil, a large dog and a toadstool cottage?"

"How'd you know?"

"It wasn't a hallucination. I was there too." I showed him the bruise on my arm, from where he had smacked me with his walking stick. "I think we just did our first sabbatic ritual together."

Sabbatic rituals were usually done in dreamscape. It was something Gus had been wanting us to try for awhile.

Gus whooped. "How freaking cool is that! It just goes to show you that what you do in the sabbatic landscape has consequences in this one."

"That's what makes me nervous." I said and shivered, afraid of what potential consequences we had just let ourselves in for.

He unzipped the thigh pocket of his shorty wetsuit and pulled out a small bone. "Ha! I still have it. We went into the sabbatic landscape and bested the Devil."

"Good for you," I said. "We should start heading back to the house."

"You don't have to ask me twice. I'm freezing my garbanzo beans off out here. How about you?"

I nodded. It was cold—dang cold. And it was getting colder by the minute.

All of a sudden, I realized what was going on. "Gus! Winter's returning! You did it. You completed the combined rituals."

He grinned. "We did it together! How cool is that? So much for your Aunt Tillie's ridiculous warnings. Dire fate my ass. Let's go home and celebrate. I have a bottle of sparkling cider in the fridge."

We had to walk slow, since Gus was still limping from his knee getting bashed around. As we neared the old cemetery, the wind picked up, clouds covered the moon, and in the dead of night, it started hailing. But it wasn't hard, glowing white snowballs. It was more like big, wet, dark, squishy blobs that bounced off us and onto the ground.

Even after the weird hailstorm stopped, the footing was getting increasingly more treacherous. The ground was slippery with mud and weirdly squishy. With the moon obscured, it was difficult to see anything. I tried to pick my way through more solid spots, but the ground kept shifting on me.

When Gus slipped and landed facedown in a mud-puddle, we were finally able to see why. It wasn't hail we were being bombarded with. It was toads. There were hundreds of toads throughout the cemetery, obscuring the ground.

I braced myself on tombstones and tiptoed over graves, trying not to squish any of the dazed amphibians. My dad would be flipping out—he believed that you never step on anyone's grave. And here I was, trampling all over my ancestors, like they weren't even here, so I wouldn't squish random toads.

I expected Gus to make some kind of gleeful wisecrack or start pocketing toads, but instead, he grabbed my arm and sat down on a rounded tombstone, taking shallow, rapid breaths.

"Are you okay?"

He shook his head. "I can't breathe."

"What do you mean, you can't breathe? Is it an asthma attack?"

"I don't know," Gus looked at me, helpless. "It's like my mid-section is swollen and I can't get air into the bottom of my lungs."

"So you can still breathe, you just can't breathe well?"

"I'm not turning blue and keeling over, if that's what you're asking."

"Could it be a panic attack?"

"I don't know." Gus said, aggravated. "I've never felt like this before. It's freaking me out."

"Can you stand up?" As I helped him to his feet, a swirling portal opened in the sky above us, and a murder of crows descended into our world.

One of the crows spotted a hopping toad. It dove down, piercing the amphibian hide with its beak, and emerged with a brown glob that it quickly swallowed. The toad puffed up and exploded, spraying its organs out into the sky.

"Did you see that?!" I yelled.

"Holy. Fuck." Gus panted.

Now that one crow had shown the way, the others swooped down, digging toad livers out of their little bodies with surgical precision. Toad after toad exploded, making the ground even slipperier, covering it (and us) with blood and entrails.

"We've got to get out of here," I said.

A phalanx of crows peeled off the main group and came after us. They attacked Gus, tearing through his shirt and pecking bits of flesh off his mid-section, trying to dig into his organs.

I didn't know if they could do the same thing to him that they were doing to the toads, and I didn't want to find out. I didn't want to see Gus explode.

I picked up a handful of stones and whipped them at the crows, trying to drive them away. "Leave him alone!"

It worked for a moment, although I accidentally hit Gus a few times. As we kept moving, I randomly continued throwing stones at the crows, backing them off. My aim was terrible, but avoiding my mini-missiles slowed them down a bit. Which was good, because between Gus's precarious breathing, his limp, and how slippery the ground was, we were forced to go slow, making pretty easy targets.

When Gus stumbled and fell, a bird came diving down at him. Since I was out of stones, I dug into my pockets and started throwing loose change at it. A quarter hit it in the chest and it pulled up, squawking its displeasure as it flew away. We were clear for the moment.

I bent down to help Gus up and suddenly realized what we were standing in. J.J. had come very close to finding his stash—he just needed to go deeper into the cemetery. I almost laughed I was so relieved. I was going to put a new twist on *stone the crows*.

"Does your lighter still work?" I asked.

"It should," Gus said, clutching his mid-section. "Shit, that hurts."

"It's going to hurt a lot more if we don't get out of here. Hand me the lighter."

He dug into his pocket and tossed it to me. "What are you going to do with it? Throw it at them?"

The black cloud returned as crows swooped in for another attack. Gus tried to hobble towards me and fell, hitting his bad knee on a tombstone. "Fuck!" he swore, hissing in pain. "Mara, run! Get out of here."

"I'm not leaving you," I said. "Protect your liver. I don't want to see you suffer the same fate as the toads."

Gus curled up in a ball, head tucked in, arms protecting the back of his neck, as the birds took turns dive-bombing him. "Whatever you're doing, hurry!"

I flicked opened the top of the lighter and held the flame to one of J.J.'s missing marijuana plants, but the leaves just weakly smoldered. They were too wet. *Shit.*

I picked up some more small stones and whipped them at the

crows. "Go away!" I screamed.

My efforts weren't going to hold them off for long. There were more crows poised to attack, than I had stones. And with Gus not very mobile, we were going to be screwed.

"Remember, you're a witch. Act like one." Aunt Tillie's voice said, inside my head.

Of course! *Hekate's fire!*

I pulled dragon energy up from the earth, through my feet, into my body and into my lungs. I could feel astral wings form on my back, as my spirit started to expand. It was as if I was turning into a dragon.

Then I reached up to the sky, and focused on gathering whatever residual electrical energy I could. There wasn't enough left to create a lightning strike, but there was enough that every hair on my body stood on end and every cell of my skin started vibrating.

I combined the dragon energy and the electrical energy within me, forcing the heated exchange through my blood and into my lungs, until I couldn't hold it any longer. I exhaled with all my might on the crops, sending a small heat wave searing through the pot plants, drying up the leaves.

I inhaled again, driving Hekate's fire deep into my body. My temperature started to rise. I could feel heat searing the inside of my lungs when I exhaled.

I took another deep breath in and clicked open the lighter. When I exhaled into the flame, it shot forward like a blazing torch, over the entire spread of marijuana plants. This time, the leaves hungrily grabbed onto the flames. Soon, all the pot plants were burning, enveloping the birds in thick smoke, blocking their view.

The astral wings pulled back into my body and vanished. I was back to myself again. Just a normal witch girl.

I coughed and I could feel my lungs burning. That must be the residual after-effects of breathing dragon fire. Hopefully, I hadn't done any permanent damage. But we needed to get out of here, while the crows were still disoriented and crashing into each other.

I hurried to help Gus up.

He was looking at me, awestruck. "Are you... getting the... Devil's minions... high?" he asked, grinning. "That... was awesome. I didn't... know you could... do that."

"Neither did I," I said, smiling. "It's one way of stoning the crows. Now, let's get out of here before they get the munchies."

I helped him up. A crow dropped out of the sky in front of us, looking blissful and uncaring. Gus eyeballed him, and I could tell he was thinking about kicking the crow or taking it hostage, in revenge.

"Leave it be," I said. "Don't give the Devil another reason to come after you."

I coughed again. The smoke was so thick, I couldn't tell which way the cottage was. I wondered how high we were going to be from the pot cloud, by the time we got out of the cemetery. Then, the spirit of Grundleshanks appeared, looked at us, and started hopping away, like he was trying to lead us somewhere.

"Come on, Gus!" I coughed, and urged him along. "Follow that toad!"

Chapter 46

We followed Grundleshanks back to the cottage, before he vanished. There was a clap of thunder and it started to rain again. I hoped the rain would stay heavy enough to put out the fire in the cemetery and send the demonic crows scurrying back to hell.

Gus and I were both shivering, so I hit the upstairs bathroom, and let him have the downstairs one. We took hot showers and met back on the couch, in warm, clean clothes, sipping cups of tea.

"Where's the toad bone?" I asked.

Gus pointed to a leather pouch hanging on his neck, and then tucked it out of sight inside his shirt.

"How are you?" I asked. "Are you breathing any better?"

He carefully shook his head. "I'm... not," he said, taking a slow breath between each word.

I felt a chill crawl up my spine. I had thought Gus would be fine, once we got back to the cottage.

"How...did...you..." he mimed giant wings with his hands.

I knew what he was talking about. It was that weird dragon metamorphosis. It wasn't like my exterior body had changed, but it's what my astral body had changed into, and Gus was tuned-in enough that he had been able to see it.

"I don't know," I said. "It was like... a part of me woke up. It was what needed to be done and I just... did it. I didn't even think about it, really."

Gus nodded, either not able or not willing to speak.

I extended my 'sight' over his astral body, and was shocked to find his entire midsection, from his chest to his waist, had turned black, as if his organs had been replaced with the darkness of the void.

I put my teacup down. "Let's go."

He looked at me, questioningly.

"We're going to the new Medical Center in Oldfield. There's an Emergency Room there. I don't know what's wrong with you, but if you can't get enough air into your lungs to have a conversation, it's getting worse."

He nodded, and within minutes, we were in Zed and I was driving as fast as I dared down the rain-slicked roads.

*   *   *

The medical center had an Emergency Room, a Surgical Center, various doctors' offices, and an Urgent Care Center about a block further down. There were a few rooms with beds, but half the place was still under construction. It really didn't inspire much confidence, but it was the closest E.R. we could get to at three in the morning. By the time we got there, Gus's left arm and face had gone numb, and he was still having problems breathing.

In the Emergency Room, they were able to see Gus pretty quickly. The perks of a small town.

They ran an EKG in case he was having a heart attack, and said his heart was fine. They gave him a nebulizer treatment and while it worked a little, it didn't work as much as it should have. They gave him a spritz of nitroglycerin under his tongue, and that seemed to work better, for a little while. And then he couldn't breathe again.

His one leg was swollen, and I wondered if it was because he had hit the tombstone in the cemetery with the same knee that had taken a pounding earlier. Because of it though, they couldn't give him a physical stress test, and they didn't have the equipment to give him a chemically-induced stress test with a 3-D heart imaging system. They suggested we put that on our to-do list.

They asked me about the trauma around his midsection, and I told them he fell in a rocky stream. I didn't think they'd believe me if I said it was the result of a demonic crow attack. They ultrasounded him for blood clots, since his leg was swollen, but didn't find any. They also MRI'd his knee, and confirmed what I had suspected about the meniscal injury.

Since Gus still couldn't breathe, they sent him for a CT scan of his lungs, but it took five tries to get the IV contrast in. Poor Gus. His arms looked like they had been beaten with a baseball bat by the time the procedure was done.

*   *   *

Eventually, a doctor brought down the paperwork from the CT scan and said he hadn't seen anything that would cause the breathing problem. He wanted to release Gus.

Something nudged me and I asked to see the report. He shrugged and left it with me.

"What...is...it?" Gus panted.

I held up my finger and read over the entire report. Everything seemed normal, until I got to the end. There was a phrase I didn't recognize. Dependent Atelectasis. I pulled out my iPhone and looked it up.

"I know why you can't breathe." I said.

"The... doctor... didn't..."

I interrupted him. I didn't want him to waste precious oxygen on talking. I showed him the report. "Look here, see this bottom paragraph? Where it says dependent atelectasis?"

He shook his head. "Eyes. Blurry."

Great. A new problem. This all had to be related. "Okay, well, it means the bottom lobe of your lungs have collapsed. That's why you can't breathe, and why none of the asthma meds are working."

Gus gave me a thumbs up, signaling he understood, then raised two fingers, ticking off a question on each one. "Why? How fix?"

"I don't know how to fix it. And I don't know the why. Most of all, I don't know why the doctor missed that part of the report. They want to release you, but I'm not going to let them. Are you going to

235

be okay? I need to go find a doctor and discuss this with them."

A panicked look came into Gus's eyes, and I had to weigh which one was more important—keeping him calm, or tracking down a doctor and beating them over the head with the report until they coughed up the answer to those two questions: Why and How Fix.

"I'll be right back. You'll be okay. It's not a big place. I have my phone. Text me if you start to freak and I'll drop everything and run back to you."

* * *

I walked through the corridors, looking for one of Gus's doctors. I stopped at a diagram of the human body, and looked at the organ layout. From what I read, pressure from the other organs could cause dependent atelectasis. And the largest organ under the lungs was the liver. *It figured.*

I should have realized we were dealing with a liver problem. Was it related to the crows trying to peck Gus's liver out in the cemetery? Did they cause the liver to swell? Or were they drawn to Gus because his liver was swollen?

I started walking faster. I was pretty sure I had the why, but now I wanted the why behind that. Why was the liver swollen and pressing on the lungs?

I finally tracked down the female doctor who had ordered the CT scan and ultrasounds. That was fine with me, because I thought the male doctor who showed up to give us his misreading of the CT results was an idiot.

I pointed out the dependent atelectasis phrase, and she gave me a blank look. I swear, it was like they were all being blocked from seeing what was going on.

Blocked. Of course. They probably were. The Devil said that Gus would be begging him to take the toad bone in exchange for the mercy of death. The Devil had to be behind this entire thing. I was going to have to take a different approach.

"Can you scan his liver? It wasn't included in the lung scan. I think it's swollen and that's what's causing his lungs to partially collapse."

She grabbed the report from me and looked it over. "Sure. I don't want to send him for another CT, but we can ultrasound his liver."

"Great. Let's do it."

* * *

I went back to tell Gus he was going in for another test, and found Forrest there, sitting in my chair, sipping on a cup of coffee from the local diner, with Gus's iPad on his lap. It was morning in the outside world, and Forrest was bright and fresh, ready to face a new day. And clearly, he hadn't given a thought to bringing any coffee for anyone else.

"What are you doing here?" I asked coldly, oddly annoyed at his lack of exhaustion after what had to be the longest night of my life.

"I got a text from Gus," he said, flashing his smarmy, lounge lizard grin at me. "I thought I'd come and see if he was okay."

"Let me save you the guesswork. Of course, he's not okay," I snapped. "Otherwise, why would we be here? Now that you know, feel free to leave."

Gus frowned at me.

"You're going in for another ultrasound," I told him.

Gus rolled his eyes, but he didn't say anything. Then he pointedly looked over to Forrest and back to me.

"I'm not the enemy," Forrest said. "Gus left his iPad at my place and I brought it here, thinking he could use it to spend the time. Would a bad guy do that?"

I sighed. "Fine, I'm sorry for being snappish. I'm tired. I've been up all night. I'm worried sick about Gus, and you look like you're abut to go spend the day crooning with Dean Martin and Frank Sinatra. So, unless it's to entertain me with some tunes, you probably shouldn't talk to me right now."

Forrest chuckled and handed me the iPad. "I admire a woman who speaks her mind."

* * *

After they took Gus for his ultrasound, Forrest and I sat and stared at each other.

"You don't like me," Forrest finally said.

"No, I don't think I do." I said.

"Why? People usually like me. I'm told I can be quite charming. Is it because you think I'm going to take Gus away from you?"

"No," I said. But why didn't I like him? I was so tired, I couldn't really remember when my dislike had started. I tried to poke in his mind, to see what he was thinking, but all I got was a smooth darkness, like volcanic glass. My 'sight' slid off it and I was no closer to uncovering his secrets than I had been when we first met.

I finally said. "I don't trust you. You're always so guarded. Makes me wonder what you're hiding."

"Me? I'm an open book," he protested.

I snorted.

*　　*　　*

When Gus came back from his ultrasound, we had another piece of the puzzle. His lungs had partially collapsed because his liver was swollen to almost twice its normal size. But they still wanted to discharge him, so he could go see his regular doctor.

"No," I said. "We're not going anywhere, until you find out why his liver is swollen."

"I'm sure the doctors know what they're doing," Forrest argued. "If they want to discharge him, there's got to be a good reason."

"Forget it," I snapped. "You can take your opinion and shove it. Why don't you go home?"

"Because I'm his significant other. You're just his roommate."

"I thought you were his sister," the nurse said, glaring at me. Then she turned to Forrest, sweet as saccharine. "Do you mind signing these papers? We need the space for incoming patients."

"I don't... feel... good." Gus said, barely able to get the words out.

Instinctively, I put my hand on his forehead.

He was burning up.

Chapter 47

Forrest made an excuse about why he had to leave and said he'd be back later. I ignored him and watched as the nurse took Gus's temperature. It was 103.

A few minutes later, a new doctor came into the room. He felt Gus's throat, commented on how swollen his lymph nodes were, and asked the nurse to schedule an ultrasound of his thyroid.

I was ready to scream. I believed that Gus's lymph nodes were swollen, but I was sure everything was centered in his liver. And with the parade of different doctors that were coming through, I wasn't at all sure they would be communicating with each other.

"Why... so... upset?" Gus asked, when we were alone again.

"Because," I said, trying to hold my anger in check. "It shouldn't be up to *me* to diagnose you. I didn't go to medical school. I don't know what I'm doing. I don't know why they can't work together to figure out what's going on. I don't know whey can't even read their own freaking reports."

"Devil... block," Gus said.

"Yeah. I think it is. Why don't you just give the Devil back the stupid toad bone?"

"Never," Gus croaked. "I won... fair and... square."

*   *   *

While Gus was moved from the Emergency Room cubicle to an

239

actual room, I called Paul, told him where the spare key was and asked him to look after the dogs. I knew he was leery of spending time at the cottage, so I asked if he could take the Dobes to his house.

"It's only for a few days, just until Gus gets out of the hospital."

"You're going to owe me for this, big time," he said.

"Whatever happened to joint dog custody?"

Silence on his end.

"Fine, whatever. I'll owe you. Absolutely. We'll settle up later. I'll buy you lunch. Gotta go." I said, hanging up before he could change his mind.

After scouring the Internet on Gus's iPad, to figure out what kind of doctor he most needed to see, I was finally able to track down an Infectious Disease Specialist. Mainly by 'accidentally' walking into every department and office in the Medical Center, until I found one who would talk to me.

I told the doctor what was going on with Gus, and my suspicion that it was all centered in his liver. I convinced her to run blood tests for anything that could possibly lead to a swollen liver and gave her a run-down of everything and everyone Gus had been exposed to, from flu vaccines to Grundleshanks and the cats, to me and Forrest.

* * *

Forrest came back later that day, wearing a Santa hat and rubbing sanitizer gel into his hands. "You've got to watch out for flesh-eating disease on hospital toilets. I once met a lady, had half her ass eaten off."

"That's disgusting," I said.

A new nurse came in, took seven vials of blood from Gus and left.

Gus was exhausted and wavering in and out of consciousness. I wasn't sure he knew either of us were there.

Forrest puttered around a little, turning the TV on and off, before saying, "I don't know about you, but I'm feeling a little peckish. You want anything from the diner?"

"No," I snapped. "I have a better idea. Why don't you go treat yourself to a really long lunch? Followed by a spa treatment. Maybe even a vacation. Come back next week."

"You're not the only one who cares about Gus," he said, sounding sincere.

If that tone of voice had come out of anyone else, I'd have believed them. But not Forrest. I shot him a dirty look.

"It's amazing how crabby you get when your blood sugar bottoms out," he said. "I think you'd feel a lot better if you ate something."

"I'll grab a candy bar from the vending machine."

He shrugged. "Your funeral."

My head snapped around and I glared at him so hard, I thought my eyes would bore holes through him. "Excuse me?"

He backed away, his hands in the air. "It's a phrase... a saying. I didn't mean anything by it."

"I don't care. I don't like it. Considering the situation, it's insensitive and inappropriate. Why don't you just go back to whatever rock you crawled out from under and stay there?"

"Mara!" Gus weakly protested, waking up.

"I apologize if I offended the lady." Forrest said to Gus. "She's very protective of you. So... how did the toad bone ritual go? Did you get it? Can I see it?"

Gus was about to pull the pouch out of his bedside table and show Forrest, but I stopped him. "No. We couldn't finish it. Gus got sick."

Gus frowned.

But every time I looked at Forrest, inside my head, I could hear a tiny whispered voice saying: *Don't trust.*

Over and over again.

⁎   ⁑   ⁎

Forrest finally left, although I knew he'd be back. While Gus slept, I sat and researched everything I could about partially collapsed lungs and any kind of illness that would affect the liver, until my eyes were stinging and swollen, and I was starting to go into hypochondriac mode.

By nightfall, my stomach was burning from all the vending

machine food. But Gus looked so pitiful, hooked up to all the machines and the IV drip, with the oxygen cannules in his nostrils, that I just couldn't leave him. Thankfully, the room was private and it had a couch, so I was able to catch a catnap.

When the nurses came to clear the floor, they assumed Gus was the father of my child and let me stay. The nurse on the late shift even gave me a blanket and a pillow.

Throughout the night, Gus grumbled about being woken up every couple of hours to have his vitals checked. But I was glad they did it. Every grumble meant that he was still alive.

The morning nurse took pity on me, and gave me a spare breakfast tray.

Once Gus was awake, I ran home to shower, change my clothes and give Duke Gronwy fresh food and water.

*   *   *

When I returned to the Medical Center, the Infectious Disease Specialist came in and told us that Gus had tested positive for active infections of both toxoplasmosis and cytomegalovirus. Between the two of them, that's what caused his liver and lymph nodes to swell, his lungs to partially collapse, and what was fueling the fever.

"That's insane," I said. "What causes that?"

"CMV is a highly contagious virus, in the herpes family. Over half of the population carries it, but most are asymptomatic. About eighty percent have been exposed. You're really only at risk when you have a compromised immune system."

"Is it sexually transmitted?"

"It can be, but not necessarily. He may have had it for years, if he had mononucleosis or Guillain-Barre when he was younger. He may have even gotten it from his mother when he was born. In this case, the toxoplasmosis, which is a parasite, weakened his immune system, triggering an acute recurrence of the CMV and allowing it to run rampant. The good news is that Gus is HIV negative, or he'd be in a world of hurt right now."

"Toxoplasmosis?" That one sounded familiar, but I was too tired for my brain to function properly. One thought bumped into another one, until it triggered my memory. "Isn't that why pregnant women aren't supposed to clean litter boxes?"

"That's right," the doctor nodded. "Toxoplasmosis is a parasite that is spread through raw meat and cat feces. It's dangerous to pregnant women and people with compromised immune systems. Everything seems to be coming back to a compromised immune system, but I'm not sure what caused his immune system to become that vulnerable, to begin with."

Suddenly, I remembered the plum that made him ill—the plum that had fallen into the garbage disposal and the horrible stomach issues that resulted. I filled the doctor in on it.

She nodded her head. "It sounds like a perfect storm. My guess is that he picked up a bacterial infection from that plum, which depressed his immune system and left him open to a parasitic infection from the cats. That then reactivated the dormant viral infection and sent it into acute mode. He's lucky to be alive."

Bacterial infection, parasitical infection, viral infection. *Fuck!* Talk about a rolling snowball of hellfire and brimstone.

"In fact, since you live together, we should probably test you as well. Especially in your condition."

I nodded, acutely aware of the danger my baby could be in, if I was affected. "Wouldn't I be sick though, if I was positive?"

"Not if you have a healthy immune system."

"Okay, then. Sign me up."

She nodded and then made a notation on his chart. "I'm going to put Gus on an antibiotic drip and an antiviral treatment. I'll keep him here for a week, but then he'll have to continue taking meds at home. I have to warn you though, you should not come in contact with the meds we're putting him on. Not even skin contact. The antiviral is fairly toxic."

"But it'll cure him, right? I asked. "We'll never have to go through this again?"

The doctor shook her head. "He's always going to carry Toxo and he may continue to carry CMV as well. It all depends on his reaction to the meds. We'll cure what we can, but our main goal is to get everything back into a dormant state, so his liver and lungs can return to normal. If his immune system gets run down again though, this acute level of infection could happen all over again. In fact, when he gets old and is less able to fight it, it will probably be what kills him."

Son of a bitch.

Chapter 48

While Gus slept, I sat and thought about everything that had happened. And every thought led me back to Forrest.

Aunt Tillie had said that the Devil had to play by certain rules. That he could exploit existing weaknesses to cause other weaknesses. In this case, Gus had a weakness in his immune system, and what had exploited that was Forrest's cats. The cats that were too sick to go to Forrest's stepsister, so Gus had to take care of them. The cats that were infected with toxoplasmosis and were the size of small leopards.

Had Forrest been in league with the Devil, this entire time?

When I had first met Forrest, he had looked so familiar. But I couldn't quite place him. And J.J. and I had been looking at Forrest and the Sheriff when J.J. freaked out and had either vanished or been turned into a rat.

Was Forrest capable of doing something like that? Did he have that kind of power? Was Forrest one of the Devil's demons? Some kind of advance guard that's sent out when a witch begins the process of the Toad Bone Ritual?

What was it the Devil had said in the cemetery? That Gus and I were a *hoot*.

Where else had I heard that phrase recently?

I thought back, and pulled up a vague memory of Forrest calling me a *hoot* during the dinner in the cemetery.

My blood ran cold. I suddenly realized where I had seen Forrest before, and why he would have wanted to get J.J. out of the picture. But if I wanted to prove any of my suspicions to Gus, I was going to need to get out of this hospital and track down the evidence.

*   *   *

I ran home and took Gronwy out of his cage. He chittered at me as he gnawed on a slice of carrot.

"If I need to get into J.J.'s apartment, where can I find a key?" I asked   , then I tried to look into his mind for the answer.

Carrots, pumpkin seeds, rocks, grass, more rocks, pieces of watermelon.

I gave up and put Gronwy back into his cage. I needed to get my hands on that picture of J.J.'s great-great-grandfather. It was the one that used to be on display at The Trading Post, but last time I was there, I had noticed it was missing. Maybe it had fallen. Or, maybe, since there was a new employee there who seemed pretty savvy, she had taken it to be restored and framed, since it was part of the Trading Post's history.

*   *   *

Anna was working behind the counter when I walked in. She seemed a little frazzled, and her bouncy blonde hair was lifeless, hanging in clumpy strands. She rang up a customer and slammed the cash register drawer shut, looking frustrated, as I walked up to the counter.

"Any word from J.J.?" I asked, trying my best to hide my inner agitation behind a carefully-constructed, casually-concerned front.

"No," she growled, in her soft southern accent. "If you find him, tell him I'm gonna kill him."

"The police don't have any leads?"

"No," she snorted. "I'm not worried. J.J.'s always going off on a bender and not coming back for a week or two. That boy's walkin' on a permanent slant. I'm surprised there's a brain cell left in that smoked-out chamber he calls his noggin. But this time, I am done."

"Are you his girlfriend?" I asked, surprised.

"As if. We're cousins. That's why I'm working both our shifts. You can report bad employers to OSHA, but when it's your own family working you to the bone, you're freakin' stuck. I should have stayed in Louisiana."

"I thought OSHA was just for health and safety violations."

"Well, me working all these hours is not very healthful. Or safe, either. For anybody. If one more customer mouths off about anything—prices, politics, immigration—I don't care what, I will knock them upside the head with a cast iron skillet."

"I'll keep that in mind," I said. "Hey, do you remember that picture J.J. had by the register? It was his great-great-grandfather, Jarvis, posing with a couple of other men? It was really old and kind of faded?"

"Are you kidding me right now? I'm on my last nerve, and you're fixin' to grill me about some dang photo?"

I grimaced. "Before you start sizing up skillets, let me remind you I'm pregnant."

"That's the only thing saving your ass right now," she said.

"And I'm a customer, so I think you're supposed to be nice to me."

"Do you really think that holds any truck with me?"

"Tell you what, I'll get you whatever you want for lunch, from the diner. That should earn me some 'let the pregnant lady live' points, right?"

Anna snorted. "All right, funny lady. What do you want?"

"I need that photo. I promised J.J. I would get it restored and framed, and I'd like to get it done for him, before he gets back."

"Then, you'll need to find J.J. Last time I saw him, I was just comin' on my shift, when he grabbed the photo, shouted *'that's him!'* and took off, lickety-split. Haven't seen him since. Freakin' no-account, air-headed moron. That boy ain't got the sense God gave a June bug."

"Do you think he took the photo home?"

She shrugged, having lost interest. "Who the hell knows. Why don't you go to his place and take a look? He keeps a spare key in a hide-a-rock, for when he's too stoned to remember how to get in. I'd say don't steal anything, but I doubt the imbecile has anything worth stealing."

A hide-a-rock, of course! That's what Gronwy was trying to tell me, with his little rat brain.

As I turned to leave, Anna called after me: "Don't forget my lunch. I want a Po' Boy, completely dressed, with fried okra."

"Do they even have that?" I asked.

"If they don't, you'd best find me somethin' similar. I am a woman on the edge."

"I'll have it delivered," I said.

I was already on my cell phone with the diner by the time I got back to the car. By some miracle, they had the Poor Boy, but they were out of okra. But they had mustard greens and pecan pie. So I hoped those substitutions would do. If they didn't, the next time I walked into the Trading Post, I'd need to wear a helmet.

*   *   *

Once I got to J.J.'s apartment building, I was able to find the hide-a-rock and get inside. His place was small and dark. The bedroom had piles of laundry on the floor. In the bathroom, a rank-looking, maroon-colored towel hung on a bar by the shower.

It was pretty much as I had pictured it, only the stench was even worse, after the dirty clothes had been marinating for a week in the locked-up apartment.

I covered my nose and mouth with my shirt and tried not to hurl. Coroners dealt with the smell of dead bodies by putting a menthol rub under their nostrils. If I had any VapoRub on me, I would have totally tried it out.

Well, that was an idea. I rummaged through J.J's bathroom and scored a tiny jar of Vick's VapoRub. I quickly smeared some under my nose, and put the jar in my pocket. I'd buy him a new one, if he ever turned back into a human.

Oh, thank goodness. That made the place bearable. But I didn't want to stay here any longer than I had to.

So I quickly searched through the tiny apartment.

I finally found the picture, at the bottom of an overflowing mail tray. I held the photo to the light, and there, standing behind J.J's great-great-grandfather and his two friends, was Forrest.

Chapter 49

I wanted to run to the hospital and show Gus the picture, but for once, I didn't act on my first impulse. Instead, I stopped and thought. Before I did anything, there was still a lot I needed to figure out. And the person who had the answers—at least, a heck of a lot more answers than I did—was my Aunt Tillie.

As much as I didn't want to go into Gus's room, I had a feeling everything I needed was in there. I reapplied the VapoRub under my nose, tied a bandana around my face to filter the air, then pulled on a pair of latex gloves and went in.

*   *   *

Gus was on every esoteric mailing list and had even more books than I did. While I wasn't into the darker side of magick—I wasn't all that interested in calling up, compelling or canning demons or delving into possessions and exorcisms (my adventure with Lisette and Lucien had pretty much cured me of a lot of my curiosity)—Gus was interested in everything supernatural. And the more dangerous the better.

What I was looking for was Gus's Grimoire. His personal Book of Shadows. I knew Gus had gone through a ceremonial magick phase where he had done all sorts of research in how to exert power over the spirit realms. And knowing Gus, that probably led to more than a little experimentation. I needed to find the ritual details and the list of results.

Unfortunately, he either hid his Grimoire extraordinarily well, or he didn't keep one. Not every witch did. I tried, when I was younger, but I kept forgetting to write things down.

Okay… if I couldn't rely on his magic, I'd have to rely on my own. I left Gus's room, took the mask and the gloves off, and thought about what I could do.

* * *

After a quick trip to the butcher shop, I went down to Aunt Tillie's grave. It had been snowing off and on all day, and the snow made the cemetery look normal. Although, when it melted, I wasn't sure if we'd have a cemetery full of dead toads, or if they'd have vanished as magickally as they appeared.

I created a circle around Aunt Tillie's grave with white candles and a handful of black crow feathers, then consecrated it as sacred space. I opened my sight and built up energy, calling upon the Keeper of the Keys to the Underworld, until I felt that mixture of unbearable dread and ethereal excitement that signaled Hekate's presence.

I never in my life thought I'd ever do what I was about to do. But I pushed down my unease, raised my arms and called on Hekate's powers to help me bind the Spirits of the Dead. Specifically one Tillie MacDougal.

Pouring bull's blood in a circle, so that it connected the candles and the feathers, I chanted:
Tillie MacDougal, tell me true
So I may share your secrets with you
By the blood of the bull, the wings of the crow
By the tongues of the Fae, these seeds I sow.
Tillie MacDougal, I call you here, bound to me.
Speak only the truth, for if you lie to me
Tonight, you will burn in hell for me.
I finished pouring the blood. The ground shook. Thunder clapped in the sky. And suddenly, Aunt Tillie was standing there, in the middle of the circle.

"What kind of spell is that to spring on a defenseless old lady?" she asked, clearly agitated. "You have a real mean streak. You undo that little ditty right now. Break this circle and send me back."

I snorted. "If you were a little more forthcoming, I wouldn't have needed to resort to this. I want to know exactly what's going on. The full truth, not some half-assed whitewash of truth."

"You can't handle the truth," she cackled. "I've always wanted to say that."

"Or you could stay right here for the next twenty years, waiting for me to release you."

She gasped. "You little ingrate. Do you know what happens to spirits who rat the D-bag out? I tried to warn you. I've left you hints. I thought you'd figure it out with the radio playing relevant songs when your visitor was in the cottage. But you're as dense as a two-headed woodpecker, staring at a pencil."

I glared at her. "I'm not kidding around, Aunt Tillie. Gus is in serious trouble. I need you to tell me the truth."

"The truth is you and your non-boyfriend are a huge pain in my arthritic ass. You're menaces, the two of you. You should have both been raised as mortals and stripped of your magic for your own good, and the good of everyone around you!"

"That's your opinion."

She snorted. "No, that's my truth. You want a specific truth, you need to come up with better questions. I'll give you five questions and that's it. Five. That's more than generous. After five, you send me back or I will sit here in silence for the next century, and you can kiss my granny-panty-covered ass before I talk to you again."

"Fine. Is Forrest the—"

She gasped. "—Don't say his name, lest you invoke him! Are you not paying attention to how much I've been trying to avoid that?!"

"I'll take that as a yes."

"Four questions left."

"No! That should *not* count as one of my questions. You didn't even answer it, really."

"Letter of the law."

I gave a cross sigh. "Fine. Why does the fact that the toad housed Lucien make such a difference? Who is Lucien? *Is* he a demon, like we think he is? Wait! Don't answer all of those. Let's just go with... who or what is Lucien?"

She rolled her eyes. "Lucien is a nickname for one of the fallen angels. He was cursed to walk in a mortal's body, so he could feel their pain. He was almost set free by Matthew Gilardi, but then he was unexpectedly imprisoned in a skull by your ancestor, the witch Lisette. Isn't that rich? Neither one of those idiots realized what they were doing. Matthew thought he was killing a savage, Lisette thought she was rescuing her lover. She was just as stupid and impulsive as you, back then. Three questions left."

Wow. That was insane. "So... Lucien... Lucifer?"

She gave me a questioning look and opened her mouth.

"Wait! Stop! Don't answer that. I have other questions and I don't really care about that one."

Boy, did I have a lot to think about.

"Is that why Gus hasn't been able to sense you, or any spirit, for that matter? Because the De... his new boyfriend is blocking him?"

"That would be my guess. The last thing he'd want is Gus to be able to sense the truth about anything having to do with the spirit realms. Now you're down to two questions."

"Wait! That shouldn't even count! *I* answered that question, you just confirmed it—and it wasn't even a hard confirm, more like a soft maybe."

"You win some, you lose some," she said, shrugging.

I bit my lip and tried to think of a way to phrase my next question. "And the toad bone..."

"What a ridiculous ritual. I can't believe anyone's still stupid enough to try it. Idiot-boy would have been in trouble with that one anyway. But boy, howdy, did he pick the wrong toad."

"What does that mean? Why is Grundleshanks so different?"

Aunt Tillie clucked. "I swear you two are perfectly matched, in the impulsive but brainless department."

"Aunt Tillie! By the power of Hekate, I compel you to give me the answer—the full answer—to what exactly the deal is with this toad bone and why it's so special."

"And then you'll let me go?"

"No! Nice try, Aunt Tillie. I still have one more question left. Answer my last two questions, then I'll break the circle and let you go—but only if you give me full answers."

She sighed. "Grundleshanks was not a normal toad."

"No, he wasn't," I agreed. "It was like he was a witch in a toad's body."

"Mmmm. What does the toad bone normally confer?" she asked me.

"Dominion over horses."

"And what is a horse?"

"An animal," I said slowly, wondering where she was going. Then I gasped. "Is that what the problem is? Because it's Grundleshanks's bone, it confers dominion over the entire animal kingdom, instead of just horses?"

Aunt Tillie nodded. "You *do* have a brain. But thanks to Lucien's influence, this particular toad bone gives dominion over the spirit realms as well the earthly realm. The D-bag will never let Gus have that bone. He wants it for himself, to increase his scope of power. And if he gets it, there's no telling what he'll do with it. Suffice it to say, it will probably amuse him while harming everyone else."

"But why doesn't he just take it? He's the Devil."

She glared at me. "I told you not to say his name. And this makes question five. Even the D-bag has to play by certain rules. He can't take anything against your will. It has to be a willing sacrifice on your part. Even if it means the D-bag manipulates the extenuating circumstances to encourage you to be willing. Which he will do, so don't trust him. After you make an agreement with him, he can enforce it however he wants. There you go. That was your last answer. Now break the circle, or I will cause you every misery known to mankind and then some."

I broke the circle and grounded it.

Wow. What was I going to do?

I had to stop the Devil, but I had to stop Gus, too. Neither one of them could have that bone.

How was a little ol' witch like me supposed to stop those two freight trains from colliding?

*   *   *

I drove to the hospital as fast as I could, with the picture of Forrest in hand. Gus was going to freak when I told him everything that was going on. When I got to his room, one of the nurses was sitting there, eating her dinner and watching CNN.

"Where's Gus?" I asked.

"Discharged. That nice, older gentleman took him about an hour ago."

"What?!" I screeched. "What happened to the antibiotic drip? Or the antiviral meds? Or the staying in the hospital for a week?"

She shrugged. "He was with his gentleman friend all day and then tonight, he insisted on signing himself out. Not much we can do. We gave him prescription meds to take home."

I swore under my breath, then hurriedly backtracked to my car and raced home. Hopefully, they'd be at the cottage. Because the only address I had for Forrest, was Hell.

Chapter 50

I banged open the door and stormed into the cottage. Gus was on the couch, looking a little green.

"What the hell are you doing here? You should be in the hospital!"

"I felt fine," Gus said, not looking at me. "I was back to normal. So I left."

"And now, you're clearly not," I said. "Get in the car. We're going back."

He shook his head. "No. Hospitals are dangerous places. Forrest has been telling me all about the latest hospital super-bugs."

"I'll just bet he has." At least Gus sounded better than he had yesterday. The meds must have done some good. "Where is he, anyway?"

"Upstairs, in the bathroom. He was looking for a nail file."

"Good. You and I need to talk." I pulled the picture out of my purse and handed it to Gus. "Look at this. See that guy in the back? Does he look familiar?"

Gus squinted at the photo.

I turned on all the lights in the room, so he could get a better look. Then I sighed and got a magnifying glass from the desk. "We need to get you to an eye doctor. The CMV is affecting your sight."

He peered through the magnifying glass. "Is that... Forrest?"

I nodded. "With J.J.'s great-great-grandfather. Not looking a day younger than he does now. Too bad that photo was taken in the late 1800's."

"What are you saying? That Forrest is 150 years old? *Damn,* he looks good for an old geezer."

"No, you idiot. I'm saying that Forrest is the Devil. Think about it. Forrest's leopards got you sick. When Forrest thought J.J. was going to show me this picture, he turned him into Gronwy the rat. He's been trying to get his hands on the toad bone ever since he showed up. And he called me a *hoot.* Who even says that anymore? You know who else called us a hoot? *The Devil.*"

"That's the most ridiculous thing I've ever heard," Forrest said, laughing, as he came down the stairs. He tossed a folded up newspaper on the table. "Lack of sleep is obviously making you loopy. You're confusing reality with some nightmare you had."

But Gus kept looking at the picture and comparing it to Forrest.

Forrest rolled his eyes. "Just because I look like some guy who lived a couple centuries ago…"

"Not like," Gus said. "Exact. This isn't a resemblance. This is you."

"Thank you," I glared at Forrest, triumphant, then turned back to Gus. "And now that he's finished filing down his talons, and reading our newspaper, I think it's time for the Devil to leave, and for me to get you back to the hospital."

Forrest grew taller, radiating light and danger. "If you think I am leaving without that bone, you're a bigger idiot than that little snot, J.J."

Forrest snapped his fingers, and Gus grabbed at his midsection, struggling to breathe.

"Stop that!" I said. "You're killing him!"

"He's killing himself. All he has to do, to make it stop, is give me the bone."

"Never," Gus spat out.

Forrest looked at Gus and made a small squeezing motion with his fingers. "Whether I take it from you now or post-mortem, makes no difference to me."

Gus groaned in agony. "Fucker," he spat out. "You played me… this entire… time? Go to… hell."

Forrest laughed. "Not without you."

"Stop it! There's no need to do this," I said. "We're witches and you're the Devil. We can be civilized. There's no need to keep hurting Gus."

"You expect me to believe that you want to have a civilized conversation with me?" Forrest asked, laughing.

"Look, I know we've had our share of problems. I didn't trust you, because I knew you were hiding something. It was driving me crazy. But now, I know who you really are, so there's no reason not to be civilized." I said.

I knew, Forrest, as the Father of Lies, would sniff out any falsehood in a red-hot second and he'd take it out on Gus. So I tried to hold onto the small kernel of truth within my words and believe what I was saying.

Forrest narrowed his eyes and looked at me, suspicious.

"Consider it professional courtesy. I may not like you, but I respect your Office. You are the Opposer, the Forge that tests the mettle of men's souls. Before now, you were just Gus's lying boyfriend. Big difference."

I poured Forrest a drink and handed it to him. "I talked to the doctor, and the string of coincidences that needed to happen, to take Gus down… was a work of art."

Forrest inclined his head and smiled. "I'm not a butcher. I take pride in my craft. I originally thought I could get to him through you, but that was a dead end."

"But you *did* get to him through me. That plum I dropped…"

He laughed. "That was beautiful. The timing had to be impeccable, to start that snowball rolling. Once that was set, the rest was easy."

I shook my head. "A perfect storm. A simultaneous bacterial, viral and parasitic infection. I don't know what to say."

"I know… what to say. Fuck you." Gus gasped.

Forrest made a motion, and Gus went flying across the room,

bouncing off the armchair and hitting the floor with a groan.

"I would already have the bone, if it wasn't for you," Forrest said to me. "Don't think I'll forget that. You took my perfectly crafted jigsaw puzzle and kept rearranging the pieces. You were the wild card I had to keep dealing with."

"What are you talking about?" I asked, confused.

"I couldn't quite contain you," he said. "As you figured out, I was able to block Gus from seeing the truth about me—or any spirit. I was able to block the doctors from seeing what was wrong with him. But then *you* waltzed in, pulled their blindfolds off and got Gus back on his feet. Thankfully, you weren't there today. And by the end of this evening, he'll be dead, your mind will have snapped with grief and I'll have the toad bone."

Chapter 51

I remembered what Aunt Tillie had said and shook my head. "You can't take the toad bone. It has to be given. A willing sacrifice. What you're doing now is outright coercion. It won't stand up in any kind of Court, much less an Otherworldly one."

Forrest narrowed his eyes. "You've been talking to your Aunt too much. She's turning into a regular Chatty Cathy."

"Have you met my Aunt Tillie? She's the polar opposite of chatty."

He snorted. "If she likes you Mouth-Breathers so much, she can stay here with you."

Forrest snapped his fingers.

The eye sockets, on the skull we kept on the fireplace mantle, lit up.

"What did you just do?" I asked, panicked.

"You'll find out."

Aunt Tillie's face appeared on Bertha's skull, looking frightened and enraged.

"Stop that! It wasn't her fault! I compelled her to talk! But she didn't tell me anywhere near as much as you think she did!"

We had worked so hard to cross Aunt Tillie over, I didn't want her to be stuck here again. Not to mention, she got a little homicidal when she got cranky.

"To truly hide something, cast no shadow. Instead, your Aunt Tillie cast one big mucking shadow around *me* and then pointed arrows at it. I'm not a very forgiving deity."

"How do you even have dominion over her? I thought she was in the Summerlands." I said.

I was guessing at the last part because really, I had no idea how the balance of Aunt Tillie's soul had played out once she crossed over.

He shrugged. "She interfered in my business. Which makes her subject to *my* punishment. We have rules and laws, just as you do. And she violated them."

No wonder Aunt Tillie hadn't been keen on talking to me. The last person you'd want to cross, if you were dead, was the Devil. Especially if it gave him permission to mete out your punishment.

I looked at Aunt Tillie and mouthed *"I'm sorry."*

She didn't look like she was going to be forgiving me any time soon.

"So the rat... *is* J.J.?" Gus asked, coughing, as he climbed up on the armchair.

Forrest snorted. "Stupid kid. I thought enough time had passed for me to reappear in this guise. For a kid with three brain cells left, who'd have thought he'd be that familiar with that picture?"

Gus shrugged. "Good thing... he's a rat. He'd be pissed... about us... burning his pot plants."

Forrest laughed. "I do so enjoy my time with the two of you. I'll make sure you're situated in my entourage, in the Underworld."

I suppressed a grimace and tried to change the subject. "What were you even doing here back then?" I asked. "Was there a reason you were hanging out in the mortal realm?"

"That would be Eleanor." Forrest paused, his smile widening. "You wouldn't know it to look at her progeny, but Eleanor was heartstoppingly beautiful. Smart, funny, adventurous. She was wasted on Jarvis."

"J.J.'s great-great-grandfather?" I asked.

Forrest nodded. "You humans have such pitifully short lives. I offered her eternity. I offered to make her my queen."

"But she wanted Jarvis?"

"She wanted off-spring and the not-so-wonderful joys of growing old. She wanted a family. Even if it was with a carousing drunkard. She said he made her laugh."

"She turned down the Devil? What did you do?" I asked.

He shrugged. "I could never deny her anything. I let her have what she wanted. And once she was past child-bearing age," his face grew hard, "I turned that son-of-a-bitch into a tree. In the end, she lost us both. And she was able to experience every single joy of growing old, all by herself."

"That was you?!" I asked. "I thought that was my cottage."

He turned and looked at me. "It's *my* cottage. This entire town is an homage to *me*. Hell and damnation, girl, look at the name. Devil's Point. You are allowed to live here by my grace. Cross me, and you will make lovely shrubbery."

"I thought it was named Devil's Point after a rock formation that looked like a pitchfork."

"Exactly. And guess who you have to thank for that? Now, about that bone…"

"I'm not… giving it up… to you," Gus said. "I'll destroy it… first."

"It's time to put an end to this." Forrest said. "Whether you're alive or dead, I will get that bone. Even if it's from a confused morgue attendant."

He squeezed his fist and Gus fell back onto the floor, screaming with pain.

"This is so stupid! Gus, you can't keep the bone. He'll straight up kill you." I yelled.

"He. Can. Try." Gus spit out.

I rolled my eyes. "He's the *Devil*. He can do more than try." I turned to Forrest. "Look, you of all people—or entities—should know how stubborn Gus gets. He absolutely will destroy the bone before he gives it to you. Can't we figure out some kind of compromise?"

Forrest eased up on Gus. "A barter? Is that what you're

proposing?"

In the skull, Aunt Tillie's eyes flared and it looked like she was about to say something, but Forrest dipped his fingers in a sewing motion, and little lines appeared across her mouth, as if someone had sewn it shut.

"I don't know what I'm proposing," I said. "Personally, I don't care what happens to the bone, I just know I want Gus to stay alive."

Forrest thought about it. "Maybe there *is* something we could work out."

"No," Gus said, and then promptly screamed. Sweat started pouring off his forehead, and he panted with pain.

"If I hear the word 'no' from you again, I will turn your liver into pate," Forrest snapped.

"I'll give the bone to Mara before I'll give it to a backstabbing asshat like you," Gus ground out.

Forrest gave a sly, evil grin. "I accept your deal."

Chapter 52

"What?! Wait. What?" I asked.

"If it's all right with the lady, of course." Forrest inclined his head towards me.

"Back that truck up, buddy," I said. "What *deal?*"

"Obviously, I can't trust Gus with the power in that particular bone. I'm sure your Aunt told you why. But you... you don't have quite the same ambitions he does. I will allow you to be Switzerland and hold the bone. If you're willing."

I looked at Gus, groaning on the floor, holding his mid-section. His eyes rolled back as he went in and out of consciousness.

"So, all I'm doing is holding it?"

"Yes," Forrest said.

"And you'll let Gus go?"

"Absolutely."

"Not good enough."

"Excuse me?" Forrest asked, looking distinctly chilly.

"I have a rat upstairs, who should be human. I have a roommate who's having his organs pulverized. I have an Aunt who's being tormented. I have a tree who used to be a man. I have a baby on the way and no income. I need all of that fixed. And I don't mean by taking away the baby."

"I'm not a savage," Forrest said, clearly offended.

"That's a matter of opinion." I glanced at Gus, whose breathing was shallow and labored.

"Let the negotiations begin," Forrest laughed. "I underestimated you. This is going to be fun."

"For you, maybe. Where do you want to start?"

"You really don't want me putting Jarvis back in his old body. It would turn into a pile of dust and ash."

"You're the Devil. Magick him up a new body."

"Mara, don't you understand? Jarvis has been a tree for a hell of a lot longer than he ever was a man. He wouldn't know what to do as a man anymore. His identity is tree. His soul is *tree*. He'd probably try to stand in buckets of water and dirt, and take root. And what about his family? Do you know the chaos it would cause for Jarvis to not only come back from the dead, but come back acting like a tree?"

I thought about it. "You have a point."

Gus and I believed that humans have both a spirit and a soul inside of them. The spirit evolves, growing ever closer to Divine Bliss. But the soul goes back into the fabric of the world.

"His soul may be *tree*, but his spirit is still *man*. Let his spirit move on. Stop keeping it trapped with his soul, in the tree."

Forrest smiled in his unsettling way. "Fine. Consider it done."

"And Aunt Tillie?" I asked him.

"I promise not to torment her for *all* of eternity."

"Don't torment her at all," I said.

"My dear girl. She'll be living with you. That will be *your* job. Torment her or not, I'm out of it."

"I don't want her trapped here, either."

"Once she loses all interest in humanity, I'll release her. Do we have a deal?" Forrest asked, smiling.

"Fulfill the rest of my requirements, and we do."

Forrest snapped his fingers. Upstairs, I heard a crash and J.J.'s voice yelling, "What the hell?!"

On the floor, Gus stopped writhing in pain. Soon, he was even able to sit up and lean against the chair, as he tried to catch his breath.

On the skull, the black threads holding Aunt Tillie's mouth

shut, vanished. "Mara, don't believe him!" she hollered.

When Forrest snapped his fingers again, the pouch around Gus's neck opened, and the toad bone shot into Forrest's hand. Forrest pressed down on it and crushed the bone into powder.

"Hey!" I said. "I thought you didn't want it destroyed."

He gave me a wicked grin. "I don't. But trust me, you're going to thank me."

Then he threw the toad bone powder at my belly. Each particle carved its way through my skin, like tiny diamond-tipped razors. I screamed with the intense, searing pain and dropped to my knees. The bone dust penetrated my skin, my tissues, it even went through the placental wall and into the baby.

Within me, the baby screamed in pain.

"Fuck!" I hollered. "What did you do?!"

"You should be thanking me. If you thought that was painful, the bone in its entirety would have severed your spine."

"I said I would hold it. *I*. Not the baby." I said, as soon as I could speak again.

"Until birth, the mother and child are one entity. Anything you agree to, you agree to on both your behalf's. There is no separation between you, until the umbilical cord is cut."

"But why?" I asked, desperately holding onto the tears that were trying to fall. "Why would you do that to an innocent baby?"

Forrest laughed, a deep, booming laugh. "I have been waiting for that baby, for a long, long time. I should thank you. I thought I was going to have to work a lot harder."

And with that, he was gone.

Chapter 53

"You stupid, stupid girl," Aunt Tillie said, clearly furious.

"I didn't know he was after the baby!" I yelled, frustrated.

"Of course, you didn't. No one ever knows the Devil's end game. But if you had trusted me to begin with, you could have avoided this whole mess."

I looked over at Gus. He was getting his color back.

"It's not Mara's fault," Gus said. "I was the idiot. I couldn't see you, I couldn't hear you, I couldn't even sense you. So I stopped believing her."

"Why does the Devil want my baby, anyway?" I asked.

"Don't you understand?" Aunt Tillie asked. "Haven't you noticed your magick getting stronger? That's the baby. The baby's heritage. That baby is part human, part witch and part Lucien. The Devil couldn't block you because the baby kept him from it. You may be forming its DNA, but that baby's also been changing yours. The power you've been showing? That's the *baby's* gift to you. "

As I thought about it, a chill ran up my spine. "But what happens now that the baby's got the toad bone in its blood?"

"I don't know," Aunt Tillie admitted. "But if it's what the Devil wanted, it can't be good. Not for you, not for the baby, not for any of us. After every warning I gave you, you made a deal with the Devil. And now we're all beholden to him."

Just then, J.J. came crashing down the stairs, a towel wrapped around his naked body, his feet crammed into my slippers.

As soon as he saw me, he started screaming. "I told you this house was evil!"

He slammed out the front door and ran as fast as he could in too-small bunny slippers.

We watched him go, in complete silence.

Finally, I closed the door and turned to Gus. "Well, *that* happened."

Gus grinned. "Never a dull moment."

"What is wrong with the two of you?" Aunt Tillie snapped. "None of this is funny!"

*   *   *

As the days went by, Aunt Tillie grew used to being in residence in the skull. She could still cross the veil, but she said it was like she was a scarlet woman on the other side. The Devil had left his mark on her, and while she could go for brief visits, she wasn't welcome to stay. Which aggravated her to no end. But, considering her other option could have been *'being tormented in Hell until the Devil got over his annoyance'*, I thought being stuck with us Breathers was the better end of the deal. I don't know if she agreed with me, though.

Gus went back to the hospital for regular check-ups and took his meds, even though he hated them. Without the Devil's interference, he was able to get healthy again and even regain his sense of humor.

I got tested for Toxo and CMV and by some miracle, I was negative.

As Gus's health improved, I picked Aramis up from Paul, but he asked if he could hang on to Apollo a little longer. Considering he was almost back to his cheerful, sweet, funny self, I was fine with that. Having the Dobies around obviously agreed with him.

*   *   *

J.J. finally calmed down, once his memories of rat-hood faded. Oddly enough though, he actually started exhibiting better hygiene. I was able to go into the Trading Post and talk to him, without using a menthol rub under my nose. And once he started washing his hair and taking better care of himself, he actually landed his first girlfriend.

After he returned to work, Anna, his cousin, smacked him on the backside with a skillet, leaving a generously-sized bruise. Then she promptly left town on an extended vacation.

I finally did have that dinner with Daniel and Raoul, and Raoul's pregnant wife. I had it catered, and we shared it with the other residents of the nursing home. I'm currently their favorite visitor.

*   *   *

When it came to the baby, Gus and I still couldn't agree on male versus female. I think the baby was enjoying the debate, so it was deliberately keeping that information to itself.

But ever since the ordeal with the Devil and the intense pain the toad bone transfer had caused, the baby had reached a new level of self-awareness. I hoped it wasn't developing as quickly physically as it was mentally, or else I was going to be in trouble. I fully expected it to walk out of the birth canal, kick the doctor's ass for evicting it from its watery womb-home, and demand my car keys.

*   *   *

I was rapidly going broke and just as I was eyeing that failure as a loophole to get out of my contract with the Devil, a letter showed up from an out-of-state bank. Apparently, Aunt Tillie had a ROTH IRA account there from when she was young, and it had been quietly growing all these years. Now it was mine, providing a monthly income of $1,500. So much for my loophole. Not a fortune, but enough to fulfill the Devil's side of the contract.

I went out and bought Hekate three fire opals with the first disbursement check. After all, you don't want to make a bargain with a deity and then bow out of it. They have a way of taking what they feel is theirs. Besides, I had a feeling I'd be needing her help again, in the near future.

Sure enough, the minute I got the opals, I was holding them on my hand, admiring their fiery colors, when a cold gust of wind blew them off my palm and they vanished. I could feel Hekate laughing

271

about how she snagged them from me, the entire drive home.

* * *

With the next disbursement check, after I paid the bills, I was going to use whatever was left to hire a private investigator to help me find my brother. I had grilled Aunt Tillie and my mom about his whereabouts, but they were no help. I wasn't sure though, if they were really as clueless as they claimed, or if they were being intentionally obtuse.

* * *

The toad bone skeleton I ordered arrived from China just after New Year's. I thought long and hard about what to do with it. I didn't want Gus to find it and try another toad bone ritual. So I shellacked the entire thing to make sure the bones would stay together and then I posed it, super-glued it onto a miniature skateboard, with a skull-shaped bead in the toad's outstretched hand, and put it in the library as a decoration.

Grundleshanks was still hanging around, in an uneasy truce with his stuffed doppelganger—until yesterday, when the UPS guy arrived with an overnight shipment. Andwyn had sent us another toad from the Grundleshanks line. Unfortunately, the little guy didn't do well with our extended winter and the shipping process, and died soon after arrival. But our Grundleshanks was more than happy to slide into the vacated body.

Now, we have Zombieshanks—as Gus sometimes calls him. Thankfully, the only type of brains he's interested in eating belong to crickets.

* * *

While the rest of the world is looking forward to the arrival of spring, we're deep into winter. The snow has reached epic proportions, and it doesn't look like we'll be out of it, anytime soon. The weather's getting colder every day. And the snow! We have snow banks the size of small mountains. Everyone in Devil's Point is paying for Gus's brief stint of shifting summer into winter. While the rest of the nation is warming up, our entire town is blanketed in snow and we're making the national weather news again, this time for cold temperatures and snowfall.

Aunt Tillie's been bugging me to leave town and go somewhere warm with Gus, until the weather gets back on track and the baby's born. Today, we got an S.O.S. from Mama Lua, the Voodoo Queen who runs the Crooked Pantry in Los Angeles. She says she's being plagued by vampires and demons, and needs our help. So, it looks like Aunt Tillie may get her wish after all.

About the Author

Christiana Miller is a novelist, screenwriter and mom who's led an unusual life. In addition to writing for General Hospital: Night Shift and General Hospital, she's had her DNA shot into space (where she's currently cohabiting in a drawer with Stephen Colbert and Stephen Hawking), she's been serenaded by Klingons, and she's been the voices of all the female warriors in Mortal Kombat II and III. If her life was a TV show, it would be a wacky dramedy filled with eccentric characters who get themselves into bizarre situations. She enjoys hanging out with her kids and writing stories with a supernatural twist.

Made in the USA
Middletown, DE
14 August 2015